Back in the mid-eighties, I wrote *Texas Anthem*. It was the first of a family saga set against the western frontier from the end of the Mexican-American War to the turn of the century. *Texas Born* soon followed and carried us forward several years from the events chronicled in *Texas Anthem*. We've watched Big John Anthem become a successful and respected rancher and carve his own empire out of the wilds of West Texas. He has sired two sons and a daughter, all of them mavericks, and a real challenge for their parents as we've discovered. I am pleased that St. Martin's Press is reprinting all five novels in the series.

The Anthem family is a robust collection of men and women shaped by the land, a strong and independent breed, often flawed and perhaps too headstrong, but the kind of folks who will stand for justice, live life to the fullest, and cast a tall shadow.

In *Creed's Law* young Billy Anthem, Big John Anthem's youngest son, has set out in search of adventure and his place in the world. Now Billy isn't looking for trouble when he rides his big bay up the coast of the Pacific Northwest and arrives in the town of Calamity Bay, but it finds him all the same. The town's all decked out for a hanging.

Noah Creed's niece has been brutally murdered and an eccentric drifter arrested for the crime. Old Noah and his hard-driven sons want vengeance, and woe to anyone who gets in their way. But Billy suspects the jailed man is innocent and that the vicious killer walks the streets, biding his time until he can strike again.

What's an Anthem to do except stand for what's right, even if the odds are against him? Sometimes a man has to break the law to see justice done, especially when it's Creed's law.

—

I reckon this is where I'm expected to tell you how I lived a life of towering adventure, saddle-broke a hundred wild mustangs, pitched a tent in Tibet, hunted Cape buffalo, served with distinction, rode with the wind, trampled the wild places and the crooked highways . . . oh, heck with it. That's not me.

I was the kid who sat in the front row of the balcony of the movie theater and spent every Saturday afternoon with the likes of John Wayne, Burt Lancaster, Kirk Douglas, Lee Marvin, Charlton Heston, Gregory Peck, and the list goes on; a kid who thrilled to the sight of charging Comanches, saloon brawls, and shoot-outs in dusty streets, not to mention sword fights, heroic last stands, dueling pirate ships, and chariot races. And when I wasn't at the theater, I was reading the same, yondering by way of the written word, finding the lost and lonely places, and dreaming I would one day be the tale-teller, spinning legends on the wheel of my imagination.

Sure, I've done some things, been some places. But so have you. All that matters now, my friend, is the story we share. I have tried to craft these books with a sense of legend as well as history; finding just the right blend of thrills, drama, romance, and a dash of wit. Whether or not I have succeeded is in your hands.

KERRY NEWCOMB
DECEMBER, 2001

"Kerry Newcomb is one of those writers who lets you know from his very first lines that you're in for a ride. And he keeps his promise. THE RED RIPPER bounds along with unrelenting vigor. This is historical fiction crafted by a writer who never loses his sense of pace, drama, adventure, and fun. Kerry Newcomb knows what he is doing, and does it enviably well."

—Cameron Judd, Golden Spur Award–nominated author of TEXAS FREEDOM

"A compelling mix of passion, revenge, and a gallant people's quest for freedom. With the historical accuracy of a L'Amour novel, the characters are well drawn, leaving the reader to feel the openness and harsh challenges of the Texas frontier . . . Don't expect to get any sleep when you start this one."   —John J. Gobbell,
Bestselling author of THE LAST LIEUTENANT

PRAISE FOR

MAD MORGAN:

"Colorful, old fashioned adventure . . . Awash with treachery and romance, this well-spun yarn fairly crackles with danger and suspense. Vigorous historical fiction."   —*Booklist*

"Swashbuckling adventure!"   —*Indianapolis Star*

CREED'S LAW

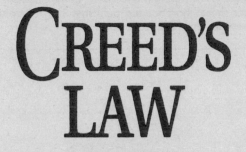

KERRY NEWCOMB

(PREVIOUSLY PUBLISHED UNDER THE
PSEUDONYM JAMES RENO)

St. Martin's Paperbacks

PUBLISHER'S NOTE

This book is a work of fiction. Names, characters, places, and incidents either are the product of the author's imagination or are used fictitiously, and any resemblance to actual persons, living or dead, events, or locales is entirely coincidental.

CREED'S LAW

Copyright © 1988 by James Reno.
"Just a Note from the Author" copyright © 2001 by Kerry Newcomb.

ISBN: 0-312-98128-7

Printed in the United States of America

Signet edition / November 1988
St. Martin's Paperbacks edition / December 2001

St. Martin's Paperbacks are published by St. Martin's Press, 175 Fifth Avenue, New York, NY 10010.

10 9 8 7 6 5 4 3 2 1

For Patty and Amy Rose and P.J.
For Ann and Paul and Jimmy
With Love

Thank you, Maureen Baron and Matt Sartwell, for cutting the fences and giving the Anthems room to ride.

Thank you, Roy and Dale, for living the myth and singing the songs and giving a Fort Worth boy room to dream.

PROLOGUE

★

It was the rain spilling from the eternally gray sky that caused Billy Anthem to think of home. Back in West Texas things were just the opposite. In that arid landscape of desert mounts and wild chino grass and cactus, a man looked at the sky and prayed for rain.

On the northwest coast of Washington Territory with winter just ending, the rains fell and men prayed for a break in the clouds. They endured a dampness that a man could shake from neither clothes nor bones.

Billy Anthem spit into his fire, tossed the dregs of his thrice-boiled coffee into a nearby puddle. He should have listened when they told him that only a damned fool would try to ride something as puny as a mere horse up the Pacific coast. A bear might do, or maybe a mule, but not a horse, not through all those miles of rain-soaked forest, and over the dozens of swollen creeks.

But Billy didn't come from stock that listened to such as "can't." Billy's father, Big John Anthem, hadn't put up with that kind of talk when he'd carved an empire out of the wilds of West Texas. And Billy Anthem had learned his lesson well. So, when the boys at the bar in the Black's

Luck Saloon on the south bank of the Columbia had told
him he couldn't, Billy Anthem's eyes had gotten hard and
his lips had set in a tight, determined grin.

"A man can do anything if he sets his mind to it," he
told them.

"You talk like a preacher's son," someone muttered.

"Hardly." Billy laughed, thinking of his family. "Nope.
No Bible-thumpers among the Anthems."

"Anthem, huh," a grizzled and toothless old river rat
said. "Well, now, that's a name of a song, ain't it? Likely
you'll fiddle a different one when that poor excuse of a
horse you got tied up out there dies of the mildew."

"We'll see," Billy said, downing a final shot of Black
Luck Holy Water, the local brew that Joe Black, the owner,
had carefully aged for at least a day. "Gents," he added,
brushing a hand through his curly blond hair. His brown
eyes betrayed little of the hard edge hidden by his gentle
demeanor as he cordially tipped his hat. "My ride across
yon river awaits me, I believe."

It was the kind of talk you could expect from a man
who'd been on the trail for a month without a drop of
whiskey. Worse than that, for he'd eaten poorly after leaving San Francisco with little more than a saddlebag full of
beans and bacon. Not real smart for a man in strange territory, but then Billy Anthem was a man on the run from
bad memories, and figured he could always make do one
way or other.

Live and learn, Billy thought now, leaning forward to
poke up his fire. He shuddered when a trickle of the cold
water leaking through the makeshift roof overhead found
the gap between his slouch hat and the collar of his coat.
He'd been so all-fired curious to follow the coast that he'd
taken the old man's warning as a challenge, saddled Rosie,
and ridden away with his belly still burning from Black's
bad liquor.

Billy had ridden the big-barreled, surefooted mare up

from San Francisco. She was a strong, hearty animal with plenty of spirit, and he had confidently pointed her north. After they'd crossed the Columbia, he veered inland around William's Bay and Gray's Harbor. Then it was back to the coast and a wet, slow, noisy hundred-plus miles north to Ozette Lake, making cold camps along the way. After a couple of days on the trail, Billy had found a small meadow between the lake and the forest, and there he'd stopped to rest.

Rosie, who was on the verge of wearing out, grazed happily on the sweet grasses. Billy gorged himself on a plump young elk he had shot and killed. I might drown in this country, he thought, but I sure as hell won't starve.

Sunrise and sunset at home on Luminaria, the vast and sprawling ranch Big John Anthem had forged from an empty and hostile land, had always been Billy's favorite times. Sunrise—when the first faint hint of light spread a breathless, expectant hush over the earth. Sunset—when a long day's work was winding down and the sky turned the colors of an artist's palette and a faint breeze sprang up to begin the business of chasing away the day's heat. Here on the coast of Washington Territory, the mountains to the east blocked the sunrise, and the roiling clouds paid the same favor to the sunset. It grew light, it rained, it turned dark and rained some more.

Grease dripped from the elkmeat steak hung over the fire. Billy reckoned the meat was cooked enough. He cut a morsel with his knife and plopped it in his mouth. Weary from doing nothing for the past three days, he rose, snared an oiled sack from where he'd hung it in a relatively dry spot under the lean-to roof, and headed for Rosie.

The horse, a pretty bay, watched him coming out of the corner of her eye. He'd built a roof for her too, and though it wasn't much, it offered some shelter and she stayed under it most of the time, grazing off the grass underfoot until bare earth showed.

"Don't look at me that way," Billy said, pouring a bait of oats into her canvas feed bucket. "I know they're mildewed, but beggars can't be choosers. If it makes you feel any better," he added, shaking out the bag, "those are the last, so you won't have to eat any more of them."

Billy trotted back to his fire and squatted down to eat. He plopped the steak onto his tin plate. "And the last of the salt, too," he said aloud, sprinkling the final grains of seasoning over the meat before he bit into it. No salt, no coffee, and no beans. As much as Anthem wasn't all eaten up with the desire to share the pleasures of civilization again, he was going to have to.

His map was crudely drawn, water-stained, and almost impossible to read in the lengthening shadows of night. Still, Billy had looked at it often enough that he didn't really need to. Rosie nearby to warn him of any trouble that might come during the night—the only thing he could think of in that godforsaken country was a bear or a big cat—he unrolled his ground cloth, shook out his soggy bedroll, and with his saddle for a pillow, lay down to try to sleep.

The next morning, he'd be on his way north, cross country to the Juan de Fuca Strait, east along the coast, and back south in the direction of Seattle. He'd find work somewhere, work to numb his body and mind as much as solitude did. And once he had a grubstake and a belly full of people, he'd be on his way again.

Almost a year had passed since he'd seen his parents, Big John and Rose, his sister, Rachel, and his brother, Cole. They hadn't tried to stop him or talk him out of leaving.

And why should they? At twenty-five, he was his own man. He cast a man's shadow, did a man's work. And deep in his heart, he carried a man's grief.

Billy rolled on his side, his back to the fire, closed his eyes, and listened to the rhythmic patter of the rain . . . and prayed, tonight, he wouldn't dream.

1

★

The bullet whipped past Billy's ear and fanned his cheek. A cat couldn't have reacted any faster. His right foot slid out of the stirrup before Rosie could shy. His right had jerked the Winchester '73 from its saddle holster. Billy dropped the reins and launched himself to the left in a fluid movement that pushed his horse to the right and sent the animal galloping down the trail.

A half-second later, a second slug tore through the empty space six inches above the saddle. A third bullet richocheted off a moss-covered boulder. The shrill scream of the deformed slug stopped abruptly when it slammed into a tree. There was no fourth because there was no target. Only the empty, soggy landscape somewhere on the northern slope of Hurricane Ridge.

The world was green and brown, moss and mud. Billy shook his head, spit out a mouthful of dirt, and wiped his sleeve across his nose and mouth. The firing had stopped. An uneasy stillness lay over the sun-drenched land. Steam rose from the earth, making judging distances all the more uncertain. Billy's senses gradually returned to normal. His heartbeat and breathing slowed. He became aware of a sharp pain in his side where, he guessed, he'd landed on his rifle butt. The only sound was the drip-drip-drip of water trickling off the overhanging boulder that shielded him from his attacker. The droplets landed in the rapidly filling shallow hole he'd dug with his face. It was one hell of a way to dismount.

"If there's no time to think, act," Big John Anthem had preached. "There's a time to consider the possibles and a time to haul leather and let the devil take the hindmost."

The lesson had been drilled in since he was a child, and Billy had taken heed. He'd seen his father act with all the temper and patience of a hunter. And remembered, too, the moments when Big John rode wild-eyed, guns blazing into the situation. Now, his mind racing, Billy assessed the situation. A dozen or so yards down the gently sloping valley they'd been descending, Rosie grazed contentedly on a patch of grass.

Unlike the hills around Luminaria or the mountains of Mexico, where the echoes from a gunshot often disguised its source, the green forests of Washington Territory soaked up echoes. From the undistorted sound, the shots had come from his left-rear quarter, from somewhere on the steep slope that bound the narrow valley. The slope, more like a cliff, was high enough that the shots couldn't have come from its top; the angle was wrong. So the would-be assailant had to be below the rim. All Billy had to do was work his way to the top of the ridge and take the offensive.

Strange, the way a man's mind works in the brief lull, the one or two seconds in which he collects himself before taking action. As if he'd had an hour to study them, Billy noted the clear blue sky and the bright sun, the first he'd seen in a month. On either side, the astonishingly varied greens of the forest dazzled him. To his right, an ancient cedar felled by lightning or a slide lay rotting and covered with a bright, bottle-green moss punctuated by equally bright yellow-and-black fungus that looked like tiny hooded caps. And right in front of his nose, he saw what looked like the face of a bear outlined in the moss that grew on the boulder. But then, he'd always been the reflective son, the watcher. Brother Cole and Rachel, too, were always on the prod, ready to erupt in a dozen different directions.

Now it's my time to cut loose, Billy thought, and he sighed inwardly. He hated to leave the shadow of the boulder that had saved his life—but he crouched, gave himself a mental kick in the seat of the pants, and dived for the uncertain safety of the fallen cedar.

A shot snapped over his head, another thudded into the cedar. Billy cradled the Winchester in the crooks of his arms and dragged himself by his elbows to the end of the trunk.

"You ain't gonna make it, you back shooting bastard!"

The voice rang out loud and clear, deep and strong, like a weathered bell. Billy froze momentarily and searched for the direction.

"But come on and try. I'll take you any day. Back-shot or not, I'm still more'n a match for you and your kind." The voice drifted downslope, runted by the moisture in the air.

Back-shot?

"What the hell have I ridden into?" Billy muttered. He had entered the little valley no more than five minutes earlier, and the way the mountains and trees and soggy ground soaked up sound, a pair of armies could have waged a battle a mile away and he'd have been none the wiser. He must have missed the opening round in this confrontation.

Someone had back-shot someone else. The wounded man had lived and was now convinced he'd drawn a bead on his assailant. Now Billy would have to find this wounded rifleman and read him from the book.

A good ten yards of open space faced him. The rifle above sounded like another Winchester. So his attacker probably had plenty of lead to spare. Might as well make him use some. Billy jumped out as if to run, then dived back. Sure enough another shot, and a telltale puff of smoke. Immediately, Billy snapped off a round and was up and running, far ahead of the single shot that followed.

"Gotcha!" He grinned, landing on his feet in a narrow gully worn into the face of the steep slope by years of torrential winter rains. "And now, my friend, let's see just who you are."

The climb was steep, but easy for one who'd grown up in the dry Southwest, where every twig cracked and every pebble rolled and rattled and gave a man away.

From rock to root, now crawling and now running crouched over in order not to expose himself, Billy scrambled to the top of what he'd thought was a ridge but was in reality a wide terrace cut in the face of the mountain. And along that lay a logging road.

A road meant people, so Billy took his time. Flat on his belly, his head barely sticking above the flat ground, he inspected the open area and found nothing more menacing than a huge gray jack mule standing about fifty yards to his left. At last, keeping an eye peeled, he ventured out and, at a crouched run, headed for the mule.

The animal gave him a baleful glance and went about its business of demolishing a clump of grass. Sure enough, a few yards farther on, Billy found a groove in the mud and a broken sapling where a man had gone over the edge.

Going down wasn't as easy as going up had been. The ground was slippery, the angle more like a cliff than a slope. Billy moved silently from tree to tree, digging in his heels to avoid dislodging any rocks or starting even the semblance of a slide. He worked his way downhill, and at last spotted a pair of boots. Slowing, then, he took his time picking the quietest path to a huge boulder, and then, after checking his back-trail one last time, he stepped out with rifle at the ready.

The man was lying on his stomach twenty feet away on a ledge no bigger than a bunkhouse table. His left shoulder, evident even under the heavy wool fabric of his coat, was humped awkwardly and his left arm lay straight along his body. His right arm held a rifle propped on a broken branch and still aiming downhill. His right leg was bent at a grotesque angle. He was bareheaded, his hat lying some yards upslope, and his shoulder-length, salt-and-pepper hair was matted with mud and pine needles. His black wool clothes were soaked and stained with mud.

Billy studied the man and after a moment's scrutiny realized that what he'd taken for a tear in the coat was a bullet hole, and that the color around it was the dull, ugly red of blood mixed with mud.

Billy shouldered his rifle and sighted on the rifleman below. He thumbed back the hammer on his rifle. The audible click, though muted, was as effective as a shout. The rifleman in front of Billy jerked as if shot, and tensed, waiting for the shock of a slug tearing into his back.

"If you're thinking that I could possibly miss," Billy said laconically, "think again, friend."

"What do I have to lose?" the man asked, his voice hoarse and bitter. "You back-shot me once and I don't doubt you'd slither like a snake to do it again. Least I can do is take you with me, you son of a bitch, so make—"

The older man might have been fast, at another time, but not under those conditions. His head rose and he tried to roll onto his back, but a dull popping sound in his shoulder brought him up short before he could move more than a few inches. Without a shot fired, he groaned once as his rifle dropped out of his hand. He collapsed in a dead faint.

Billy sighed, shook his head in wonder at the courage, and foolhardiness, of the man. "Well, you got my vote, mister," he softly said, and eased down to the fallen man. Wary of a trick, Billy drew his Colt .45, cocked it, then set aside his Winchester and kicked his assailant's rifle out of reach.

"You playin' possum, friend?" he asked, nudging the man's ribs near the bloodstained bullet hole with his toe.

Not a wiggle, not a move. He was out like a candle in a sandstorm. Reassured, Billy eased the hammer off cock, holstered his pistol, and set to work. Whoever the man was, he'd come prepared. Billy removed a revolver like his own from the man's holster. One boot held an over-and-under .25 derringer, the other a sheathed double-bladed throwing knife.

"Okay, pardner," he said at last, taking the unconscious man by the shoulder and belt. "Over we go, and let's see what a feller with so much salt looks like."

He was forty, maybe fifty. His mud-streaked face tended to roundness, but the strength and determination and grit written in its lines dispelled any notion of softness, even in his unconscious state. He wore a thick mustache that sloped down almost to his chin and was, unlike his hair, almost totally gray. His shoulders and chest were burly and broad in the extreme, and sloped to slim hips and spindly legs, as if he'd been cast together from two different molds.

Billy stepped back from the man and softly whistled. "What the hell," he growled, more perplexed than ever before.

The man's coat had fallen open to reveal a gray flannel shirt and, pinned to the pocket, a five-pointed star, mud-streaked but gleaming in the sun. Anthem read the engraving aloud.

"Town Marshal, Calamity Bay." Billy Anthem's would-be killer was a man of the law.

2

★

Human target one minute, a makeshift doctor the next, Billy knelt and inspected the unconscious form of the lawman. He then manhandled his coat off and opened his shirt. As he'd thought, the bullet wound wasn't bad. The slug had struck a rib, flattened, and cut a six-inch-long, jagged tear as it exited. The rib was no doubt broken and painful as sin, but the wound would heal with little more than an ugly scar to show for it.

The marshal's leg forgotten for the moment, Billy concentrated on the grotesquely distorted right shoulder. He had seen but one dislocated shoulder in his life, and that when he was fifteen.

The mottled gray-and-black Indian pony had looked docile enough when they'd taken him on a trade from a band of wandering, down on their luck Comanche, but that sleepy look had disappeared the instant Pete Lucas, one of the Luminaria hands, had climbed on him. After one second in the saddle and a few in the air, Pete had landed on his elbow. Everyone around the corral heard the pop as his shoulder went out. And the sight was one that Billy hadn't forgotten. Neither had he forgotten the way Chapo Almendáriz, the Luminaria segundo, had fixed Pete's shoulder.

Billy had to work fast, before the lawman regained consciousness and tensed his muscles, which would make the job well nigh impossible. Quickly, Billy sat at his patient's side, grabbed the man's wrist, and stuck a booted foot in his armpit. Sweating, hoping he was doing it right and not causing more damage, Anthem levered the upper arm out and away from the shoulder, pulled straight down, then let the muscles and tendons pull the ball in toward the body. To his relief, he was rewarded by the faint *snick* of the ball slipping into the socket.

"I'll be damned." Billy chuckled, pleased with himself. "Might just as well set the leg while he's still out."

Legs were easy for anyone who'd grown up on a working ranch, where breaks were common. With a practiced hand, Billy pulled off the man's boot and slit his trouser leg up to the knee. The break wasn't bad: no bone showed through the skin and the leg was only slightly bent. Wood was plentiful, and it was but a matter of a couple of minutes to fashion four splints. Using his knife, he cut strips from the man's shirt and already torn trousers, pulled the leg straight, and lashed the splints to it.

And then, what? As Billy squatted at the lawman's side and considered his next move, the man stirred. Quickly, before he could hurt his shoulder, Billy held his patient's upper arm and wrist. "You awake?" Anthem asked.

The man's eyes fluttered and he concentrated on focusing on Billy. "I guess," he groaned, "I hurt too damn much to be dead. Who the hell are you?"

"The man you tried to kill. What kind of law you got around here? I thought a man was supposed to be wanted for something before he was eligible for shooting."

"Don't look to me like you're dead," the marshal dryly observed.

"No thanks to you. You got a name, Marshall?"

"Rhodes. Go by Hank. You?"

"Billy Anthem. Looks like I rode all the way from Texas just to be at your service, fool that I am."

Rhodes chuckled, winced, and turned white with the pain in his side. "I do appreciate it, Billy Anthem from Texas," he said weakly. "As long as you ain't the one who back-shot me in the first place."

"You'd be dead if I was, and that's a fact. I sure as hell wouldn't have taken the trouble to doctor you."

"Can't argue with you there. Just one question, though." He glanced down to where Billy was holding his arm and wrist. "You sweet on me or something?"

Billy reddened, almost let go, but didn't. "Just making sure you didn't wave it around when you came to," he explained. "I popped that shoulder back in, and the last thing you need is to move it before it has a chance to heal."

Rhodes groaned in disgust, lay his head down, and closed his eyes to gather himself against the pain.

"You all right?" Billy asked, letting go the arm.

"Shit, no, I ain't all right. It don't rain without pouring."

"So I've noticed," Billy said with a chuckle. "In more ways than one. At least you picked a good day for bad luck."

Rhodes looked up at the young man whom he'd mistaken for his assassin, and liked what he saw. In his middle twenties, perhaps, Anthem was lean and hard looking as a plank. His dark blond hair was shaggy and his clothes looked lived-in, as if he'd been on the trail for some time. His eyes were brown and open, without rancor, the eyes of a peaceable man, and yet, somehow, not a man who would be dominated or ridden over. An inch of light-brown beard, darker than the rest of his hair, covered the lower half of his face, but couldn't disguise the sharp, square lines of his jaw. "Or a bad day for good luck," the lawman said. "You easy could have rode off, and the hell with me. There's those who would've."

"Well, I'll tell you straight," Billy said with a grin. "I figure that any man who can hold on to a rifle as you did after being back-shot and tumbling down two hundred feet

of cliff and in the process dislocating a shoulder and breaking a leg is probably worth taking a minute or two on. The
only problem is, what the hell we gonna do with you now?"

It was a good question. Up or down, they'd have to find
a way to move to a spot where they could start a fire and
boil some water to clean Rhodes' wound and cook some
food to put in their bellies. Either way, Billy thought dole-
fully as he looked first up and then over the edge of the
small terrace and down the almost impossible slope, was
going to be a chore.

"Rope me down, I'd guess," Hank said, struggling to sit
up. "If we can figure out just where the hell to tie on to
me."

Billy considered the possibilities. "That your mule up
there?"

"You mean it hung around?" Rhodes asked, surprised.
"I'll be damned. Would have figured it'd be halfway home
by now."

"If you got a rope on it, we could haul you up, maybe."

"Oh, I got a rope, all right."

"Well, then—"

"But it ain't no two hundred foot long."

In the end, it took them almost three hours. Billy
climbed up, caught, and hobbled Absalom, the mule, then
slithered back down with Rhodes' saddlebag, bedroll, and
rope. He dulled both edges of the lawman's hideaway knife
in the process of cutting Rhodes' blanket into strips that
they used to bandage his wound and immobilize his shoulder.

Getting the marshal down would have been funny if the
trip hadn't been so painful. The line in his left hand, with
Billy Anthem half-holding and half-carrying him, Rhodes
worked his way twenty feet at a time from tree to tree,
down over three hundred feet of wet rocks, sharp ledges,
slippery pine needles, fallen trees, and every other obstacle
a determined forest and mountain could throw in his path.

By the time they reached the valley, Rhodes was white and trembling with pain and shock, and both men were soaked to the skin, covered with mud, and dead-tired.

And still there was no rest for Billy. He caught his own horse, then made up a pallet for the injured Rhodes. He started a fire, boiled water to wash out the bullet wound, and made a pot of coffee from Rhodes' supplies. And finally, when the lawman was comfortable, Anthem rode six miles back up and around the valley to the log road, found the mule, and led the obstinate animal back to camp. It was nearly dark when he got back, but for once, the sky had remained clear.

Rhodes had slept and was rested, but still in pain whenever he moved. "You see anybody up there?" he asked as Billy slid from his horse. "Any tracks?"

Billy tethered Rosie and Absalom to separate trees, staggered to the fire, and sagged down on a tree trunk. "Not a soul," he said, pouring the last of the coffee. It was a black and evil brew, but he drank it down gratefully before rising to build up the fire and refill the pot from a nearby freshet. "As far as any tracks, it'd take a dozen Comanche trackers working all day and night for a year to figure out anything up there, with that road and all." He snagged Rhodes' saddlebag and opened it. "You got anything else to eat in here?"

There wasn't much. A chunk of corn bread, a half pound of cooked beef, a small wedge of rat cheese, and a mysterious mess of something mashed into an empty peach tin. Billy inspected his find in dismay. "You sure as hell travel light, for a lawman. This is it?"

"I didn't plan on no camping out," Rhodes snapped.

"Apple pie!" Billy exclaimed, scooping a fingerful out of the peach tin. He grinned at Rhodes. "Now, isn't that grand? Hank, you travel light, but in style."

Rhodes scowled back at him. "I guess," he said, not used

to being made fun of, "that bein' from Texas, you never heard of apple pie."

Billy smiled around a mouthful, and his eyes closed in absolute bliss. "Oh, we heard of it, all right," he said, savoring the indescribable sweetness of sugar and cinnamon. "My mother makes the best pies in Davis County."

"Well, I hope mine will do, since your ma ain't nearby."

"Indeed." Billy grinned. "You want some?"

"No. No. You just help yourself," Rhodes said, his voice heavy with sarcasm. "There's a fork somewhere in that saddlebag too, if you can stand to use one."

It was a poor supper for a long, hard day. The night, too, promised to be long, with Rhodes' bedroll having been cut up for bandages. Billy dug a hole in front of the felled cedar, filled it with fire, and installed Rhodes, complete with his blanket, nearby. For himself, he made do by laying a bed of cedar branches and wrapping himself in his ground cloth. It wasn't much, he explained to the lawman, but it beat hell out of being kicked in the head by a mule.

The April night, after the warm sun of the day, rapidly turned cold. Sometime later, the coffee gone except for a half-pot they saved for the next morning, Billy banked the fire and turned in. "You need anything, holler," he told Rhodes.

The lawman coughed and winced in pain as the ends of his broken rib grated together. "I'll make do," he said weakly. "Anthem?"

"Yo."

"Thanks, uh, for what you done. I, uh, well, appreciate it."

Billy chuckled. "Don't thank me too much yet. We got tomorrow to go, don't forget. You reckon you'll be up to riding?"

"Up to?" Rhodes snorted. "Up to! Hell, yes, I'll be up to. What the hell do you take me for?"

"Kind of a cantankerous old fart, I guess," Billy said

with a smile, digging himself deeper into the cedar tips. "You and my pa share the same bark. Back-shot, broke leg, stove-up shoulder and all, I reckon you'd ride through hell. As for me, I'm going to sleep."

Rhodes almost laughed, but the rib wouldn't let him. The leg and shoulder he could live with, but that blasted rib was a damnation. Whoever had back-shot him—and he thought he had a pretty good idea whom to blame—had left him for dead. Rightly so, if Anthem hadn't come along.

Rhodes turned his head to look at the fire. Using an old trick of the mind, thinking about one thing to forget another, he concentrated on the youth across the way.

Billy Anthem had been on the trail a long time, if he had come from Texas. He was a might pale for someone who claimed to be from the Southwest. And Hank had to consider the possibility that Anthem was recently out of prison. At the same time, the youth had given him back his guns, and that same sixth sense Rhodes had picked up being a sheriff and marshal in half a dozen towns along the West Coast for nearly twenty years told him that there wasn't a lawbreaking bone in the young man's body. He'd merely been in the Northwest for a few months. Still, Hank found himself itching to ask and knew he wouldn't sleep until he'd heard it from Billy himself.

"You still awake?"

Half-dozing, Billy jerked awake. "Huh?"

"Gotta know," the marshal said. "You ain't runnin' from the law, are you?"

"Law?" Billy sighed, stared at the stars, the first he'd seen in weeks, high overhead. Unbidden, images of hair as black as night, of soft red lips, and of a name—"Laura . . . Laura . . ."—whispered as sweetly as the wind soughing in the tall trees, dimmed and then blurred the stars. And with that image, overriding it, covering with a black veil, a gravestone he'd visited and viewed only once, that stood alone, alone in the shade of an ancient, sad oak tree.

"Law?" he asked again, his voice as forlorn as the dreams that had hounded and followed him from Texas. "I wish I was."

3

★

Instinct Valley, as Rhodes called it, angled slightly to the northeast and descended in gentle arcs and turns to the Strait of Juan de Fuca, that broad waterway that connected the Pacific Ocean to a veritable inland sea that extended from Tacoma, Washington Territory, in the south, to the fiftieth parallel and beyond to the north.

They rode in silence, William Michael Anthem and Henry Worden Rhodes. Around them, squirrels played in the red and yellow cedar, the yew and alder, and the great stands of Douglas fir. Jays screamed raucously, and once, taken by surprise, an elk thundered down the valley away from them. The sky was cloudless for the second day in a row—a miracle, as far as Billy was concerned. He'd forgotten what it felt like to be dry.

Rhodes had told him little of their destination and what to expect when they arrived. Only that Calamity Bay was run by Noah Creed, who with his three sons controlled the lumbering trade, through it all local shipping, and soon, with the money he was pouring into a pair of mines a few miles to the southwest, a growing coal industry.

Rhodes hadn't said in so many words, but the implication was that Creed was behind the man or men who had bushwhacked him and left him for dead. Billy didn't need

to know the details. He knew enough to make him wary of
Creed and the majority who would bow to lick his boots.

Billy's estimation of Rhodes continued to rise. The lawman wouldn't have been shot if he hadn't had the guts to
stand up to Creed. The story was familiar, and had been
told a thousand times.

Marshal Hank Rhodes kept secret whatever thoughts
were going through his mind. Not simply because he
wanted to keep secrets from his rescuer, but because he
was a private man in the first place, and in pain in the
second. The leg throbbed, but the pain was dull and could
be discounted. The shoulder ached, but was bound tightly
enough that it didn't really bother him. The broken rib,
though, was a different matter, and every step the gray mule
took sent a stab of fire through Hank's side.

Rhodes made it a matter of principle to ignore pain.
He'd taken a .44 slug in the shoulder once. Now he couldn't
even remember the name of the mining town in Colorado,
but he had stayed in the game long enough to kill his first
man and win the day. Two years later, on a long ride and
while asleep in the saddle, Hank had fallen heavily across
the remains of a washstand discarded by some westering
pioneer family when his horse stepped in a ground squirrel
hole and snapped its leg. He darn near broke his back on
that one and had crawled seven miles before he found help.
Another time, with a bullet hole in his arm and an arrow
in his buttock, he'd lain silently and motionless on an ant-
hill until a band of Blackfoot had ridden out of sight. He
could take pain. But Lord almighty, he never ever wanted
another broken rib.

"Where's that lead?" Billy had asked an hour after
they'd started, pointing to a trail that snaked up the western
side of Instinct Valley.

The answer was that it led straight over the hill to Klallam Creek and on to Calamity Bay, but the climb and de-
scent were so precipitous that Hank was loathe to try it in

his condition. "An old gold mine," he'd lied, wincing with the effort. "Dead end. Keep going."

And keep going they had, for almost four hours with but one break, and that to trade mounts because Absalom's gait had become too much for Rhodes to take, and the mare was an easier ride.

The sun was shining high noon when they reached Instinct Bay, a narrow, shallow, inhospitable cove on the shore of the Strait of Juan de Fuca. From there they turned west and, avoiding the rocky, windswept shore of the strait, walked their mounts up the gently sloping bluffs that overlooked Calamity Bay

"You see what I see?"

The speaker was J. D., the only name he went by, a once-upon-a-time sailor and gold-miner who had struck it lucky and had enough sense not to gamble or whore his money away. J. D. had long since retired to spend the last of his days drinking himself into a stupor, whenever and wherever he wanted. For the past year, his poison of choice had been Sophie Barrett's Klallam Kounty Kocktail Klub, as potent a brew as he'd been privileged to savor in many a year. He slept in Sophie's garret, where a bottle was never farther away than an easy fall down a short staircase.

J. D. spent his days, when it wasn't raining, tilted back in a chair on the rickety back porch of Sophie's establishment, watching the water in the bay change color, the gulls swoop and fight, and the ships come and go. Nothing missed his good right eye, and there were those who swore he could see as well out of the painted glass ball he wore in the empty left socket.

Amstel, his drinking partner for the past three months, tilted his chair forward and peered drunkenly in the direction of J. D.'s pointed finger. "Well, blast me," he said, and almost fell out of the chair. "First time I ever seen moose on this coast. Didn't know they lived here."

J. D. whipped off his hat, slapped Amstel up aside the head with it. "Moose, hell," he snorted. "You're drunk, ya old coot. A man can't hold his liquor shouldn't be drinking this time of day."

"Looks like a moose to me," Amstel insisted lamely.

"It is a mule and a horse," J. D. said as if talking to a child. "Hank Rhodes' Absalom, by my guess, only that ain't him on deck."

Amstel squinted down the beach at what still looked like a moose to him. "It ain't, huh?"

"Nope. Appears that Hank's on the mare, and stove up, I believe. Well," he grunted, pushing himself out of the chair and hiking up his trousers, which as usual were in danger of falling. "I reckon maybe I better go find Doc Bannon. Looks like ol' Hank's gonna need him for sure."

J. D. wasn't the only one who had seen the travelers skylined on the bluffs. In his father-in-law's freight office, Jared Krait, Calamity Bay's deputy marshal, peered intently at the pair of riders through a powerful glass set on a tripod.

"Shit!" Krait said, despondently fingering his badge and sagging into a high-backed leather chair. "Damn Hank Rhodes and whoever's with him to hell."

So the marshal had made it home. A fine plate of shoe-leather steak that was. I'll be a goddamn deputy forever if I stay, Krait thought. Why fight it anymore? Better to give in, let his wife have her way, and go to work for her daddy. At least he wouldn't have to risk getting shot at or knifed every Saturday night. Which left just a couple of chores. The first, turning in his badge, would be easy. The thought of the second left his mouth dry and his knees weak. Because Noah Creed, his boss and the man who had promised him the marshal's job when Rhodes was gone, was not a man to take bad news lightly.

Billy couldn't remember a prettier scene. Most small towns in Texas, when seen from a distance, were drab, unpainted affairs stuck in a barren landscape. Calamity Bay was a gem, in contrast. The water of the bay itself was as blue as the sky it reflected, broken by dashes of whitecaps. A half-dozen small sails leaning away from the wind scurried across the water in the direction of a larger ship sitting long and sleek on the windswept surface of the bay. Men scurried like ants in the rigging, hauling in all but one or two smaller sails as the craft quartered across the bay.

The town nestled in a broad valley that was bound by Cameron Bluffs on the east, another, forested ridge on the west, the bay to the north, and a towering rise of mountains behind it to the south. Great sheds and warehouses on the western shore were unpainted, but most of the houses in the town had been given a coat of white that, in the sun and framed by the blue of water and emerald trees, literally glowed.

The bluffs, hard and sharp but a few hundred yards inland, sloped gently nearer the water's edge and, from their crown, gave a panoramic view of Noah Creed's empire. The entrance to the strait was wide. The undeveloped eastern shore run directly south for a quarter-mile, then arced a full mile inland, where it might have been an arrow pointing to the town that lay there. The western shore dipped briefly inland before running northwest to a dead-end cove, then cut back on itself and due north to the strait.

They stopped on the crown of the bluff, sitting easily side by side on their mounts. "Sawmill, warehouses, docks," Rhodes said, pointing with his good left arm to a sprawling complex of unpainted buildings on the western shore. "All Creed's, of course. His mills, coal mines, fishing boats, and ships account for almost all the work in Calamity Bay. If folks don't work for the Creeds, they own businesses that depend on the incomes of them that do. Yep, Captain Noah Creed owns everything and everyone. Creed founded the place. You might say he planted the garden and owns everything that growed."

"Even you?" Billy asked.

The lawman chuckled despite the pain in his rib. "Let's just say it wouldn't be a garden without at least one thorn."

One large building, obviously unfinished, stood at the back of the western cove at the end of a likewise unfinished pier that jutted far out into the water.

"What's that?" Billy asked.

"Coal warehouse and dock. Hell of a market in San Francisco. Costs like sin to ship it there, but the quality makes up the difference in cost. Creed's first fortune was in lumber. He's got another on the way in coal. He'll own half the damned coast by the time he's finished."

"Nice being rich," Billy allowed.

"You might say," the lawman admitted, his lips drawn into a thin, disapproving line. "Trouble is, it costs."

"Oh? Who?"

"Everybody who ain't," Rhodes said shortly. Changing the subject, he nodded in the direction of the town. "Same name as the bay, and same owner. Shopkeepers and well-to-do live there to our left," he said, indicating the sparsely inhabited slopes of Cameron Bluff. "Water Street along the bay, Broadway running down to it. Business section there in the middle, with the workin' stiffs pretty much kept to the west side of Klallam Creek. Usual dives an' whore shops along the water. An' that—"

"Don't tell me," Billy said, his eye following Broadway to its end, where a large white house like some great old frigate rode the crest of a high knoll. "Creed's. The people on the hill."

"You got it." Rhodes hated for folks to see him stove up, but there was nothing to be done about it. "Well, let's get this over with."

"It can't be too soon," Billy replied, short of temper. He sat forward on the McClellan saddle and rubbed his aching buttock.

"I've had about all of this mule that I want to take. The

sooner I clear him out from under my britches, the happier I'll be."

Absalom brayed as if it shared an equally poor opinion of Billy Anthem.

Word spread fast, and by the time Rhodes and Billy had descended the bluffs and were halfway across the broad meadow that ended at the eastern end of Water Street, a half-dozen riders were approaching. These were working-men, loggers and a few dockhands wearing knit hats or caps and dressed in brown Levi's or overalls and plaid coats.

"Hey, Marshal! What the hell?"

"You run into a bear, Hank?"

The questions flew thick and fast. Breathing alone was difficult enough without having to talk, and Rhodes grew visibly weaker with each response. At last, as the ragtag parade turned off Water Street onto Helena Street, Billy took over and waved them away. "You heard the most of it," he told them, riding closer to Hank in case the lawman passed out. "You'll get the details later."

"Who the blazes are you, his nurse?" someone called out.

"The man took a bullet in the ribs," Billy explained. "What he needs is a doctor, not a pack of busybodies yapping at him."

"Busybody, hell!" the same voice gruffly complained.

"Pack it in your saddlebag and tie it down, friend," Billy warned, his temper fraying. "Now, where's that doctor?"

"Doc Bannon's out to Cedar Crest," an old-timer offered. "Can't no way make it back afore tomorrow."

The parade had come to Pine Street. To his left, halfway down the block to Broadway, Billy saw a sign that read WICK'S HOTEL. "Reckon that hotel's the place for him, then," he said, reaching for the mare's halter.

"The hell," Rhodes said, his voice weak but commanding. "Home, dammit. Take me to the jail."

Home was to the right, on the corner of Pine and Mount Olive. The sign over the front door read CALAMITY BAY— MARSHAL, and underneath, in crudely drawn letters, JAIL. A half-dozen willing hands lifted Hank off Billy's horse and carried him inside. Billy took up the rear.

The marshal's office was a good-sized room about ten paces square. The front half was given over to an enormous potbellied stove, a cot, a desk, a bookcase filled with piles of loose paper, a coatrack, and a gunrack. The rear was divided into three cells, each with a bunk, a rickety table, and a chamber pot. Only the middle cell was occupied, and that with a frail-looking, scruffy man who clutched the bars and shook his head. "I told him not to go," the man said to no one in particular. "I told him he was being set up, but he wouldn't listen."

"Shut your murdering mouth," one of the men snarled at the prisoner, and pushed him away from the bars. The rest ignored him.

Hank was carried into his living quarters, a large room connected to the west side of the office, where he was helped into his bed. Everyone helped. A trio of volunteers took the mare and mule to the stable built on the rear of the jail. The animals were given food and water. A boy was sent out for laudanum. An older man built up the fire in the office potbelly and put on water to boil for coffee. Someone else went for food, and returned ten minutes later with a tray laden with bowls of stew and great slabs of freshly baked bread slathered with healthy dollops of butter.

At last, full to the gills, bone-tired, and lightly drugged, Hank chased everyone except Billy out, and fell asleep.

Mount Olive Street began across Water Street from a sprawling building in which were made and warehoused CREED'S CEDAR SHAKES, *Superior Quality*. A half-block before it intersected Pine Street, on the front porch of an unpainted single-story house, Jared Krait kept a nervous

watch on the corner of Pine and Mount Olive. His brow
was furrowed, his look worried. When the last of Rhodes'
visitors disappeared down Pine Street, he rose and, keeping
an eye out for newcomers, walked up the street to the marshal's office and jail, and entered.

"Lookin' for somebody?"

Krait stopped just inside the door. A trailworn stranger
stood in the doorway to Rhodes' private quarters. He was
a string bean and looked as hard as he was tired. A Navy
Colt rode low on his right thigh. His boots were of the
cowboy type and out of character for lumbering country.
They looked as if they'd seen more miles than Klallam
County had trees. "You the feller who found him?"

"That's right."

"The whole town's obliged. I'm Deputy Marshal Jared
Krait."

Billy introduced himself, playing down his part in saving
marshal Rhodes. "Anybody would've done the same," he
said modestly.

"Can I see him?"

Young Anthem shrugged. "I reckon. But that's about all.
He's about done in after a couple of rough days. Taken
laudanum. Maybe you've a mind to come back." He
grinned. "Hell, from what I seen of him, he'll probably be
healed by then and up to a day's work."

Krait laughed weakly. "That's Hank, all right. Tough as
a cedar knot." He paused, and his eyes shifted nervously
away from Billy. "Which makes what I got to do kind of
hard. But I got to."

"Oh?" Billy asked. "What's that?"

Krait opened his coat, fumbled at the badge he wore on
his shirt pocket. "Been mean doings of late. My wife's
heard about Hank. She's been skittish as is. Anyway, she
has laid down the law," he explained, finally managing to
free the badge. He walked hesitantly to the desk and laid
the shiny piece of metal on the edge. "Her an' her folks

been tryin' to get me her daddy's freighting business for some time now, an' what with the marshal bein' shot up an' all, she says the time is ripe fer me to get out a' law work."

Jared craned his neck to look through the door into Rhodes' private room, and caught a glimpse of the sleeping man. Satisfied then, he sidled away from the desk, his back aimed for the door. "Yup. Her daddy has the contract to supply stock to haul coal from the new mine, an'—"

"Noah Creed's, I reckon," Billy interrupted.

"Well, yeah. Who else?"

"Right."

"So you'll, ah,"—his hand fumbled behind him for the door—"ah, tell Hank, huh? I mean, that I'm resignin'?"

"You ashamed to tell him yourself?"

The question was like a slap across the face. "Now wait a minute," Krait bridled. "I didn't say that."

"I did," Billy persisted, his voice cold. He repeated the question. "You ashamed to tell him yourself?"

Krait's eyes met Billy's, but quickly darted away. The Texan had shifted his weight so he lounged against the doorway to Rhodes' quarters. His right arm hung loosely at his side, his hand relaxed except for his little finger, which twitched almost hypnotically.

Krait started to say something, but his throat was dry with fear. The fear angered him. Who the hell did this Billy Anthem think he was to judge a man? What did he know of Noah Creed and the power he wielded? The Creeds would wipe that holier-than-thou look off Anthem's face. And quick too. If Anthem stayed around, the Creeds would break him every bit as fast as they'd broken Jared Krait. And with any luck I'll be there to see it, he thought.

" 'Course I ain't afraid," Jared said at last, regaining his courage. "Just I hate to burden him more, what with him bein' stove up an' all. Well . . ." He opened the door. "See you around, pardner," Krait said, his voice tinged with sarcasm as he closed the door behind him.

Billy relaxed, wondered how a man of Rhodes' ability and character could have chosen a man like Krait. Then again, maybe Krait was the best of the lot.

"Welcome to Calamity Bay," a voice said, breaking the Texan's reverie.

Billy had forgotten the prisoner. His hand near his gun, he spun toward the voice and discovered a dark-skinned, black-haired man staring at him through the bars.

"Ah, ah, ah!" the prisoner said, holding up a drawing tablet as if to ward off violence. "Please! I am the soul of peace. An artist." His eyes twinkling, he stepped back and gave a small, mock bow. "Angelo Goretti at your service, my young friend. A musical name, yes. Not like Krait. Now there *is* a name. Do you know what it means?"

"I reckon you'll tell me," Billy said, walking back to the cell.

"Of course I will tell you," the prisoner exclaimed, waving his finger in admonition. "A krait, my dear young man, is a cobralike poisonous snake indigenous to the jungles of India and sometimes found"—he allowed a dramatic pause—"in the alleys of Calamity Bay."

4

★

The sound of gunfire split the air. Flames from a roaring bonfire lit the dusk as sparks flew skyward. More than twenty men, each with a bottle to call his own, hooped and hollered and danced around the towering flames. They had done it. They had brought in Creed Number One, and they were being rewarded.

Noah Creed and his sons stood in the small cabin built some twenty yards from the mouth of the mine and watched the last light of day fade and the fire brighten. Two days earlier, the first man had emerged from the hole in the face of the mountain with a chunk of the hard black gold. Just that afternoon the last load of rock had been removed and the last timber hammered into place. Now, at the end of the short tunnel, the thick black seam glimmered richly in the light of a single lamp. Tomorrow, Sunday, would be a day of rest as this day, Saturday, had been one of celebration. Monday morning, they would bring out the first carload.

Noah Creed was pleased. He sipped on the sweet Kentucky bourbon that had traveled around the Horn at tremendous cost, and contemplated the riches that would soon flow into his coffers. The road from the Creed Number One to Calamity Bay was almost finished. Two coal ships had been ordered and would arrive by the end of the month. By the first of May, the first shipment would be on the high seas on its way to San Francisco. Creed had every reason to celebrate. So did his sons, Aden, Ebeneezer, and Timothy, for their father's fortune would one day be theirs.

As yet unseen—and in truth, unexpected—Jared Krait guided his horse up the unfinished road. The going was tricky. True, it hadn't rained for two days, but the passage of stock and wagons had made the road muddy and treacherous. At last, weary after the ten-mile ride that required a third as many hours, he broke into the circle of firelight and was greeted by the revelers.

"If it ain't Jared Krait!" a voice hooted.

"Drink up, Deputy," a tall, black-bearded man said, handing him a bottle. "We brung her in!"

"Where's Mr. Creed?" Krait asked, tilting the bottle to his lips for a badly needed drink. He'd need more, he knew, after he told Creed the news.

"In the cabin yonder. Happy as a boy with a new toy, by damn!"

"He won't be for long," Krait muttered, helping himself to another fortifying swig. He handed back the bottle and kneed the black gelding into motion. "Back with you boys shortly. I hope," he added forlornly.

A man needed a great deal of courage to carry bad news to Noah Creed. Jared Krait thought himself a brave man, but not that brave. The job had to be done, though, and he was grateful for the whiskey that warmed his belly and steeled his nerves. And one other thing, he thought, swinging down from the gelding and tying him to the post. It wasn't, after all, his fault that Hank Rhodes was alive.

Billy Anthem was a new man. With Hank Rhodes resting peacefully, he had left the jail and followed Angelo Goretti's directions to Ah Sing's Oriental Baths. He ordered the works, beginning with a shampoo and haircut. Next, Ah

Sing chopped off his beard, wrapped his face in steaming hot towels, lathered him with a thick layer of hot, rich suds, and gave him his first shave in a month.

The most luxurious bath he could remember followed. Billy stripped, surrendered his clothes to Ah Sing's wife for cleaning, and gingerly lowered himself into a steaming tub full of hot soapy water.

For a man who has been on the trail for a month, there are few pleasures to compare to a hot bath. Billy scrubbed himself until he was pink. He wallowed, splashed like a boy, and called for more water. He lay back and felt the dull ache that comes from riding countless miles melt out of his muscles and bones. And at last, arms dangling over the sides, his chin on his chest, he fell dead asleep.

Ah Sing woke him when the town bells rang six o'clock. So relaxed it took him a minute to get his legs under him, Billy dressed in clean clothes. The works had cost him a five-dollar gold piece, but he had no complaints, he decided as he checked himself in the mirror. Boots shined, hat cleaned and blocked, clothes washed and pressed, himself shaved and shorn, with a faint air of cologne for a finishing touch, he felt very much the dandy as he thanked Ah Sing and strolled out into the night.

The look of the men who thronged the streets on Saturday night in Calamity Bay was different than those Billy was used to in Texas, but the difference was only skin-deep. They were hard, proud men, and in search of the same fiery drink, female companionship, and wild release from day's drudgeries that workingmen everywhere seek. Billy Anthem had simpler pleasures in mind.

Following his nose and the aroma of fresh cooking, he headed for Wick's Hotel and a real meal. He chose well. Wick's steak was thick and tender, the potatoes mashed without any lumps, the bread hot out of the oven. The crowder peas had been cooked with a smoked hock and were delicious. The meal was well worth the last of his money.

Hunger is the best seasoning, Billy mused as he strolled back to the jail with a basket of food for the marshal and his prisoner. Many a time the chuck during roundups was often cold and greasy, barely edible were it not for the near starvation after a dozen hours in the saddle. He didn't even like to remember the terrible excuse for food that the Varelas had given him when he was imprisoned in their Mexican stronghold. He frowned, for the memory was linked to the death of his bride-to-be. It took effort, but he forced the painful images from his mind. No doubt about it, he brightened. I might be broke, but I'm living high on the hog. At least for a few days.

Billy's spirits faded quickly when he arrived back at the jail and found Rhodes writhing in agony with a fever. A broken bone was one thing, but he was unsure of how to treat a fever. "Where'll I find that sawbones everybody was talking about?" he asked, walking back to the cells.

"What is the matter?" the diminutive Italian asked, sitting upright on his cot.

"Rhodes is burning up. Where'll—?"

"You won't. Not at this hour if he's up at Cedar Crest. He can't possibly return before noon tomorrow."

"Damn!" Billy slammed his hand against one of the bars, looked around helplessly. "Well, what about somebody else? There another doc in these parts?"

"There was, until he drowned last week," Goretti said. He shrugged. "A shame. Hadn't been here three days, and he fell through a hole on the new coal dock. If you'll let me out of here, though, I'll see what I can do."

"The hell," Billy said. "I'm not lettin' a murderer out."

"And who, my friend," Goretti asked, "said I was a murderer?"

"Seems I heard it mentioned when I brought Rhodes in."

Goretti's laugh took Billy by surprise. "Ah, my gullible

young friend," he said. "You heard. Someone said. Someone also wants everybody in this magnificent city"—he
waved his hand in an almost flowery gesture—"to think I
am a murderer. But I ask you." His eyes glittered with
intent as they bored into Billy's. "Do I look like a murderer?"

Billy had, in truth, never seen anyone quite like the
brash, cocksure Italian. Angelo Goretti looked like a ne'er-
do-well gypsy. Somewhere in his forties, he was as thin as
a reed. His thick, curly hair was jet-black, his eyes as dark
and crinkled with good nature in spite of his predicament.
His skin was a swarthy hue, almost matching that of the
many Mexican nationals who rode for Big John Anthem's
Slash A brand.

"I've seen all kinds of hard cases and some of them a
lot more innocent-looking than you. 'Sides, what do you
know about doctorin', anyway?"

Goretti's smile faded. A brief frown darkened his features as he looked down at his hands, which he clenched
and opened, clenched and opened. "I could tell you things,
Billy Anthem," he said, his voice subdued. "The many men
I have seen die needlessly. The arms and legs I have am-
putated, the bullets I have dug from torn flesh, the fevers
and starvation that I have seen waste away thousands in the
flower of manhood."

The Italian's eyes searched Billy's. "Have you seen so
much death, my friend, that you have grown sick even unto
death?"

"I don't know what you're talking about," Billy said, his
voice hushed by the horror that seemed to have shrunk
Goretti into himself.

"I'm talking about Gettysburg, my friend," Goretti whispered. "I'm talking about the Wilderness Campaign and,
worse, the prison ships where men died like flies."

"Prison ships?" Billy asked, recalling the same horror in
his brother Cole's voice when he recounted the hell of the

ships and the men who died there. "You were in the prison ships in New York? Did you ever meet a Cole Anthem? He's my brother, and he—"

"In?" Goretti's laugh was haunted. "Not as a prisoner, my friend. I was a Yankee. A bluecoat doctor." The corner of his mouth twitched. "Your brother, you say?"

Rhodes was forgotten. Billy's gorge rose, and in that instant he might have killed Goretti, had not the Italian sunk onto his cot and fixed his hands with that same empty stare.

"Think what you will. But there are some of us, not many, but some, who tried. We argued, we pleaded, we begged. We literally got down on our knees and begged." His laugh was hollow. "Oh, we saved a great many. Just as did some of the Confederate doctors who served at Andersonville, the Confederate prison that stank every bit as much of death as the ships. But there was never enough food or medicine, the conditions never more than inhuman. But we did try."

"Is that supposed to make me think you're some kind of a hero?" Billy said, remembering the accounts of sickness and disease, of filth and death Cole had endured.

"Hero?" Goretti asked, his voice a whisper. "Hero? No, my friend. I was not then a hero, I am not now a hero. I am a simple man who threw away the tools of his trade lest they betray me again, and took up a pen and brush instead. I stand before you, an itinerant painter and portraitist, and that is all."

"A portraitist isn't going to help Marshal Rhodes," Billy remarked.

Goretti rose from his cot, threw off his sadness, and patted Billy's hand where it clenched the bars. "Open the door, my dear young man. Open the door. I promise you I will not try to run away."

Billy glanced around as if emerging from a dream. "You know where he keeps the keys?"

Goretti's laugh was once again genuine. "On the peg

there by the desk, my friend. And hurry, eh? A fever is no man's friend."

A springlike breeze wafted the sound of the Baptist church bell striking midnight through the open window. Closer by, from the bars and bordellos along Water Street, came the rowdier, lustier noise of merrymaking, the louder this night for the lack of a marshal.

Back at the jail Billy rubbed the fatigue from his eyes and muttered, "Well?"

"The fever is broken," Goretti said. He removed the cool damp cloth from Hank Rhodes' forehead, dipped it in a basin of water, wrung it out, and lay it on the table next to Rhodes' bed. "A good night's sleep, and he will be himself again, eh?"

Goretti's hands had been sure, his every movement certain. He had removed the makeshift bandages Billy had applied in Instinct Valley, and revealed a red, swollen, and pustulent wound. After washing and heating Billy's knife in the candle, he had wielded it quickly and tenderly.

Rhodes had groaned in his feverish sleep, but the ex-surgeon hadn't hesitated or slowed his pace. The knife had flashed and blood had spilled. The work had been brutal, but the dead and decaying flesh had to be removed and the wound washed out.

That had been over two hours earlier. Now, after a fresh salt compress every fifteen minutes to leach out the poisons, and what seemed like innumerable glasses of fresh water that Rhodes had been forced to drink, and had then as quickly voided into a bucket, the job was done.

"You sure?" Billy asked.

Angelo Goretti's shrug was characteristic. "Nothing is sure, my friend. But I think so, yes. And now we, too, could use some sleep, eh?"

They could, but sleep wasn't something that came easily after such a chore. Tired and lazy, the two men sat in the office with the lamp turned low. Billy poured coffee, and they talked quietly, sipping the dark brew laced with the whiskey they'd found in the bottom drawer of Rhodes' desk.

"What?" Billy said, jerking awake. He had dozed off.

Goretti chuckled. "I said, I think I will be able to sleep now."

The room was warm from the balmy weather and the fire in the potbelly. "Right," Billy said with a yawn, rising and going to the cot. "Me too."

Goretti pushed himself out of his chair. "You going to lock me up?"

Billy found a blanket on a shelf, threw it on the cot. It had a real pillow and he couldn't wait to use it. "You gonna go somewhere if I don't?" he asked, tossing his coat onto a chair.

Goretti appeared to think about it. "Would I get very far?"

Billy's shirt, boots, and trousers followed his coat. "Nope."

"Then I suppose not."

Billy lay down and wrapped the blanket around him. "Far as I'm concerned, then, you can lock yourself up."

And bone-tired, too tired to worry about the dreams that had followed him from Texas to this northwest coast, Billy drifted into a deep sleep and didn't even hear the cell door close.

5

★

Noah Creed was up well before sunrise. He ate a wealthy man's breakfast of freshly boiled coffee, eggs fried in butter, slices of ham, and flapjacks slathered with honey.

The revelry outside the mouth of the mine had gone on into the wee hours. The men had known better than to make much noise once Krait passed the word that Mr. Creed wanted to sleep, though. So they'd drunk quietly and swapped tall tales and lies about their previous lives in Kansas and New Jersey and a dozen other faraway cities and states.

Only one, an orphan boy employed to carry water to the men in the mines, was a native Washingtonian, and he was too young to drink or have had any exciting escapades, so he sat and listened wide-eyed until he fell asleep. He was the only one who was awake to see the Creeds ride out.

Noah Creed was approaching sixty, but was he still man enough to ride the best-blooded horse in Calamity Bay. Trafalgar was a massive black stallion with a white blaze on its forehead. A spirited animal, it allowed only Noah to ride it, and became dangerously vicious if anyone other than the master or Creed's longtime houseboy, Chi Lo, attempted to so much as touch him. It had sired the three horses Creed's sons rode.

Noah and Trafalgar, as was their way, led the small band of riders down the mountain. Next in line rode Aden, Noah's eldest at thirty-three, followed by Eb, at twenty-nine, and Timothy, at twenty-three. Behind them, leading the packhorse that carried the luxuries that Noah Creed insisted on carrying with him, rode Chi Lo. Last in the small procession, Krait stewed over having to ride behind a mere houseboy, and a Chinese at that, but kept his peace. Jared Krait had never been known for his intellectual accomplishments, but he was smart enough not to shoot himself in his own foot. If Noah Creed had told him to walk backward down the mountain, he would have.

Billy Anthem woke to darkness. No lamp glowed inside the jail to lighten the scene. He might have been alone in a universe of his own, had not Rhodes' rasping snores cut the silence.

It was a darkness of a stark loneliness, of the hellish ashes of love, of the depths of a grave, where no light enters, only dreams, cruel dreams.

He relived fragments of the past. Sweet softness first and the taste of Laura's kiss, then the inward war of powerful desires, love's joyousness. Words. Questions. "Marry me?" "Yes, I would love to be Mrs. William Anthem." Now rain, a blinding torrent, Laura and Billy trying to outrace a storm. Suddenly the carriage pitching out of control, bodies flung like rag dolls to the ground. An image of Billy trying desperately to crawl to the torn and broken body of his beloved Laura and breathe life into her. Life where there was none.

Billy groaned. The cot in the marshal's office had left him stiff and cramped after sleeping on the ground for a month. If he'd had any money, and if he hadn't feared leaving Rhodes alone, he would have stayed at Wick's Hotel, and at least had a decent bed.

The day creaked into life like an old wrangler who's

been thrown a dozen times too often and worked too many roundups.

Billy built a fire in the cast-iron stove and boiled coffee, fresh for once, and savory. He paid a visit to the privy and then fed and watered Rosie and Absalom. Breakfast came from Openeer's Dutch Boy Restaurant, where the city fathers kept a tab for the town marshal and his prisoners. Openeer's daughter, a doe-eyed blonde, walked down from the corner of Green and Water. She appeared at the door to the jail with a couple of wooden trays crowded with breakfast plates.

They ate thin, tough steaks, overcooked eggs, and bowls of glutinous porridge sweetened with molasses. The coffee helped weight the meal and send it down to the gut. Billy didn't know what the city fathers paid for such a repast, but it was too much.

Rhodes, tough as sharkskin, as he liked to say, had improved remarkably overnight. His fever had broken, but he was still weak and listless. Goretti was Goretti. Pale and wan, his lungs racked by the morning damp chill, yet ready with a wry comment when Billy took up his tray.

"I'm a lucky man, Billy Anthem," he said, chuckling, and then paused to cough. "Three thousand miles, not counting north and south, to be unjustly charged with the heinous crime of murdering that poor child." He noticed Billy's reaction. "Ah. You hadn't heard the whole charge? Noah Creed's niece. A young maid fresh in the bloom of womanhood. Murdered, yes. But not by me," Goretti added. Then, changing the subject once more, he held up his plate of scraps. "I should like to see the cow that steak was carved from." Goretti opened his cell—he had kept the keys overnight—and followed Billy into the marshal's living quarters.

"Just make sure you lock yourself up before I leave here," Billy warned.

"What's that?" Rhodes said, adjusting his position in the

bed. "Look, son. Your news about Krait weren't hard to take 'cause I figured you'd stay on. Gimme another couple of days, at least," he said, groaning as Angelo stripped off the bandages binding his wound. "Leastways until I can get around on a crutch. Hell, I'll pay you for your trouble. Enough to see you to Seattle, anyway."

Billy hadn't liked what little he'd heard about the Creeds and had no desire to make enemies or get involved in Goretti's problems. But, dammit, Rhodes reminded Billy too much of Big John Anthem to desert him. Both were men of character, decent men without any backdown in them.

"I'll stay, then," the Texan finally said, against his better judgment. "But only for three or four days. Come Wednesday, the latest, you'd best be gettin' around on a crutch or learn to hop like a frog, 'cause I'll be gone."

Rhodes' wound had drained well during the night. Goretti cut off the dying skin with Rhodes' razor, thoroughly cleaned the wound, and rebandaged it. After fashioning new and smoother splints, he removed the old and examined the marshal's broken leg. "Very well done, Billy Anthem," he announced, moving the leg up and down to make sure the bones were joined evenly.

"Great jumping Jehosophat!" Hank roared. His face turned white. Drops of sweat stood out on his forehead and rolled down his cheek to collect in his silvery mustache. "What the hell're you doing?"

"A necessary step, my doughty marshal," Goretti said, elevating the leg on a pillow before resplinting it. "You wouldn't want it to heal crooked, would you?"

"Crooked would beat hell out of bein' tortured half to death," Rhodes allowed.

Goretti laughed. "Ah, they all say that, my friend. And they all thank me in the end."

"You can get your damned hands off my leg, or I'll thank you with the workin' end of my twelve-guage scattergun," Rhodes threatened, gritting his teeth.

"Yes, yes. Of course. Here," Angelo said, showing Billy how to hold the leg. Paying no attention to his patient's fulminations, he began to replace the bandages and splints. "We'll want the swelling to go down first, and then you can be up and about. With a crutch, of course. Then, in six or seven weeks, you'll be as good as—"

A malevolent voice thundered in the front office.

"Where's Goretti? What in Sam Hill is going on here?"

Boots thumped heavily on the wooden flooring; then, a second later, a man who could only be Noah Creed filled the doorway and stepped uninvited into Rhodes' room.

Billy stood back and appraised the patriarch of Calamity Bay as he towered over the bed. Creed looked like the drawing of Abraham in the Anthem family Bible. A huge man, he towered a good six inches over six feet. Long silver hair swept in a mane down to his shoulders, and a fierce beard of the same color covered his neck and hung like a shining scimitar six inches down his chest. He wore a black slouch hat, a black wool frock coat and vest, black trousers of the same material, and knee-high mud-spattered black boots. His complexion was ruddy and his eyes blazed with an explosive combination of indignation and fury.

Behind him, fanning out, stood the three Creed brothers, whom Billy recognized from Goretti's descriptions. Each seemed a distillation of some particular characteristic of his father. Aden, the eldest, was lean, and a good half-foot shorter than his father. He was already balding and his thinning hair was tinged with gray at the temples. Dressed much like his father, with the addition of a holstered Colt .45 riding high on his waist, he held himself aloof and watchful. His were the dangerously predatory eyes of a wolf. He stood as a reflection of his father's intellectual side.

Eb was a hulking specimen, the physical side of his father, dressed in corduroy trousers, a heavy plaid shirt, and a sheepskin vest, the garb of a lumberman. He was broad-faced and homely, and his huge head sat on a short neck that slanted into thick, broad shoulders that were literally wide enough to touch both sides of the door. Everything about him was big. Bulging arms ended in the biggest hands Billy had ever seen. A chest and stomach large enough to fill a shirt big enough for a man and a half were supported by thick thighs that could no doubt match a mule's for strength.

The third son, Timothy, was a mystery, until Billy remembered hearing his father once say, that a strong man is often plagued by weaknesses that he dare not let come to light, and that he takes great care to hide. Timothy was the smallest of the three brothers, dressed like his father but with a frilled shirtfront. He, too, was armed, though with his gun tied farther down his leg. He was a handsome young man, as Billy supposed women would find him. Curly jet-black hair flowed in waves to his shoulders. His eyes were dark and wild, his skin pale, his cheeks and chin sculpted like a statue's.

Billy returned his gaze to Noah Creed. Here was a blunt, strong-willed man who radiated an aura of rigid shadow, as if mirroring some darker aspect of the family's proud achievements.

"And what, might I ask," Noah Creed demanded, pointing at Goretti, "is the meaning of this?"

"Good to see you, Creed," Rhodes said, summoning more strength than Billy had given him credit for having. "Word was you weren't due back until Monday."

"I heard you'd been attacked. I was concerned," Noah said. His burning eyes never left Goretti.

"Concerned, eh?" The marshal propped himself up on his good elbow. "A coincidence, I suppose. See, I was concerned too, Creed." His eyes met Noah's without flinching. "Now, why do you suppose someone would send me a note asking to meet me at Hemlock Camp and then bushwhack me along the way?"

Creed bridled. "If that, sir, is an insinuation, I resent it. As much," he added, returning to Goretti, "as your laxity with this murdering son of a bitch."

"He's my prisoner, Creed. I'll handle him as I see fit. Don't worry, he won't run. Especially," he added with a touch of sarcasm as he indicated Creed's sons, "with the hounds on hand to track him down."

Unperturbed, Goretti tied the final knot on the bandages holding the splints in place and stepped away from Rhodes. "That should do it, Marshal. You'll want to readjust them every eight hours until the swelling is gone. As much as you can, keep the leg elevated until then."

"Thanks," Rhodes told him, and then, stroking his mustache, the town marshall looked at Creed. "Amazing how hard it is to find good help, ain't it, Mr. Creed? You take that feller that bushwhacked me, now." He shook his head sadly. "Seems like the kind of job a man ought to have done right the first time."

"Perhaps he did," Aden Creed interjected in a smooth, level voice. "Perhaps your assailant didn't mean to kill you, Marshal. Perhaps he was a citizen tired of your procrastination, your protection of a woman-killer. Maybe it was meant as a warning, from your friends in town."

Rhodes wasn't fazed. "A woman-killer? Goretti?" He chuckled. "Well, that's for a court of law to decide. He gets trial by jury. Until then, he's just a man innocent as me. Or you, Mr. Creed."

"An unbecoming attitude, Marshal," Aden said. He sounded like a barrister. "My cousin was found raped and murdered. Articles of her clothing were found in a trunk in Goretti's room, and blood on some of his clothes. We have learned that she had been seen sneaking up to the man's hotel room, and they were also seen unchaperoned in the woods, where the bastard was purportedly giving her 'art' lessons."

"A closed case, then, in your lights," Rhodes observed blandly.

"Dammit, man," Timothy said. "We ought to string him up here and now."

Aden silenced his younger brother with a wave of his hand. "The man can't say where he was the night of the murder. He has no alibi. He is guilty as hell, and you know it!"

"That may be," the marshal said, tired of the game. "Tell you what. Soon as a jury agrees, you'll have your hangin'. That good enough for you?"

"The bastard doesn't deserve a trial." Pale, his voice shaking, Timothy took two steps and grabbed Goretti by the arm. "Hang him, I say, and be done with it."

Rhodes' good hand dipped beneath his blanket and a second later reappeared with his Colt revolver, which he held rock-steady on Timothy. "Let him go, Creed," he ordered, his voice steel.

Aden Creed, when Rhodes' gun appeared, flipped back his coat for faster access to his gun. In the same instant, Billy, to Rhodes' left and nearest to Aden, pivoted so he faced him. His hand, the little finger twitching slowly, ominously, hovered near his own weapon. "Don't," he said quietly. "Don't even touch it."

For a moment, all eyes focused on him, the stranger in the room who had gone unnoticed until now. His body was coiled tight, poised to strike. If there was gunplay in such a closed space, a lot of men were going to die.

Timothy released Goretti's arm and stepped carefully back. At the same time his father drew himself to his full height and moved between Aden and Billy. "I won't let you or any other man draw a weapon on my son," Noah said coldly

"You own most everything around here, but not this jail, Mr. Creed. Now, thanks for your . . . concern. Maybe you better take your sons and go," Rhodes drawled. He acknowledged Billy's gesture with a nod and lowered his gun to the sweat-stained bedding. "Goretti is my prisoner. He's under my protection."

Noah Creed's face was white with fury. "I assume, then, sir, that you will lead your prisoner back to his cell."

"No, my deputy will."

"Ha!" Creed snorted. "You forget, Marshal. Your deputy resigned yesterday."

"News travels quick, don't it?" Rhodes chuckled. "Where'd you leave Jared, outside watching the horses like a good lackey?"

"Jared Krait is of no importance."

"Looks like nobody is, to you," Billy said, unable to curb his tongue.

Creed refused the bait. "This prisoner is important to me. His hands are red with the blood of my family." Noah's features grew flushed; he paused to bring himself under control. "May I suggest, Marshal, that since you are unable to discharge your duties, you swear in my son, Ebeneezer. He has had, you might know, some experience in the law."

Rhodes glanced beyond Noah Creed to his son Eb. Strangely enough, he would have made a good deputy under different conditions, for he was as loyal as he was powerful—the problem being that his loyalty was first to his father. "Got no problem with Eb," Hank said, careful not to give offense. "He's a good man. But I already got a deputy."

"Oh?" Noah sneered. "Who?"

"Why, Billy Anthem, here," the lawman replied, nodding in the young Texan's direction.

Billy was as surprised as the Creeds, and too stunned to speak.

Noah Creed recovered quickly, gave Billy a withering look. "He's a stranger."

"So was I, when you hired me," Rhodes pointed out.

"More's the pity," Aden muttered.

" 'Sides, he saved my life. And knows how to handle himself. And he was a deputy sheriff down in Texas, in, ah, what'd you say the name of that town was, Billy?"

"Ah, Luminaria," Anthem blurted out, naming the family ranch when nothing else came to mind. He tried to display more confidence than he felt.

"Right. Luminaria. A rough cattle town, as I hear," Rhodes lied. "He ain't got nothing to lose whether Goretti goes free or hangs."

Nothing to lose but my life, Billy thought, considering the array of firepower the Creeds could bring against him.

"I don't like this, Rhodes," Noah warned.

Rhodes lay his head back, closed his eyes. "Didn't hire on to please you, Mr. Creed," he said tiredly. "Deputy? Escort the prisoner to his cell, eh? And dammit, pin that badge on like I told you, hear?"

"Yes, sir," Billy said, quickly moving to Goretti's side. Might as well play the bluff out, he figured. Gunplay with the Creeds held as much appeal as smallpox. Now, Brother Cole, he liked nothing better than riding into trouble. He was a bounty-hunter, and gunplay was his meat. Billy liked to think of himself as peaceable. And there was nothing more fun than running a bluff, unless you got called.

For once, the Creeds had nothing to say. Silent, they stood aside and watched Billy escort Goretti out of Rhodes' private quarters. Seconds later, as if energized by the sound of the cell door slamming shut, they turned as one and, with Noah Creed leading the way, stomped out. Timothy was the last to leave; he turned in the doorway, pointed at Anthem, and mimed a gun being fired. He blew imaginary smoke from his fingertip.

"You find that badge, bring it back when you come," Rhodes called weakly from his bed.

Krait's badge was lying where he'd left it on the desk. Not at all sure why he was obeying, Billy picked it up and carried it to the marshal's bed. For such a little piece of tin, it felt heavy in his hand. "It was fun for a while," he said, dropping it on the bed, "but I won't wear this, you know."

"Why not?" Rhodes asked, feeling for the badge with his fingers and picking it up. "You got anything better to do?"

"Yeah. Live, to begin with."

"Hah!" Rhodes winced, caught his breath. "You're doing that. But lookee here, everybody's got to die sometime."

"Not tomorrow," Billy said. "Not me."

Rhodes shrugged. "Creeds're like most others. Ninety percent bluff. You bluff 'em back, they fold."

Billy pulled up a chair, straddled it next to the bed. "Poker, huh. You know what? I'll bet you draw to inside straights."

"Sometimes. When I got the feelin'. You gotta help, Billy Anthem from Texas. Creed owns everyone else, one way or other. A man like you can't tuck tail an' run. It ain't in your possibles." He cocked his head to one side, eyebrows arched, fixed on Billy, and held out the badge. "Well, you gonna pin it on, or do I have to do it for you?"

Billy sat motionless for a moment. He'd been running in the darkness for more than a year. Maybe it was time to stand in the light for a while. He took the badge, gave it a quick polish on his shirt sleeve, and pinned it on. "Well, Hank," he said, "looks like you drew to another straight."

"Ace high, boy," the marshal replied wearily. "And I expect you to live up to it."

Live up to it. Words Big John Anthem might have said.

The marshal's eyes had closed and his chest rose and fell gently. Quietly, Billy Anthem rose and walked to the door, hesitated briefly, and then said softly, "I will."

Creed Manor perched majestically on Creed's Knob and overlooked Calamity Bay. The view from the front-parlor windows was serene, a sleepy town on this Sunday afternoon, nestled in the hollows of the mountains. Smoke curled lazily from chimneys. The laughter of children occasionally floated on the sea breeze that blew across the sparkling blue waters of the bay. It was a day of worship for those so inclined, a day of rest for the others, before they returned to yet another week of hard, productive labor for Noah Creed. On Sunday, peace reigned in the valley.

But not in that fabled front parlor where Noah Creed sat as one enthroned, surrounded by luxuries unknown to most of Calamity Bay's good citizens.

The grim quartet, Noah and his sons, had ridden single-file down Pine Street and turned south on Broadway. A stately procession, with Krait dismissed and Chi Lo bringing up the rear, they had ascended Creed Knob, dismounted, and handed over their mounts to Chi, who led them to the stables in the rear of the house.

Noah, Aden, Eb, and Timothy—in that order, as always—ascended the wide front steps, crossed the open veranda, and entered the foyer. As one, they removed their coats and hung them on the hall tree. In line again, they trooped into the front parlor just as the Seth Thomas on the mantel struck eleven of the morning.

And then, with the mellow sound of the chimes fading, Noah whirled and struck Timothy with a backhanded blow across his face.

Timothy reeled backward, striking his head against the edge of the open door. "Hey!" he exclaimed. His jaw numb, the back of his head exploding in pain, he stared uncomprehendingly at his father. A trickle of blood formed at the corner of his mouth. "Wha—?"

"Idiot! Dolt! Incompetent ass!" Noah thundered, advancing on his son. The old man's cheeks turned a mottled red above his silver beard.

"What'd I do?" Timothy asked, cringing before the enraged patriarch.

Noah Creed picked up his son by his lapels, turned, and pinned him against the Wall. "You saw him as well as I did."

"Who?" Timothy pleaded. "Who?"

"Rhodes, damn your incompetent soul to hell." Noah dropped Timothy, turned, and strode to the window overlooking the town. "Rhodes. Lying there in that damned bed of his."

"Don't blame me," Timothy blustered. "Bushwhacking the marshal was Aden's idea. Not mine."

"Fool!" Noah spat, not bothering to turn to face his son.

It was always his fault. No matter what he did, it was his fault. Near tears, Timothy approached his father. "But what'd I do wrong, Pa?" he begged. "You told me to go on and shoot him. You said so yourself, so I did."

"And missed!" Noah thundered.

"Missed, hell! You seen him yourself, all stove up so he can't even walk to the privy by himself. What more do you want?"

"I wanted the marshal's office," the patriarch said, his voice dropping, now ominously low. Noah's reflection filled the window and covered the town below in the transparent image of himself. "I wanted Hank Rhodes dead."

6

★

It was unnatural for a woman as pretty as Penelope Swain to remain a spinster at the ripe old age of twenty-five. She had arrived in Calamity Bay three years earlier, in 1873. In her possession were a purse in which she carried her last twenty dollars, a single trunk filled with clothes, one certificate that said she had completed a course of instruction at a Mrs. Howlitzer's School for Girls in Boston, and another that attested to three years as a teacher in the small town of Milford, Connecticut. Her credentials as good as gold as far as the town fathers were concerned, she had been hired immediately to take the place of Mildred Smithwood, one of Calamity Bay's two teachers, who had gotten married and pregnant, which of course immediately disqualified her for the post.

The town fathers had reason to be pleased with Penelope Swain. Her appearance was immaculate. Her morals were beyond question: she attended the Congregational church and served diligently on its Women's Auxiliary Missionary Board. She neither drank spirits nor associated with unruly or questionable men. She ruled her classes with a gentle hand, but was not above applying the switch to her charges when necessary. She had quickly won the trust of the townspeople. Storekeepers' and millworkers' wives alike were pleased to send their children to her for learning.

Penelope was blessed with a warm smile and a musical laugh. Folks considered her friendly and outgoing. Her ash-blonde hair hung far down her back when not rolled in a more modest bun. Her eyes were as blue as Calamity Bay on a sunny afternoon. Some said her jaw was too square and her skin too ruddy for a true beauty, but beauty was hardly a consideration in a land of few unattached women, so it was no surprise that she was considered a prize catch and had been courted by almost every eligible bachelor in town.

For a spinster teacher to carry a basket lunch to the jail might have been considered unseemly in the East. Not in the wilder, less-tamed far Northwest, especially when the marshal was also single and every busybody in town had been trying for the past two years to marry him off. And so it came to pass, on that Sunday, in consideration of Hank Rhodes' injuries and the members' concern for his well-being, the Congregationalist church voted to send him a basket lunch. Penelope, upon due election by the Women's Auxiliary Missionary Board, had been commissioned to de-liver it.

Billy Anthem was sitting at the desk and leafing through Hank's log and the last six months' arrest reports in an effort to get a handle on his new job when the door opened behind him. "Help you?" he asked, swiveling his chair and stopping, wide-eyed, at the woman who stood in the door-way.

"You are the new deputy, I presume?"

"Yes, ma'am," Billy said, bounding to his feet. "Some-thing I, ah, can do to help you, ma'am?"

"The Congregationalist church heard about Marshal Rhodes' injuries and sends its regards." She held out the basket. "And dinner."

She was dressed in black from a small round hat to the tips of her shoes, whose toes peeked out from under her full skirt when she walked toward him. Sunlight streamed in through the doorway and framed her in its golden rays.

Billy held out the arrest ledger to her before he remembered he was holding it. "Sorry," he said, quickly replacing it on the desk before reaching for the basket. "It's mighty nice of you."

"Penny!"

"Hello, Angelo," Penelope said, leaving Billy and going to the cell where the Italian was held. She stopped, touched his hand where it clenched a bar. When she spoke, her voice seemed lower . . . and richer. "How are you?"

"As of this moment, I think I will survive. And you, my dear? What a delight to see you."

Billy wasn't sure what to make of this. The woman had said she had come to see Marshal Rhodes, but was treating his prisoner like a long-lost friend. He set the basket on the desk, peeked into Hank's room to see if he was awake.

"I was worried about you, Angelo. I'm relieved to see you are still here, and in good health." A frown clouded her face as she turned to Billy. "Do you really believe this gentleman is guilty of murder?"

"I don't believe anything, Miss, ah . . ." Billy said, a bit put out by her attack. "But like the marshal says, he's the only suspect we have. And he won't even tell us where he was the night of the killing . . ." Billy paused realizing he didn't need to defend himself just for doing his job.

"Ah, forgive my manners, Billy," Goretti broke in, interrupting an uncomfortable situation. "If I may? Miss Penelope Swain, may I introduce Mr. Billy Anthem. Mr. Anthem, Miss Swain."

Billy tipped his hat. "My pleasure, Miss Swain."

"Good morning," came the response in a cold and formal voice.

"Ah, Penny," Goretti chided. "None of that, my dear. He is a friend, and has already rescued me from the clutches of our dear friends the Creeds. So be a good girl and give him a smile."

She glanced at Goretti, then the frown melted into a smile that lit the room. "Forgive me, please, Mr. Anthem," she said in the same honeyed voice she had used to greet Angelo. She held out one tiny gloved hand.

Billy gingerly took her hand. "Billy, to my friends," he said.

"And Penny to mine," Penelope said, allowing only a fleeting touch.

"She instructs the heathen youth of Calamity Bay," Goretti offered. "And she allows them no sloth."

"In that case, I'll be sure to watch my Ps and Qs," Billy said, grinning widely.

"You better," came the voice of Hank Rhodes from his private room, "or she'll take a switch to your britches. Is that pretty gal gonna stand around out there yackin' forever, or come in an' say hello to a poor ol' shot-up marshal?"

That poor ol' shot-up marshal was healing remarkably fast, Billy thought, amazed by the man's progress. Obviously pleased to see Penny, he was in a jovial mood. Penny piled pillows behind him and hiked him into a sitting position while Billy moved the table to the side of his bed.

"I'm hungry as a bear in springtime," Rhodes announced, keenly eyeing the basket as Penny opened it. "Haven't et—"

"Eaten," Penny corrected with a laugh.

"Et," Rhodes pointedly said, "in must be . . . years." He chuckled at his own wit.

His eyes positively twinkled as Penny removed a pumpkin pie and a platter of fried chicken from the basket. She brought out a bowl of steamed rice, another of cooked carrots glazed with butter and honey, and a tureen full of giblet gravy. Fresh-baked rolls with butter to spare completed the meal.

Rhodes groaned in anticipation. "Better let Angelo out

of his cell. It'd be a shame to put any of these fixin's behind bars." Billy nodded, left the room, and returned a minute later with Goretti. The artist bowed to Penny and then took a place at the table. Billy returned to his seat and helped himself to the splendid repast.

"You did pretty good for a one-armed man," Billy dryly observed as the marshal wiped his plate with a morsel of bread and plopped it in his mouth.

"It has been my privilige to observe," Rhodes said, pausing a moment to chew and swallow, "that Congregationalists beat the Methodists and Presbyterians, both, every time, when it comes to cookin'."

"If you aren't careful, you'll add bloat to all your other ills." Billy laughed. "Then we'll have to put you down for sure." He cocked his head to one side and looked at the schoolmarm. Billy caught her studying him. She blushed and looked away.

Billy sighed and leaned back in his chair. There were worse things than being Rhodes' deputy. And much worse than watching the schoolteacher move fluidly around the room as she cleaned up and repacked the bowls and plates in the basket.

"And so what *are* you going to do about the Creeds?"

Penny's questions brought Billy wide awake, and he listened tensely for the answer.

Rhodes shrugged his good shoulder. "That's what I hired Billy here for," he said, half-asleep himself. "Keep an eye out till Judge Robbins rides through. Keep a lynch rope from findin' its way 'round Angelo's neck. You ain't no killer, Angelo. Trouble is, you ain't much of a talker either. All this secret stuff about havin' an alibi but not tellin' what it is ain't gonna cut it in court. So you better find your tongue, my friend."

A plate crashed to the floor, and the men at the table jumped in spite of themselves. "Stupid of me," Penelope muttered, and stooped to pick up the pieces. By the time she finished Hank had settled in for a nap and Billy had returned Goretti to his cell.

"It's been a pleasure," he said, escorting Penny to the door. "Be obliged if you'd thank the good women for us."

"I will." Her brow furrowed, she lightly touched Billy's arm. "Take care of them, Billy Anthem," she said, worried. "They're good men. Calamity Bay needs both of them. Noah Creed is accustomed to having his own way. His sons, too. They want Angelo to pay for a crime he didn't commit."

"I hope your trust isn't misplaced, ma'am."

"I trust you, Billy, to do what's right," Penelope said. "Be careful. The Creeds can push hard."

"Don't worry. We Texas Anthems are born stubborn. We don't have much give in us."

"That can be dangerous." Her eyes flashed as she gave him her hand. There was a hardness in his voice that belied his youthful years and caused her to reappraise Rhodes' new deputy. "And now goodbye. Until the next time?" Her lips parted a moment. Billy was tempted to kiss her but managed to control himself. The front door of the town marshal's office was neither the proper time nor the place.

"Hasta la vista," Billy said, in the Spanish that he spoke nearly as well as his native English. *"Vaya con Dios."*

Penny turned and started down the street.

Intrigued, Billy watched her leave. Seldom had he known a woman quite like Penelope Swain. On the surface, she was prim and spinsterly, as could be expected from a schoolmarm. But underneath, she brimmed with laughter and a rare good humor. She was bubbly and bright, a playful coquette.

"Miss Swain!"

A half-dozen steps away, Penelope paused and turned. "Yes, Mr. Anthem?"

"I'd, ah . . ." What was he doing? He hadn't so much as

looked at another woman since Laura had died. And yet, as if driven, he heard himself say the fateful words. "I'd be proud to escort you home, if you don't mind."

Her smile put the noon-day sun to shame. "Why, I'd be delighted, Billy," she said, waiting for him while he caught up with her.

Penelope lived next door to the school, only three blocks away on Helena Street. They strolled slowly, Billy carrying the empty lunch basket, and paused on the bridge over Klallam Creek for a moment to peer down at the sun-dappled waters.

"The Pacific Ocean really is something," Billy said. "We don't have a pond anywhere as big in Texas."

"And I thought everything in Texas was bigger," Penny teased.

"Most everything, for sure," Billy said, mock seriously. "You take grasshoppers, for example. Why, you couldn't hardly use them for bait, they're so big."

"Oh?"

"That's right. In fact, we rope the biggest ones, saddle break them, and keep the cutters for roundup. Nothing beats riding a grasshopper in rough brush. Of course, even the real tame ones are a might, uh, jumpy."

Penny's laughter was rich and full; she laughed with her whole body. Light at heart, she took Billy's arm as they started down the street again. She had met many men since she'd left the segregated halls of Mrs. Howlitzer's School for Girls, but none quite like this dashing young cowboy from Texas.

As for Billy, he was somewhat confused. A single woman in Texas who acted as freely as Penny risked being considered a loose woman, one to be shunned by decent people. And yet he felt in his bones that Penny's easy camaraderie with men was completely natural and unstained.

How she got away with it was a mystery to him. Perhaps because she was so open and frank. Perhaps because she was so free with her friendship and yet so guarded with her favors that no one could take her behavior amiss. In any case, it was obvious that everyone, including the women they met on the street, liked her and held her in high regard. Certainly Hank was smitten with her, whether he admitted it or not. And Angelo Goretti too. And Billy couldn't help but wonder about the artist and the schoolmarm. There had been something special between them. Nothing in the open, just an occasional glance during her visit that spoke more than words.

"Our school," Penny announced as they turned off Hemlock onto Helena Street. "Would you like to see it?"

"If you'd like to show it to me," Billy said.

He had no tales to tell about the size of Texas schools because most he'd seen were pitifully small, usually only one room. Calamity Bay's was a palace in comparison. Built from finished lumber delivered from Creed sawmills, the whitewashed structure boasted two large rooms, each with its own potbellied wood stove, slate, and rows of desks that attested to the large number of children taught there, virtually all of them the offspring of men who worked for Noah Creed.

"This is my room," Penny said, leading him through the door. "First through fourth, more or less. Mr. Breen teaches the older children through the eighth. Some beyond, if their parents will let them. But that's rare."

A schoolroom was a schoolroom, as far as Billy was concerned. The usual alphabet, in large and small letters, was strung across the top of the slate. Potted plants graced the two windows. Here were the usual maps, a pile of primers, and on the inside wall, a line of drawings, all of various aspects of Calamity Bay, all the work of young artists.

"My favorite subject," Billy said, crossing to inspect the drawings. "I always wished I could have learned proper. But such things weren't looked upon highly back at my father's ranch. Nothin' wrong with that, I suppose, but I always did wish there was more time for drawing and some for learning how to paint as well."

"Are you a painter?" the schoolteacher asked, surprised, then glimpsed, but just for a second, a mature sensitivity behind his boyish charm. "I never would have thought . . ."

"Neither'd anyone else. An Anthem was supposed to learn his reading, writing, and ciphering so he could keep books and count cattle and profits . . ." He trailed off, gazed wistfully at a drawing of a bark, cutting through Calamity Bay.

"You ever see a herd of antelope grazing on an open plain?" he asked softly. "Or the desert mountains at sundown, all gold at first, then turning blood crimson, then purple?"

"No," Penny whispered, entranced.

Images of home flooded Billy's mind. "Hell, there's even a kind of magic in a bunch of drovers taking that last cup of coffee around a fire at night after the herd's been bedded down, each man lost in his own private memories. I'd like to paint that, someday."

"Maybe you will."

Billy jerked as if awakened from a dream. "Huh? Oh, yeah," he said, embarrassed at having shown a side of himself he'd kept carefully hidden for years. He stepped back to look at the row of drawings. "Lucky bunch of kids, you teaching them color and composition and all."

"Me?" Penny laughed. "Heavens, I can't draw a stick, much less anything like those. Mr. Goretti is kind enough to give the children a few hours once a week." It was her turn to frown. "Damn Noah Creed anyway," she snapped.

Billy's eyebrows rose. She had shown another side of herself as well.

"I'm sorry. I don't talk that way in public, but it's true. Angelo is innocent. Anyone with an ounce of sense knows the man is incapable of murder."

"You're sure of that?" Billy asked.

"Of course." Unladylike, her creamy white ankles showing beneath her skirts, she perched on the edge of her desk. "He was a doctor, you know, during the war."

"He told me." Billy tried not to stare, but my-oh-my she had lovely skin.

"And the children were quite taken with him. No," she corrected herself. "Loved him. He was amazing with them, even the toughest of the tough. Surely such a man couldn't be a murderer."

"What about you?" he asked. "Are you taken with him, too?"

Penelope blushed. "Perhaps a little. Angelo can be a charming man." She toughened rapidly. "But I know—I *know* that he is innocent."

"Know, huh?" Billy said, probing.

The schoolteacher jumped down from her desk, strode toward the door. "You heard me, Mr. Anthem," she snapped.

Curious, Billy followed her outside. She was embarrassed about something and keeping back information he needed if he were to do his job well. "Sure would help if I knew just why you're so certain," he suggested, hurrying to keep up with her.

"My house," Penny said, ignoring his hint as she turned up the walk leading to the house next door. She stopped at the bottom of the steps, took the basket from him. "Thank you for walking me home, Mr. Anthem. It has been a pleasure meeting you."

"I guess I've overstayed my welcome," Billy unhappily observed. Her rapid change of mood puzzled him, but it was also a challenge. "I won't be in town that long. Be kind of nice to maybe see you again before I leave."

Her voice was coldly formal. "If you are lonely, sir, I am told there are plenty of available women along Water Street."

'I didn't say I wanted to bed you," Billy said calmly. "I

asked if I could see you again." He grinned. "Didn't reckon that'd be cause for gettin' my head snapped off."

Penelope paused, her anger melting like spring snow upon the slopes of Hurricane Ridge. "I'm afraid I need to apologize again," she said, giving him her hand. Once more, her smile was warm. "And mean it this time. Will you forgive me?"

Billy wished she hadn't put her gloves back on. "Consider it done."

"Please, help Angelo if you can." She dropped his hand and stepped onto her porch.

"Still didn't get an answer," Billy persisted to her back.

The schoolteacher's eyes flashed with amusement when she turned to face him. Sunlight in her hair gave it the look of wild heather. "Are all the Anthems so persistent?"

"It's a necessary quality when you're trying to ranch on land that's claimed by the Apache, the Comanche, and Lord knows how many bandits," Billy replied, a mischievous light in his eyes.

"My heavens," Penny said. "Well, you'll find no Apache or Comanche around here. As for the bandits . . ." Her gaze drifted to the house on Creed's Knob. Then she nodded. "Perhaps we should see each other again. I'll try not to be rude, not even once." She stepped inside her cottage and closed the door.

Billy swept the hat from his head, slapped his leg, and just managed to keep from whooping out loud. As he started back toward Klallam Creek, the day seemed brighter and the air fresher than it had in months.

7

★

Eudora Creed Crenshaw had almost everything she wanted. Thanks to her brother, Noah Creed, she lived in the most beautiful house in Washington Territory, not counting two or three in Seattle and Tacoma. Her rooms were warm and dry in the damp, bitter cold of winter, refreshingly cool during the heat of summer. She dressed impeccably in the latest fashions to reach San Francisco, but six days by sea to the south. She lived well, dined well on fare only dreamed about by the common folk of Calamity Bay. She did not, it is true, have a man, but she had grown to accept her widowhood these past eight years. Thoughts of marrying again seldom entered her mind, and even those occasional flights of fancy had ceased with the death of Melinda.

Now, the one thing Eudora wanted above all else was vengeance. It had become the great burning desire of her heart, and she was frustrated by Noah's unwillingness to do what was in his power: hang Angelo Goretti, her daughter's murderer.

Eudora's world had become a hostile, hateful place in the week since Melinda's death. The one light of her life had been cruelly snuffed out. And it had changed her. The darkness in her soul seemed to emanate from her as she performed the simplest tasks.

Checking the dinner table to make sure all was in order, she looked an entirely different person than she had a week earlier. A week ago, Eudora had borne her fifty years with regal grace.

Now she appeared haggard and worn, a mere shell of her former self. Streaks of silver were suddenly noticeable in her uncustomarily unkempt hair. Her once sharp and domineering facial features appeared to have sagged, and the lines deepened. Her granite-gray eyes, which once imposed her will on one and all, were one minute dull and lackluster, the next bright with hatred and a burning anger.

The Seth Thomas in the parlor chimed. On the final stroke, the sixth, the kitchen door opened silently and Chi Lo entered and bowed deferentially. Eudora looked up from the table. Her gaze never quite focused on the servant. Chi Lo had the uncomfortable feeling she was staring through him.

"Very well, Chi Lo," she said dully, and proceeded around the table to stand behind her chair.

Chi Lo, moving with catlike quickness, turned and disappeared into the kitchen. A moment later, a series of bells chimed through the house, one each in Noah's and his sons' rooms. The bells were followed, as always, by the clatter of footsteps upstairs and on the stairway. In due course, the double doors that led from hall to dining room swung open, and Noah, Aden, Ebeneezer, and Timothy filed in and took their places at table.

Sunday dinner at Creed Manor was a formal affair. Noah sat at the head of the table in the great, sculpted chair that had come from an English castle. Eudora faced him as matriarch in the place of his long dead wife, Cassandra. To his right, in the place of honor, Aden alone, and on Noah's left, Ebeneezer and Timothy. Eudora wore black widow's weeds. The men were dressed formally in black frock coats, vests, white shirts, black ties, and polished black boots.

His head erect, as if posed for a sculptor, Noah waited

while Chi Lo and Mrs. Amandus, the cook, took their places at the kitchen door. "Let us pray," he finally intoned when the silence was to his liking. Seven heads bowed as one.

"Heavenly Father, we thank Thee for Thy bounty. You have given us a special place in this world. We strive to prove ourselves worthy. Bless our efforts that we may prevail against the wicked. In Thy name we ask this. Amen."

And everyone answered, "Amen."

The dining room glowed from the light of a coal-oil chandelier festooned with crystal teardrops. Three candelabra graced the table, around each a dried arrangement of sea grasses and pinecones.

The Waterford crystal stemware glistened, the Oneida silver, both flatware and service, glowed with the soft luster of long use. The china was from China, bone white and translucent, with thick green trim bordered with gold leaf. Only in San Francisco, it was said, could a more elegantly set table be found on the whole of the West Coast of America.

The menu, only slightly altered, might have been taken from the mighty Baldwin Hotel in San Francisco, where Noah stayed when he traveled there.

Chi Lo served. They began with a light soup and sherry, after which appeared fresh salmon and a sauterne. The roast was of boned lamb with mint sauce, accompanied by tiny potatoes in a cream sauce, and tips of asparagus imported from San Francisco. To clear the palate, there were sliced pears.

Noah had long since decreed that dinner was not the time for business talk. The conversation revolved around more genteel subjects. They discussed the news of the territory and the nation at large as learned from the San Francisco papers that the Creed ships delivered. They chatted about friends and acquaintances in San Francisco whom they occassionally read about.

They dissected the politics and social comings-and-goings, such as they were, of Calamity Bay itself. And for the second week in a row, at Eudora's insistence and against Noah's will, they had discussed Melinda's murder.

Tonight, she was furious about the news she had heard through the grapevine that ran from Jared Krait to his wife to Francine Wolf, a seamstress, to Mabel Andover, Eudora's hairdresser, and to Eudora herself: Angelo Goretti had been permitted out of his cell.

"And to imagine that you saw him yourself, Noah, and allowed him to remain at large," she huffed. "And alive."

"With Doc Bannon out of town," Noah replied, barely restraining his anger, "someone had to treat the marshal."

Aden stepped in to cool down what threatened to be an awkward situation. "Everything was well under control, Aunt Eudora. The man couldn't have escaped."

"Ha!" Timothy interjected. "The way Rhodes operates that jail, I'm surprised he didn't send the damned guinea out for supper. All the way to Port Angeles, maybe."

"Fat chance, with you holding a gun on him," Eb grumbled, slyly poking fun at Timothy for backing down from the new deputy so fast. "You sure had 'em treed, Tim."

"At least someone in this family seems to care." Eudora smiled at Timothy. "Others, I fear, could not care less."

Noah stabbed a piece of lamb. "I would prefer," he snapped, popping the morsel into his mouth, "that you place your confidence in one who has yet to fail you."

Eudora bristled. "I have placed my confidence in you for nine days, Noah, to no avail. Might I remind you that my daughter, your own niece, was heinously, brutally assaulted and murdered?"

"You need not remind me—"

"Am I, then, to be ignored when I wonder, as any sane person might, why my child's murderer is allowed to run about free and unpunished?"

"Ah! Been trying to remember all day," Aden broke in,

trying to change the subject before things got out of hand. "One of the men hailed the *Dora G.* on Friday. She was Seattle-bound with a dozen mail-order brides. You can bet they're having a grand party there to—"

"I am not in the mood for banter, Aden Creed!" Eudora's back was stiff and her eyes were wild with fury. "It is bad enough when your father treats me like a child. I will stand for no such nonsense from you, do you understand?" Her voice had grown shrill.

The silence could have been cut with a butter knife.

"Of course, Aunt Eudora," Aden answered soothingly. "I meant no insult."

"We wouldn't even be having this conversation if I'd had my way," Timothy boasted.

Eb guffawed. "Your way, Timmy? That new deputy would have cut you down before you could have squeezed the trigger."

"You think so?" Timothy sneered.

"He moved pretty smooth. You gotta remember, those Texas boys're sometimes pretty good with a gun." Recognizing his own limitations, Eb grinned. "Faster'n me, anyway."

"Texas, hah!" Timothy said. "Steers come from Texas, too, and we butcher them."

Noah Creed had never backed away from a fight in his life, but he too had seen how smoothly the young deputy from Texas had moved, and remembered the determination in his eyes. "Don't give yourself airs, Timothy," he said dryly. "After Friday's performance, I'd suggest that you remember you're a businessman, and obviously not a gunfighter."

Ebeneezer guffawed again, and both Timothy and Aden fixed him with a stare. "Don't look at me," the giant said. "Far as I'm concerned, Hank Rhodes is a good man, even if he is on the wrong side of this one."

"Him and that uppity deputy both," Timothy snapped.

"And don't you worry, Aunt Eudora," he added, once again including her in the conversation. "They'll get their come-uppance soon enough. And justice will be served."

"Which is what I've said all along," Noah grumbled.

"As do we all," Aden agreed. He raised his glass. "To justice, then. Don't worry, Aunt Eudora. Melinda's murderer will pay the price for his foul deed," he predicted, though to what disastrous end he could not foresee. "I assure you. He will pay the price, in full."

The lanterns were turned down, the light dim and restful. Dinner was long over, the boys gone their separate ways. Noah Creed sighed, inhaled the luxury of Napoléon brandy, and washed a small sip around in his mouth. Good boys, they were, all of them. Aden, no doubt reading in his room, was fast becoming a remarkably knowledgeable manager with a keen grasp for every aspect of the business. Without him, their costs bringing in Creed Number One would have been double at least, possibly triple.

Eb, who would be asleep, was slower and more easy-going, but he knew his timbering as well as any man in Washington Territory, and in addition he had a rare knack for getting the most work out of his men without coddling them.

As for Timothy . . . Noah shook his head. No doubt where Timothy was: on Water Street, raising holy Ned as he did at least five out of every seven nights of the week.

Timothy was special because he lived life to the hilt, the way Noah had always secretly wished he might have. It was all very well and good to work your fingers to the bone, to consider your every move, to plan and deliberate, to raise a family and make a great deal of money with which a man could buy anything he wished; but there was something to be said, too, about being brash and impudent and not giving a damn, about sailing ahead full speed—wine, women, and song—and damn the consequences.

Well, Timothy could do that. He had a rich father, a luxury Noah, who had grown up an orphan on the streets of New York, had never known.

Behind him, the door whispered open. "Nine o'clock, Master," Chi Lo said in a voice as soft and melodious as the Seth Thomas, which began, as if it had been waiting for permission, to chime.

Noah listened to the bells, counting them silently.

"Nine o'clock, then," he said. He held out the brandy snifter, felt the added weight as Chi Lo poured, and wondered, as always, how the houseboy always knew exactly what he wanted without asking. "A long day. I'll sit for a while longer. Join me on the bridge later?"

The ritual was old and cherished. Chi Lo didn't need to be asked, and didn't need to answer, but did. "As Master wishes."

Noah leaned back, let the soft leather chair enfold his weary bones. As silent as a ghost, Chi Lo cracked the windows at top and bottom to let out the cigar smoke, gathered the boys' ashtrays, and blew out the lanterns.

Nine o'clock. Aden set aside the January issue of *Harper*'s, rubbed his eyes, and blew out the lantern.

Nine o'clock. Ebeneezer slept, dead to the world.

Nine o'clock. The night was just beginning at "Sophie Barrett's Klallam Kounty Kocktail Klub—Ladies Available for Dancing." Not that the saloon was a cocktail club or that anyone had ever bought a drink by such a fancy name there, or that Sophie's girls were ladies by any definition of the word, nor did they limit themselves to dancing, as any fool could find out by opening his wallet. When it came to whisky and women, Sophie had the best of both in Calamity Bay.

The saloon dominated the riverfront street. This "palace of perdition," as the preachers were want to call it, was built of redwood timber, a massive two-story structure. The downstairs windows and the windowed panels in the massive oak doors at the entrance were of stained glass brought up from San Francisco. Rather than the lives of saints or images of suffering Christians, the windows depicted the saturnalian pleasures to be found within.

Inside, the saloon was a spacious room crowded with tables and chairs, gambling tables and wheels of fortune. Smoke clung to beams and wheel chandeliers overhead. Men jostled for a place at the bar lining one end of the room while Ham, a reed-thin black man, sat at the piano and hammered out a tinny "Timber Tallulah." Gerta, the saloon's song-bird, strutted down the bar and stopped in front of a young man sitting alone. Pulling up her skirts, she knelt in front of him, ruffled his hair, and made obscene gestures with her pelvis while she belted out the words. "Timber Tallulah, over she goes. Flat on her back, she wiggles her toes. One two three, lad, that's all you've got? Up with your trousers, and out you trot!"

The crowd roared with glee as she pushed the blushing lad away from her and drowned her out with the chorus. "With a larrupin, larrupin, larrupin lee, Timber Tallulah's the girl for me!"

Upstairs, in the front bedroom, a different tune was being played.

"Ouch! That hurts, Tim darlin'. Don't! Please don't!"

"Slut! Whore!" Naked, his pale skin glowing in the faint candlelight, Timothy knelt over Carolina Jenny and slapped her face again. "I paid good money for you and I'll do what I damned well please."

Pale welts flamed on Carolina Jenny's tear-streaked face. "I tried, Timmy. It ain't my fault if you cain't—" Her voice sounded bleak as the wind whistling forlornly through the shutters.

Again the hand struck, cutting off her words. "Don't say it, bitch. You hear me, damn you? Don't say it!"

Desperate, the girl freed her arm and began to stroke the

inside of his thigh. "I won't, Timmy," she promised. She took him with both hands. The bedsprings creaked as she shifted her weight. "I'll make it work for you, Timmy. You'll see," she crooned. "You'll see. I promise . . ."

Carolina Jenny knew her trade. Men with Timothy Creed's problem always blamed the girl, even if it wasn't her fault. These men, she knew from experience, were always angry, and guilty as hell of something. Business, though, was business.

She'd be rid of the bruises on her face a lot faster than Tim would the devils inside him, so she was willing to take his abuse and service him as long as he paid well. And bruises or no, Timothy Creed paid very well indeed. The money he'd throw on her table would make it worth the extra time and effort—even the pain, which she was used to.

It took an hour, and the prostitute never did satisfy him. At last, frightened by the blood and hoping Jenny wouldn't say anything, Timothy dressed, threw a twenty-dollar gold piece onto her table, and stalked out. A moment later, when he strolled down the stairs into the bedlam of the crowded saloon, he managed to give the impression that he was the master of his world in every way.

"If it ain't Timothy Creed," Old J. D. cackled. "Back from the dead, eh, boyo?"

Timothy wanted to leave, but appearances were important. He swaggered to the bar, where a bottle was waiting for him. "Dead, hell!" He grinned, downing a shot.

J. D. sidled up next to him in the hope of a free drink. "Wish I was still as full of piss 'n vinegar as I used to be. Three, four times, grab me a shot or two of pecker juice to stiffen me up, an' ready t' have at 'em again." He winked with appreciation as Timothy filled his glass. J. D. raised his drink in salute. "Well, Timmy me lad, here's to good times."

"Over and over again," Timothy Creed said, lying and

boasting in the same breath. He shoved the bottle across the bar, tossed a coin after it. "Fill 'em up as long as it lasts," he told Elmo, the barkeep.

A chorus of thanks came from along the bar. The men may not have had much use for Tim Creed, but they had nothing against drinking his whiskey.

Timothy was halfway to the door when Sophie called his name over the din.

"Timothy Creed, you son of a bitch!"

A sudden hush fell over the crowd. Timothy's stomach knotted, and he turned to see Sophie standing halfway down the stairs. Next to her stood Carolina Jenny, blood streaming from the gash his ring had cut in her cheek.

Tim was so busy watching the saloon's busty owner, that he didn't see the front door open and a young man dressed in gray and black and wearing a deputy-marshal badge enter.

Sophie descended the stairs, helped Carolina Jenny into a chair, and advanced on Timothy. "I told you the last time you cut one of my girls that you were on my list."

"I don't know what you're talking about," Timothy said, desperately trying to brave it out.

"You damn well do." Her red hair piled high on her head, she towered over him. "You cut my girl." Sophie's pockmarked skin was hidden behind a mask of powder and rouge, but her eyes were all ablaze.

"She said that?" Timothy asked brazenly. His lip curled in a sneer. "And I suppose you're gonna take the word of a whore over mine, am I right?"

Sophie's eyes blazed and she came dangerously close to pulling the derringer she kept in her wrist purse and firing point-blank. "Out of here, Creed," she said in a hoarse voice instead. "Me and my girls depend on Creed money as much as anybody else in this town, but yours ain't no longer needed. Your brothers come in here . . . fine. But not you. Never again."

A hush fell over the crowd.

Timothy glared at Sophie and challenged her. "You're wrong, Sophie. I'll be back whenever I damned well please. And if you know what's good for you, you'll take me and my money. People don't tell us Creeds where to walk. Not in Calamity Bay. Not anywhere."

"I just did, little man," Sophie said, her green eyes blazing with contempt. A big woman, and as often as not her own bouncer, she grabbed Timothy by one arm, spun him around, and shoved him toward the door. "Now get out of here, and don't come back."

Nobody manhandled Timothy Creed. His temper out of control, he bent over, scooped a knife from his boot, and whirled to face Sophie. "Bitch!" he snarled.

"Don't," a soft voice behind him commanded.

Timothy didn't even look back. "Stay out of it, whoever you are," he snapped.

He heard the whisper of a hand slapping leather, a gunshot exploded with a deafening boom. The knifeblade skittered across the floor, leaving Tim holding nothing but a hilt. Creed spun around, his hand reaching instinctively for the gun he had left at home in his room on Creed's Knob. Halfway through the action, he was stiff-armed and sent sprawling and left to stare up at Billy Anthem.

The crowd, which had been holding its breath, let it out as one. "Holy shit," a hushed voice whispered. "You see that?"

"If'n I did, don't know as I believe it," another answered in awe. "That boy's blue lightning with a gun."

"The lady told you to leave," Billy Anthem said evenly. He slowly holstered his .45 and kicked the knife hilt back under a faro table. "Maybe you better do that."

His face white, Timothy stared up at his attacker. His eyes widened and took on a crazed look, just for a brief second, that made Billy's flesh crawl. Tim Creed's upper lip curled back in an animalistic snarl.

"You son of a—I'll get you for this."

"Don't let your mouth write a check your fists can't cash," Billy warned in a cold voice.

Timothy's mouth went suddenly dry. He licked his lips, but wisely held his tongue.

"Good." Billy nodded in the direction of the front door. "Now get out of here." His voice never rose, but was as cold and hard as an ice saw.

Timothy crawled to his feet, dusted the sawdust from his backside, and headed for the street. Someone laughed. Creed's shoulders tightened, but he continued through the heavy oak doors.

"Durndest thing I ever seed," the man everyone called J. D. said from his place at the bar.

"Still an' all, I wouldn't wanta be the deputy," a slow-talking lumberman muttered. His head drooped forward as he stared into his glass. "I ain't afeard of no fair fight. But all Creed has to do is lift a finger, and there'll be an army in front of the jail, come morning." The lumberman drained the contents of his glass. The liquor burned his throat, warmed his belly, and made him feel alive again. "I'd be among them, too, I reckon," he added, and shuffled away from the bar toward the nearest chair.

Billy's cheeks reddened as half a dozen of Sophie's girls fussed over him and offered to show their gratitude in one of the rooms upstairs. Sophie had to fight her way through to him.

"I won't forget this," she boomed, shaking Billy's hand in that big paw of hers. "I got a real aversion to knives, and that's for true. Billy Anthem, huh?"

"Yes, ma'am," Anthem replied, glancing wistfully for a means of escape. He'd stepped into this situation before he knew what was happening. And acted on the instincts his father had engrained in him.

"Well, I'm here to tell you it's about time Hank Rhodes got hisself a deputy that was worth spit. Jared Krait was about as useful as a fart at a funeral." Beaming, she reached into her bosom and withdrew a wooden token. "And it's a fact that I by God owe you one. Here." She pressed the token into his hand. "Good for any girl on the premises. Includin' me," she added. She threw back her head and roared with laughter. The men gathered within earshot whistled.

"Yer riskin' gettin crushed, Deputy," someone hollered. "Or swallowed whole," another voice added.

"You boys pipe down an' mind your own business," Sophie roared. She threw one arm around Billy's shoulder and led him to one side and lowered her voice. She smelled of whiskey and French perfume, and the thick sweet scent of opium lingered on her breath. "Come on, honey. I'll give you something to remember till the day you die."

Billy managed to stifle an immediate protest. It wouldn't do to be rude and make an enemy when he was probably going to need all the friends he could find. "There's a few more places to check on," he said, gently extricating himself from her grasp.

Sophie's eyes glowed with an ardor she seldom felt. "Just remember, as long as I've got thighs and a belly, you've a place to curl up and sleep," she murmured huskily, as much enamored by his turning her down as she was by his obvious courage.

"Makes me warm just to think of it," Billy graciously replied. If the ranch hands at Luminaria could see him now, they'd be laughing their heads off at his discomfort. It was said that Billy Anthem, the handsomest of the Anthem brothers, had a way with the ladies. Well, Sophie sure had him treed.

"You be careful at the Flying Dragon, now, you hear?" Sophie called after him. "That's one dangerous place. Not like here."

A drunken millworker, bottle in hand, sauntered up behind the madam and grabbed a handful of hip. Sophie swirled about, grabbed the millworkers bottle, and crashed it over his head. He collapsed at her feet in a shower of glass, his body thudding off the hardwood floor.

Billy heard the commotion but never even slowed. It'd be risking more than his life to go to Sophie's rescue again.

8

★

Four bells. Ten o'clock. Creed Manor was quiet. Noah had heard Eudora stirring about upstairs a little earlier. Timothy had yet to return from sowing his wild oats.

Get it out of your system, Noah thought. The time is drawing near when you'll have to assume your share of the responsibilities, like Aden and Ebeneezer before you.

The parlor was dark save for the wan moonlight that streamed in through the front windows. A chill was on the air. Noah sighed and wearily set aside the empty brandy snifter. He pushed himself out of the deep leather chair. The dining room, immediately to his rear, was dark and empty. A thin sliver of light from the kitchen leaked under the door. Mrs. Amandus would be abed, he knew, but Chi Lo was awake, would hear him on the stairs, and follow him as dutifully and silently as ever, to the bridge.

The house seemed to breathe as he walked down the hall to the great formal staircase. It seemed to be trying to tell him something, the way a ship did when a man had sailed it through storm and calm, and knew it well. Every nerve alert, Noah passed the staircase and stepped into the ballroom which extended almost to the rear of the right side of the house.

Was someone there? Moonlight reflecting off the polished parquet floor illuminated the portraits hung along the walls. Chairs, sofas, tables, lamps, all were properly arranged. For one brief, startling moment, he thought he heard laughter, and then it came to him.

Ten years ago to the day, one week before they were to move into the great mansion that had been his dream, Noah and his wife, Cassandra, were standing in the very center of this ballroom. Noah had heard the creak of wood, but the house was too new for him to know what it portended. Suddenly, the scaffolding the painters were using gave way, and the end of a heavy plank swung down. It struck his wife on the head and killed her instantly.

Some of the purpose had gone out of Noah's life on that afternoon. He'd been a driven man before the accident— oh, yes, but only for the joy of success and accomplishment. Ever since his wife's death, the joy seemed gone, yet the drive remained.

But what else, other than money and power, was there without Cassandra? he thought, standing there, awash in memories. His sons, yes. It was for them he was determined to build an empire that, once left to them, would bring them the happiness he had lost. That was the one dream that remained, and that, he had sworn, no man would deny him.

A lantern burned in the upstairs hall. Noah stopped at the top of the stairs. To his left, from rear to front, Timothy's, Eb's, and Eudora's rooms. To his right, a guest bedroom, then Aden's, and in the front with the view of Calamity Bay and the strait, the master bedroom, where Chi Lo would have laid a fire. Timothy's room was dark. The soft sound of snoring came through Eb's closed door, as it did from Aden's.

There was something peaceful about a house asleep, Noah pondered, passing his own door on the way to the bridge. His brow furrowed, he paused at the double doors at the end of the hall and listened intently and heard the sound of weeping that issued from Eudora's room.

Noah lit one of the hall lamps, lifted it off a small round table set against the wall, and entered Eudora's bedroom without knocking.

Light flooded the chamber. Eudora, her hair unbound, sat wrapped in a blanket on the window seat, gazing out the window at the black sky and crying softly. She had heard her brother enter, but acknowledged his presence only by shielding her eyes from the light.

"Have we not had enough of these tears, Eudora?" Noah asked, kindly enough in spite of his irritation.

She turned her face away from him.

"I have suffered loss," Noah continued. "You are not alone in your grief. My wife, a son and a daughter stillborn, losses, loved ones I dearly love, I tell you, and yet I wept no more for all of them than you have for one daughter."

"She was all I had," Eudora whispered in a voice thick with pain.

"Enough, Eudora. You infect this house with an insupportable gloom. I am—we are all—weary of your tears. Why, sometimes I think you blame me for this tragedy."

Like an animal cornered, Eudora shrank against the wall. "I blame you for allowing it to continue," she hissed, and stared at her brother. Her eyes rolled up into her head, she shuddered then, sobbing, looked at her brother again. "I am in pain," she said, each word a wound that bled. "My heart is broken. I am in pain."

"I do not question your pain. The child was dear to me, and I, too, wish she were still with us."

"You cared not one whit for Melinda," Eudora snapped, lashing him with the words. "If you did, that man would be dead. Oh, God, why was I born a woman? A man could take action and exact retribution."

Noah stiffened. "A lynching must be a last resort. Especially with Rhodes around to name all the participants to the higher authorities. But mark my words, Goretti will die."

"Words, words, words," she shot back acidly. "If he had killed one of your sons, you would have killed him on the instant."

She had him, Noah admitted. Ten, even five years ago, he would have openly killed Angelo Goretti on the street without a second's hesitation. But things had changed. As the Creed interests had expanded, Calamity Bay had grown and filled with outsiders. He still ruled, yes, but precariously. Still, he was not without influence. A Creed could well become a senator when the territory became a state. To that end, Noah dare not take the law so blatantly into his own hands.

He'd been forced to try to remove Rhodes permanently in order to get him out of the way. Without Rhodes, Goretti was ripe for the taking—why, the murderer might even have taken his own life there in the confines of his cell. But what was the use in telling someone so unstable as Eudora. No, the fewer people Noah confided in, the better.

Wearying of the argument that had gone on for a week, he set the lantern on her bureau and sat on the far end of the window seat.

"For the last time, Eudora," he said. He rubbed his eyes with his fingertips and then fixed her with the piercing glare that bent all others, save her, to his will. "Melinda's murderer will pay for what he did. I promise you."

Eudora's eyes were those of a madwoman, her voice laced with bitterness. "I've choked on such promises for nine days. They are as empty as Angelo Goretti's grave."

"You will not thaw, you would not listen to reason. No answer I give will suffice. Bah, I no longer care to try," Noah said, rising to his full height. He took up his lantern, and walked toward the door.

"I will have that grave filled, my dear brother," Eudora called after him in a voice as cold as winter ice. "Filled."

Noah did not even deign to turn to look at her. "In due time, Eudora," he said flatly. "Unless you wish to fill it yourself. If you have no faith in me, and if being here has become such a torment, then I suggest you go elsewhere. And now," he said, swinging the door closed behind him and leaving her in the dark, "I wish you good night."

Chi Lo was well on his way up the stairs when he saw the light moving across the wall. A sixth sense warning him, he stopped in time to hear the mistress's door open. The master was unhappy, he knew. Noah had been unhappy since the death of the young missy whose laughter had for eight years filled the house and made it a bright and merry place to live. Chi Lo was also saddened. He grieved for Miss Melinda. He worried too, for he did not understand Master Noah. The family had been wronged. It was up to Master Noah to set things right. In the old days, the master would never have waited so long.

Chi Lo had been with Noah Creed for thirty years, ever since Creed had pulled the Chinese boy from the sea. Chi Lo had been but a sapling, a reedy youth sailing for the first time with his father to catch the fish that would sustain their family. A squall sprang up, became a full-fledged typhoon, broke their mast, and drove the fishing craft far out to sea.

Chi Lo had seen such storms on land, where they were frightening enough. At sea they were utterly terrifying. His father did the best he could, but in the end he lost his struggle with the violent crash of wind and waves and was thrown overboard, leaving Chi Lo alone to fend for himself.

Somehow, Chi Lo had survived, bailed out the battered hull, and fell into an exhausted sleep. Days and nights blended together.

He lived on raw fish and drank what little rainwater he could wring from his clothes.

He lost track of time and had resolved himself to death when one morning he glimpsed a ship on the horizon. It was no more than a tiny smear of color against the sky at first. Gradually the whaling ship came into focus. Providence had placed the boy adrift directly in the path of the vessel.

Eventually the wretched fishing boat was spotted and the boy rescued from the clutches of the sea. He'd been brought aboard the American vessel. Nearly starved, naked, nearly dead of thirst, and very frightened, Chi Lo laid eyes on Master Noah Creed for the first time.

There had been no going home, of course. Chi Lo spoke no English, had no idea of where home was. None of the white men with round eyes spoke his language. Still, they fed and clothed him and did not beat him as his father often had. He was never to see his home or surviving family again.

The strange language and stranger ways were difficult, but Chi Lo learned quickly. Each day he added new words. First, the name of his benefactor, Noah Creed. Then, mast and sail and line, whale, harpoon, and flense. Food was easily mastered—hunger and thirst were good teachers, so it was biscuit and water, beef and rum. And finally, a year later, America, and with the men drooling over the prospects of women and whiskey and solid land under their feet, San Francisco. By that time, he was Noah Creed's shadow, as he would remain for all the years that followed.

It was not a bad life. Chi Lo had met others of his kind in San Francisco and elsewhere, but Orientals were looked down upon by the round-eyed white men and forced to live in hovels. Noah Creed was different. In no way did he consider Chi Lo his equal, but Noah possessed a just and honest nature.

Chi Lo and Noah Creed had become friends, in a manner of speaking, over the years. Noah was ever the master, Chi Lo ever the servant, but they shared a mutual respect. Nowadays neither of them said much to the other. Words were little needed after thirty years. They had grown accustomed to each other's presence.

And on the death of Noah's wife, master and servant had sat alone together and smoked their pipes. Chi Lo had watched Noah change. He became harsh and sometimes cruel. He seldom laughed and bent his will to money and power instead of the joy of accomplishment for its own sake. But Chi Lo remained.

The argument was over. The mistress's door closed, the door to the bridge opened. Chi Lo waited a few moments so it would not be obvious he had been listening, and then he silently climbed the final half-dozen steps and padded along the hall.

The bridge was a railed balcony over the front portico. Noah had added it as an afterthought the year after Cassandra died, and outfitted it with captain's chairs, a tripod for a glass, and the wheel from the last ship he had mastered, the *Cassandra C.* That it was outside and subject to the weather didn't bother him at all; in fact, heat or cold, rain or snow, any change in the elements pleased him.

He sensed rather than heard the door open behind him. A moment later, Chi Lo joined the patriarch where he stood with his hands on the rail, staring out over the town, bay, straits, and the dark line of hills beyond. Chi Lo handed him a thick ceramic cup filled with black coffee. They stood together, each with his own thoughts.

There are times, Noah considered, when I'd give up everything just to weigh anchor and sail off toward the setting sun.

Tonight, a damp, chill breeze blew out of the northwest. Set a full dress of sails, keep a course of 210 degrees. Farther out, come up a little to quarter into the wind, and not drop anchor till we reached the Hawaiian Islands.

"What do women know, eh, Chi Lo?"

A wisp of a smile played fleetingly across Chi Lo's face before being replaced by the suggestion of a frown. "Vengeance, Master Noah," he said.

Noah glanced sharply at him. "Perhaps," he grunted. He

sipped his coffee, made a wry face, then shrugged in satisfaction. He'd tasted worse.

"But it is you, Master Noah, who will decide what is right and what is wrong," Chi Lo added, moving up to stand alongside the one to whom the Chinaman owed his loyalty and life.

Noah studied the bay and the strait beyond. He called back his imagination, returning to reality, to the responsibilities at hand. The irony wasn't lost on him, that when a man fulfills all his dreams yet continues to dream, to yearn for what once was, then something must be wrong.

"We are none of us as wise as we'd like to think, old friend," said Noah Creed. "None of us." He chuckled softly, mirth tinged with sorrow.

Chi Lo agreed, but was wise enough to keep silent.

9

★

Aden Creed had never eaten at Openeer's Dutch Boy Restaurant. He'd preferred to keep his record clean, but sacrifices sometimes had to be made. As far as he could tell, breakfast was the best time to find Anthem alone and feel him out.

The interior of the restaurant was dingy. Aden's nose curled as the odor of grease and the sweat of workingmen assailed his nostrils. For two cents, Aden Creed would have found another time and place, but then it was too late, because Anthem had spotted him and was eyeing him the way a gull sizes up a beached fish.

The dining room was no more than four or five paces square. The walls were lined with faded chromolithographs depicting European life of the last century. Two long trestle tables sat eight to the side, and both were nearly full. Of those who faced him, Aden recognized two or three men from the shake mill, and two more he had recently hired to work on the road from Creed Number One to the new bayside coal-loading dock.

The men crowded at the breakfast table were taken totally by surprise. The ones facing Aden saw him first, of course, and within seconds all the others had glanced over their shoulders to make sure they weren't being ribbed. Had

Aden Creed come down from his high and mighty house to take breakfast here? The rumble of conversation lessened as this newcomer moved through the room.

" 'Bout 'nuff fer me, I reckon," one grizzled hand grumbled, pushing away a plate still half-full of overcooked flapjacks and undercooked bacon.

"Yup," another opined. He finished off his coffee, belched, grabbed a handful of biscuits, and stuffed them in a side pocket. "See you boys later up to the mill."

Aden noted the animosity and resented it, yet he hid his feelings as he squeezed past the men on the ends of the benches, then along the rear of the dining room toward Anthem. Some touched their caps in sullen greeting. " 'Mornin', Mr. Creed," they said. Others merely nodded. One or two ignored him completely, which was fine with Aden.

"Deputy Anthem, what a surprise."

Billy chewed on a mouthful of buttermilk flapjacks and swallowed. " 'Mornin', Mr. Creed. I'll just bet you are." Billy wore a gray wool shirt and black string tie, a faded red plaid coat with the elbows patched and black woolen trousers tucked into his boots. His short-cropped tousled blond hair seemed in perpetual disarray. He was not the picture of prosperity.

Aden looked confused. "What? I don't understand."

"I'll bet you're surprised." The restaurant was emptying rapidly, and Billy gestured with his fork to the place opposite him. "Take a seat. Had breakfast yet?"

"Well, ah . . ."

"Flapjacks aren't bad this morning. The syrup helps. A dime'll buy you a short stack and bacon." He grinned, dabbed another pat of butter onto his plate. "Can't hardly beat that, now, can you?"

"I'll try the coffee," Aden said, sitting. "I didn't really come to eat."

Billy reached behind him to the stack of cups on the

counter, snared one, and pushed it across the table. "Didn't expect you did, somehow. Just puttin' a burr under your saddle, as we say back home." He jerked a thumb toward a large black pot halfway down the table. "Help yourself. Don't know as they have any sugar, if you take it."

Aden knew when he was being rousted, and he wasn't about to be goaded into losing his temper. As if he dined at Openeer's every day, he leaned across the table, grabbed the pot, and poured himself a cupful of evil-looking brew. "Top yours off, Deputy?" he asked pleasantly.

"Obliged," Billy said. "You can call me Billy, same as everybody else does. Let me see now. You're ..." A thoughtful frown creased his brow.

"Aden," the eldest of the Creed brothers said. He took a sip of coffee and grimaced. "Eb's the big one of us. Tim is . . . well, Tim."

"Right! I know what you mean. I ran into him last night."

"Oh? He didn't mention it this morning. Of course, he was barely awake when I left. It must not have been too important."

Billy glanced down at the cup he held and considered recounting the incident at Sophie's, then decided against it. He had seen a quality in Tim that would bear watching. Billy didn't want the hot-tempered young man to be too much on his guard.

"No. It wasn't important," Billy agreed. "But I imagine this visit is. What's on your mind?"

Now that the novelty of Creed's arrival had worn off, the conversation in the restaurant had returned to its normal level. However, Creed and Anthem were given a wide berth by those who came to eat.

"That's right." Aden Creed's smile was lazy, almost contemplative. He had come there not knowing whether to bribe or bully. But he knew now. And it was time for the gloves to come off and to get down to business. "You are, I suppose, Mr. Anthem, a reasonable man."

"Depends on what you call reasonable," Billy allowed.

"Yes, doesn't it? Let me lay my cards on the table." He glanced to his left, staring at the one lone customer who sat with an ear cocked to the conversation. "I know you," Creed said coldly. "The whistle blows any minute now up at the mine. Later this morning, I will ask if you were on time."

The man grabbed his hat and headed for the door. The remaining customers followed his example, and soon Billy and Aden Creed had Openeer's to themselves, much to the dismay of the owner.

"Must have been something you said," Billy muttered. He shoved his plate away, easing back in his chair until he balanced on the back legs. He hooked his thumbs in his gun belt.

"I'm through playing, Anthem," Creed said. "Why are you here? What do you hope to accomplish by stirring up trouble in Calamity Bay?"

It was like a game of five-card stud, and the first man who blinked lost. "Seems like trouble was already here," Billy said evenly. "I just happened to come along and throw my hat into the ring. And lucky for Hank Rhodes I did."

"I wasn't talking about Marshal Rhodes. We're all grateful to you for saving his life. He's a good man. But misguided. He is protecting a cold-blooded rapist and murderer. Now you, a complete stranger, are helping to thwart the will of the law-abiding citizens of Calamity Bay by protecting Angelo Goretti, my cousin's killer."

"Seeing to it a man gets a fair trial is what the law is about. That, and seeing justice is done."

"Where were you and your high talk of justice when my cousin was being murdered?" Aden sneered.

"The question is, where was Goretti?" Billy replied.

The same cold implacable look Billy had seen in Aden's

eyes on Sunday morning returned. The scion of the Creed
family stiffened as if he had been slapped. "My father
doesn't like you, Anthem. I don't like you. And there are
many more in this town who will agree with us without
question. This is a question of family honor. My cousin's
soul cries out for vengeance. And woe to the poor fool who
stands in our way. Do I make myself clear?" The cheek
muscles on Aden's face began to twitch.

"Perfectly," Billy answered. "But can you back it up, I
wonder."

"I don't care how good you are, Anthem." He grinned,
showing a row of white teeth. "I don't care how fast, how
smart, how brave. You can't come out a winner against a
hundred guns."

The man had a point. Even Cole, as good as he was with
that Yellowboy Winchester of his, would probably figure it
was time to turn Mother's picture to the wall and get out.

"There's only one way you can win," Aden continued.
"Go. Right now." Slowly, he opened his coat with his left
hand so Billy could see he was unarmed, reached into the
pocket, and withdrew a small leather pouch that he tossed
on the table in front of Billy. "A hundred dollars. Gold
coins. Not bad wages for two days' work."

The coins clinked together with a muted, satisfying
sound when Billy picked up the pouch, tossed it lightly two
or three times, and let it drop to the table. "So that's the
going rate for a man's life. What about for a man's conscience?"

Again, Creed pulled open his coat. "Every man has his
price, Mr. Billy Anthem. Name yours."

Big John Anthem had talked about that. *Most* men had
a price, he had said. But not the ones John Anthem chose
to respect. And if there was anything Billy wanted from his
father, even more than his love, it was his respect. Because
as hard as it may be to love, it is harder by far to respect.

"Your pockets don't go that deep." Billy dropped the

pouch, pushed it with one finger toward Aden.

Aden nodded and retrieved the gold. He had tried. So be it. "Very well," he said, thinking of how much he was going to enjoy seeing Anthem fall. "And you just talked me into helping you stay. Forever, Billy Anthem." And in the deadly calm that possesses some men in their fury, Aden stood and stalked away from the table.

"Creed," Billy called.

His face white, Aden turned. "It's too late. Too late—"

"You forgot to pay for your coffee," Billy said. In the kitchen, Mr. Openeer groaned and dove for cover.

Creed cavalierly flipped a twenty-dollar gold piece onto the table. "You can keep the change . . . for your funeral."

Monday morning was a quiet time in Calamity Bay. The men were back at work, many of the children in school. Most women were home washing and baking. Shopkeepers were using a day of little trade to get ready for the week. Billy brought breakfast back to the jail for Rhodes and Goretti and said nothing to the marshal about his run-in with Aden Creed. Billy couldn't bear the confines of the office and headed out again. He figured to use the day getting acquainted with the layout of the town.

Water Street was shut down for the day, and it wouldn't come to life again until sundown. No matter. Billy had acquainted himself with all the dens of iniquity the town had to offer the night before, including the infamous Flying Dragon, Sophie's main competition. Today, he intended to avoid the waterfront.

He had all of Calamity Bay to choose from. A maze of narrow, muddy streets on the west side of Klallam Creek housed the vast majority of the millworkers. He made the circuit around the business section of town, stopping to meet people and indulge in small talk, then strolled down Hemlock to watch the school empty at lunchtime and spend

a pleasant half-hour with Penelope before she had to return
to the classroom.

That afternoon, he saddled a horse and rode lazily
through the wider shell-paved streets on the slopes of Cameron Bluff, where the well-to-do citizens of Calamity Bay
lived, and then climbed into the mountains to the south of
and behind the town.

The mountains were lush with the new growth of spring.
Keeping a wary eye out for bushwhackers—once burned,
twice shy—Billy followed dim trails through the dusky
light of the deep forest, broke into secluded glades where,
shielded from the wind, he relished the sunlight warming
his face and back. Calamity Bay was to his right, but he
caught few glimpses of it—mere dashes of the blue of water or the white of a house. And then, with a suddenness
that took away his breath, Billy emerged onto a small pla-
teau on the edge of the mountain. And there before him,
like a painting that he wished he could commit to canvas,
lay a vista of breathtaking beauty.

He could see for miles. To east and west were the mountains, until one or another ridge cut off the view. Below
them, rolling hills were cut by creeks swollen with spring
melt that rushed to tiny bays cut into the coast of the strait.
To east and west again, the broad slash of blue-green water
that was the Strait of Juan de Fuca connected the horizons.
Beyond it, the deep green of more forested hills and mountains stretched as far as the eye could see.

Awestruck, Billy took the glass he'd borrowed from
Rhodes, dismounted, and let his horse wander and crop the
sweet spring grass. He was not the first to visit that lofty
height. Someone else with an axe had been there before,
and had fashioned a shallow seat in the bole of a Douglas
fir he had felled for that purpose. Quickly, Billy cut a
forked branch to rest the glass on, and settled in for a closer
look.

The mountain fell steeply away from his position. The

town lay some five hundred feet below and a quarter- to a half-mile to the north. He scanned the streets through the single eyepiece. There the jail, the school. There the top story of Wick's Hotel, and close by, the bridges over Klallam Creek. And there, of greatest interest, Creed Manor a little to his right, so he could see its back and west sides.

Billy took his time, studying the layout with care. Broadway snaked up the side of Creed's Knob and became a private drive that passed through a white picket fence, encircling the house, and rejoined itself behind a gatehouse.

The stable faced the drive at its farthest point to the rear of the house. To the right were servants' quarters, with what looked like four apartments.

Billy could tell little about the house itself. Smoke came from a rear chimney, so that would have to be the kitchen at that end. Blankets had been hung to air on the railings of three small balconies that graced the second story.

While he watched, a maid appeared on each in turn, shook and flipped the blankets to give the other side some sun, and disappeared again. There was little else to see.

He had just decided to head back to town when a chunk of the makeshift log seat exploded. Splinters stung his cheek and a lead slug whined by into space. A rifle shot echoed across the landscape. Billy dropped the spyglass and rolled over the edge of the log as a second shot rang out.

He broke from cover and bolted headlong into a grove of firs about twenty feet from the lookout. He drew his Colt and crouched in the emerald shadows. He strained to hear, he searched the underbrush that masked his back trail. He saw nothing of his assailant.

Anthem was willing to wait. He looked at the horse he'd left in the clearing, and was amazed that the animal hadn't spooked at the rifle shot. Thank God for small favors, Billy thought, and hefted the reassuring weight of the Colt in his hand. The sun crept westward. The surrounding forest seemed devoid of life. And why not, when death stalked the paths?

Billy shifted his aim as the faint rumbling cadence of hooves drifted across the clearing. His attacker galloping away? Maybe. The deputy's heart slowly ceased hammering in his chest. He licked his dry lips and waited another half-hour before venturing into the clearing. And even then he felt like a target.

He retrieved the spyglass and hurried over to his horse and remounted. A second glance at the bullet-marked stump brought home the precariousness of his situation. Someone in Calamity Bay had declared open season . . . on Anthem.

"Where the hell have you been?" Rhodes asked two hours later when Billy rode in after stopping at Openeer's to pick up supper for the three of them. The marshal was propped up in bed. A checkerboard was unfolded on the mattress. A bag of checkers was close at hand.

"Out. Nosin' around. Getting the lay of the land. You hungry?" Billy decided to keep the attack on the mountain to himself. Rhodes was in no condition to be riled up. Anyway, it was done with.

"Durn me for a springtime bear, but I could eat my weight. I was just about to hobble over an' let Goretti out so's we could have a game. But that can wait." He hiked up in bed, winced at the pain in his side. "What'd you bring?"

Billy set down the basket and went to release Goretti. "Pork chops, grits, and gravy. A crock of kidney beans, too."

"Every Dutch man's cuisine of choice after a hard day at the windmill," Goretti said, following Billy into the marshal's quarters.

"I ain't picky. You better not be either. If ol' Noah had his way, it'd be your last," Rhodes warned. Duly warned, the artist demurely took his seat and filled a plate.

After dinner it was time for fresh coffee with a splash of whiskey in it, and a pipe for Rhodes.

"So," the marshal said, sucking on his pipe until the tobacco in the bowl glowed a fiery red. "You nosed around. Get anything?"

"This," Billy said, dropping the change he'd pocketed from Aden's gold piece.

"Who give it to you? And what for?"

"Present from Aden Creed. For funeral expenses." He scooped up the coins and returned them to his coat pocket.

Goretti sighed. "A very bad man. Sly and crafty like a fox. The smartest of the Creeds. More so than the father, I think, in some ways."

"I wouldn't know," Billy said as Rhodes nodded in agreement. He frowned, noticing that Rhodes had a change of bandages expertly tied in place. "Goretti's handiwork?"

"Nope," the lawman snorted. He looked down at the new bandages wrapped around his shoulder and ribs. "Doc Bannon finally come back. Grouchy as an elk in rut after losin' that baby he'd gone to deliver. Took it out on me, the rough old fart."

"Neat job," Billy observed.

"And complete," Goretti added with a laugh. "He poured tincture of iodine on it, which should take care of the last of the infection."

Billy winced. "I'll bet that stung a little."

"He raised the roof," Goretti said, trying to keep a straight face.

"So what else did Creed have to say?" Rhodes interrupted, hastily changing the topic.

Billy recounted his conversation with Aden Creed, and fleshed out the rest of the day. Rhodes and Goretti broke in often with comments on one or another of the people Billy mentioned.

Rhodes too had had a long day. The session with Doc Bannon had taken a lot out of him. Since his right arm was out of commission and he couldn't write, he'd sent for Spaulding Conway, the clerk at the town hall, to take some letters for him.

They spent half the afternoon writing to the governor of the territory, the captain of the militia, and in the hopes that they could get one sooner rather than later, two circuit-riding judges.

Most wearing of all, Rhodes had spent an hour practicing with the crutch Bannon brought him. The effort had taxed his strength. He had the energy to finish his pipe, but by nine-thirty the marshal was asleep.

Billy took Goretti to the privy, then walked him back to his cell to settle the artist in for the night. For the first time that evening Billy noticed the easel in the cell. "Bannon bring that?" Billy asked.

"An act of kindness for which I will be eternally grateful," Goretti said.

He turned the easel toward the light, which Billy held up to better illuminate a large pad of rough-textured drawing paper. There, in a sketch unlike any other Billy had seen, was duplicated the wall over the marshal's desk, complete with gun rack, keys, wanted posters, and the like. Amazingly, the lines and shading, the light and shadow, made the scene appear even more real than the wall itself.

"Do you like it?" Goretti asked.

Billy glanced back and forth from wall to drawing, comparing them. "Yes," he finally said. "Not what I'd choose for a subject, but yes. The way you caught the shadows highlights the rest of the picture."

Goretti's eyes lit up. "Ah! The gunfighter is an artist as well?"

"In the first place, I'm not a gunfighter," Billy said. He scratched at his left arm and shifted his stance. His deceptively gentle eyes took on a faraway look. "As for being an artist, I guess I do kind of wish I was." He looked around as if afraid someone might overhear him. "I've tried some before. Can't make anything look near that good, of course."

"My dear young man!" Goretti exclaimed. "Why are you so embarrassed to say you wish to draw? Is it so terrible to wish to be an artist?"

Billy knew the answer. But such an avocation wasn't to be taken lightly or even discussed by a man whose father was Big John Anthem and whose brother was a bounty-hunter known far and wide as Yellowboy. "I guess," he mumbled, "that there's more important things where I come from."

"More important than beauty?" the artist asked, appalled. "Or the interpretation of life and truth? What could be more important than such as these?"

Billy pondered all of a couple of seconds. "Like figuring out how we're gonna save your life," he said, going for the keys. He unlocked the cell door and swung it open. "If it deserves saving, that is. Out. We have to talk."

They fired up the potbelly, put some water on for fresh coffee, and sat by the fire to keep off the night chill. "I spent a lot of time talking to folks today," Billy began. "Everyone has the same opinion. You won't tell where you were the night of the murder. Therefore, you must be guilty. You won't explain your whereabouts to anyone. Right?"

Goretti seemed to draw into himself. His olive-skinned features grew pensive. He leaned forward in the chair and folded his hands beneath his chin.

"Want to tell me who you were with?" Billy asked, taking a gamble. The look of abject surprise that grew suddenly composed told the deputy all he needed to know.

Another pause. "No," Goretti said. He realized how lame he sounded, but there was nothing to be done for it.

Billy nodded and helped himself to the coffee. "So it isn't as much where you were as who you were with, right?"

Goretti smiled wanly. "A reasonable man could make that assumption," he said at last.

"And I'm not gonna get it out of you."

"I can't, Billy." Goretti looked stricken. "I just can't. You must understand that."

Was he telling the truth? If so, then Goretti had been with a woman but was too much of a gentleman to clear himself at the expense of her reputation. Forthrightness seemed to work the best with the Italian. Billy resolved to continue the approach.

"Tell me about you and Melinda."

"Noah Creed's niece," Goretti said. He fished a dried black twig of a cigar from his coat pocket, lit the tip, and exhaled a pungent-smelling cloud of smoke. When he spoke, his voice seemed to come from a great distance.

"A beautiful child. I say child. Fifteen years old, straw blonde hair. Eyes a striking, light gray the color of . . ." He hesitated, thought. "Yes. Of birchbark. Skin clear as innocence, with hints of roses and peaches ripening in the summer sun. A budding form that was no longer a child's, but a woman's. She would have been a great beauty. Had she lived."

Goretti fixed Billy in his intense stare and continued, his voice stronger now. "But more than that, Billy Anthem from Texas. Much more. For she had a brain as well. A keen mind, and as keen an eye, though untrained. She wanted to be an artist. An unusual occupation for a woman, you say?" He shrugged. "There have been others in years past, and it is a great injustice that their works have been ascribed to men. She had true talent. And I was prepared to stay in this godforsaken town and teach her all I know."

"Folks said you were seeing her," Billy interjected. "And hinted that she even came to your room."

Goretti's tone grew caustic. "I am impetuous, Anthem, and I am a romantic, but I am not a fool. Seeing her, yes, of course. How else could I teach her? In my private rooms, never."

"And the forest?"

"No. Never out of sight. Not for a moment. And that I swear to you." Abruptly, he stood. "Wait."

Billy sat up, watched as the artist went to his cell, pulled a large folder out from under his cot, and returned. Sitting next to Billy, he opened the folder, leafed through it, and extracted one sheet that he handed to Billy. "Look," he said. "You would be an artist. Tell me what you see."

The paper was large and of good quality, expensive for the time and place. The drawing a charcoal sketch of a combination land and seascape. Billy held it to the light so he could see it better, and instantly recognized the shore of Calamity Bay and Cameron Bluff. And yet more than merely the land and the sea.

He had ridden to the very spot, stood at the same vantage point Melinda had used to draw the scene. But Billy felt his view seemed mundane in comparison. The work was simple, even crude in some respects, but even in black and white, the water seemed to shimmer and hint of hidden beasts within its depths. The land seemed to breathe, to lie in expectation of some event it had awaited for a long time, perhaps ages. Scrawled in the lower righthand corner, the single name, "Melinda."

Moved, Billy leaned back and closed his eyes.

"Never mind," Goretti said, replacing the sketch and closing the folder. "You do not need to try to put it in words. She was an innocent who wanted to be a great artist. I touched her but once in the year I knew her, and that when I took her hand one afternoon when she slipped and would have fallen." The artist's eyes were moist. "I saved her from a mishap. A mere fall. And could not save her from that . . . which was . . ." His voice cracked and faltered. "Forgive me. They say she—"

"I heard," Billy said, cutting him off. "In all its gory

variations. The story of her death has been passed around with considerable relish," he added bitterly, reliving again the horror of seeing his own intended bride's broken body long ago. "People."

Silence hovered over them, great and ponderous and impenetrable.

"Yes," Angelo Goretti said at last. "People. The world is too beautiful a place to be plagued with such cruel creatures. The innocent die, and how often, my friend, have you seen the guilty reap rewards for their misdeeds?"

"Too often," Billy said, remembering Laura, and then, too, the splayed and bloodied corpses of her murderers. "But not always," he added, his course clear at last. "Not always. And not this time."

10

★

"Marshal Rhodes. Marshal Rhodes."

Desperate hands worked the latch and the door flew open.

"Wa' the hell!" Bolting upright on his cot, Billy slipped his .45 from its holster where he'd hung it close at hand. "That's far enough," he said, leveling at the figure charging through the door.

"Jesus, Marshal . . . Deputy!" A ragtag boy of ten skidded to a halt, threw his arms in the air. "Don't shoot!"

A kid! Billy's heart slowed as he lowered his weapon. He shook his head to wake himself the rest of the way, then checked the pocket watch he'd dangled over a chair. He and Goretti hadn't turned in till past midnight. "What's wrong?" he managed to ask.

"You better come quick, Deputy. There's a hell of a fight brewin' down to the Flyin' Dragon. Four, five guys hoorawin' Wabash Jack, who's steamin' an' 'bout ready to blow his top. 'An if'n he does . . ." Words failed the lad: he stumbled and couldn't finish his tale.

Billy didn't have the foggiest idea of who Wabash Jack was or why he was to be so feared, but it sounded bad. Wide awake, the deputy pulled on his boots and strapped on his holster, clapped his hat on his head, and was out the

door and on his way. Behind him, Hank Rhodes demanded
to know what the hell was going on. But damned if Billy
even knew.

At six o'clock in the morning, the dives along Water Street
were shooing out the night's last customers and getting
ready to close for the day. Fights along that notorious
stretch of sin and debauchery were as common as salmon
in Klallam Creek, and usually began and ended with little
notice. Word spread quickly, though, when Wabash Jack
was involved. Billy wasn't the only one hurrying to the
Flying Dragon Saloon.

He swerved around an unconscious vagrant lying across
the narrow, mud-soaked wood sidewalk, vaulted another
sprawled facedown between two boards. Billy landed on
the slippery surface and lost his hat and almost his footing.
A sleepy whore wearing a frilly chemise that left nothing
to the imagination leaned out a window to see what was
happening. A pair of her worn and haggard sisters flattened
themselves against the plank wall of Lazy Sue's Sailors'
and Loggers' Haven as Billy raced by them.

"Better watch yourself, Deputy, honey," one called to
Billy's back, knowing he was new and hadn't seen Wabash
Jack in action. She stooped to pick up his hat. "He'll split
you into a dozen shakes before you can say Juan de Fuca!"

Billy had barely time to wonder what he'd gotten himself into, much less to register the warnings from these
soiled doves. His left arm flailing, Billy just managed to
keep his balance as he skidded to a halt in front of the
Flying Dragon.

If Sophie's Klallum Kounty Kocktail Klub was a palace
of perdition, the Flying Dragon was hell's own hovel. It
had a brooding facade. Low-ceilinged, one-story, the saloon
was built of logs with the bark on, much like the men who
no doubt visited the place. A row of narrow, foul-smelling
cribs out back offered Chinese whores, women with broken

spirits, dependent on the generosity of the men they bedded.

From inside, Billy heard a howl of anger and wood cracking. He peered over the top of the batwing doors.

A hell of a fight, as the kid had said when he'd come crashing into the jail, was a tame definition. As nearly as Billy could tell, it had started out about a dozen or so to one. And the "one," considering the bodies sprawled around the room, was doing the majority of the damage.

Billy gulped, and wished he had Cole and Big John and a dozen good riders for the Anthem brand to help him. Wabash Jack was a giant. He stood at least seven feet tall and was built strong as one of the giant redwoods Billy had passed farther south. He had a mane of shaggy brown hair and a wild scraggly beard that made him look as if he'd been sired by a wolf.

Men, bottles, chairs, and tables bounced off him like hail off a roof. Blood streamed down his face, flying off him like raindrops when a chair crashed into his back. Wabash Jack only laughed, howled another curse through broken teeth, picked up his assailant, and hurled the fool across the bar into the mirror. It splintered into a thousand pieces. Another man, this one with a knife, came in low. Wabash Jack caught him out of the corner of his eye. Billy had never seen so large a man move so fast. Somehow, he pivoted to his left. The blade missed his gut, but skewered the fleshy part of his forearm. Wabash Jack roared, picked the man up by the scruff of the neck, and hurled him toward the door.

Enough was enough. Billy ducked out of harm's way as the man went sailing past into the street. Anthem darted through the swinging doors, pulled his Colt .45, blasted a pair of holes in the floor between the combatants.

The sound was deafening. All activity came to an instant halt. One man, already groggy, turned slowly toward Billy, rolled his eyes up in his head, and crumpled, unconscious. Others froze or ducked behind overturned tables.

Wabash Jack took a step toward Billy and, with the knife sticking out of his arm and blood dripping from his fingers, peered nearsightedly at him, looking for all the world like a great bear, wounded and highly dangerous. "Who the hell are you?" he asked in a guttural voice that rumbled around in his chest like a piece of lead shot in an oak bucket.

"Name's Billy Anthem. Hank Rhodes named me deputy until he gets back on his feet. You've gotta be Wabash Jack. Well boys, it's sunup. Closing time, even for this pit."

Wabash Jack's eyes crinkled, his massive chest expanded; he made a short, deep, barking sound as he lurched forward to continue the fight with this new foe.

Billy held his ground. "That's far enough," he warned, leveling his revolver at the advancing giant. "I know your reputation. But I've got four shots left, and not even you can take that many slugs even in your hard head."

Wabash Jack cocked his head, peered quizzically at the young man sighting down the gun barrel at him. "Maybe you're right about that," Jack grunted at last, his massive head shaking slowly in agreement.

"The rest of you." Billy turned, eyed each conscious combatant in turn. "Anyone want to keep it going?"

Heads shook. A beating was bad enough, but getting a bullet between the eyes was something else entirely. "Naw," one after another grumbled. " 'Nuff for me."

Billy moved to his side, trained his weapon on a man who stood behind Wabash Jack and held, poised over the giant's head, a full bottle of whiskey. "You, friend?"

"Sumbitch knocked out two my goddamn teeth," the man slurred.

"That's two won't rot out in another year," Billy suggested. He cocked the revolver.

The man glared at Billy, briefly at Wabash Jack, and back to the gun. "Shit!" the man grumbled. "Can't have a goddamn friendly fight."

Wabash Jack reached behind him, snagged the bottle out

of the man's hand. "Well, I'm drinkin'," he said. Jack pulled the cork with his teeth and marched to the bar. "French!"

A dapper, somewhat oily-looking man Billy knew as French Goldstein, the owner of the Flying Dragon, popped up from behind the bar. He was a little man, unshaven, with rodent features and a nervous smile.

"Glasses!" Wabash Jack demanded. He jerked the knife from his arm to toss it unconcernedly to one side. "We drink. I buy." He licked the blood from his knuckles and pounded on the bar. "Quick. Glasses."

Billy heaved a sigh of relief, then slowly holstered his weapon. It was over. One by one, the men gathered at the bar in a long line, passed the bottle, and filled their glasses. "Who started this?" Anthem asked.

"Everybody," groaned one of the men at the bar.

Billy had seen his share of fights and rapid reconciliations, but nothing to compare to this. Except for the unconscious figures scattered around like chaff and the shattered furniture and mirror, a new customer might think that nothing at all was amiss.

Billy wasn't about to pit himself against the likes of Wabash Jack and his battle-worn friends by trying to arrest them. If French didn't care, neither did the law.

Again the doors creaked, this time as a tall, cadaverously thin man with a wide and floppy black hat perched on top of a great shock of white hair entered. He glanced around the room and shook his head, shifted his attention to Billy. "You must be Anthem," he said, peering at the deputy through his wire-rim spectacles. I'm Bannon. Folks just call me Doc. After all these years, it fits, I reckon. Saul," he barked over his shoulder. "Come on in."

Doc Bannon, like most of his profession in the territories, had seen it all. Nothing fazed him. With no more concern than if he'd been pulling a splinter from someone's finger, he took the black bag his manservant stepped in to hand him, picked the nearest body, and set to work. Ten minutes later, three more stood at the bar with their *compadres*, and another had been packed off to Bannon's office to have a murderous gash in his head sewed up.

"You get used to a lot of things," he told Billy, who remained at his side while the physician went about his task, "but never to Wabash. You want to see something?"

"I've already seen a lot more'n I usually do before breakfast," Billy said, instantly liking the man.

Bannon appeared to be fearless, but was at the same time no fool. Stopping out of range behind Wabash Jack, he called the man's name. When that great shaggy head turned, Bannon crooked his finger and beckoned. Surprisingly, the giant hung his head sheepishly and complied meekly. "You ain't gonna be mad at me, are ya, Doc?"

Bannon jerked his head. Saul pulled an unbroken table over and set the bag on it. "Take off your shirt, Wabash," Bannon ordered. "When the hell are you going to learn to play your damn games at a decent hour? I work half the night and then have to get up at the crack of dawn to tend some hairy beast . . ."

Wabash Jack grinned widely. "It was a good fight." He laughed, stripping off his shirt. "Nothing happened this time."

Billy had never seen anyone like him. An incredible specimen—great muscles rippled under a thick mat of black hair that was creased by lines and holes where scar tissue showed through. The man had been knifed and shot well over a dozen times; he looked like a towering redwood that had been used for target practice.

"What the hell you call this?" Bannon said, taking the giant's arm and inspecting the knife wound.

The blood was already clotting on both entrance and exit wounds. Wabash Jack paid them no more attention than a glance. "Ain't nothin'. Get better quick, eh?"

"Probably. One of these days, though, your natural resistance is going to fail you, and then we'll see how damned smart you are. Hold still."

Wabash Jack watched bemused while Saul handed Bannon a probe and a bottle of grain alcohol. A treatment he'd performed a hundred times, Bannon ran the probe through the wound, separated the tissue, and poured the alcohol straight into the front of the wound until it ran out the back.

Billy gritted his teeth and winced. Goose bumps rose on his arms. Amazingly, Wabash Jack didn't seem to feel a thing. He merely grunted when the procedure was finished, and waited placidly for Bannon to wrap the freshly bleeding wound with a clean piece of linen.

"There you go, Wabash," Bannon said. "You're all set for the next round."

Wabash Jack dipped one hand in his pocket and extracted a gold coin, which he handed Bannon. "You're a good man, a good friend, eh, Doc?"

"You bet." Bannon's eyes sparkled impishly as he jerked his head in Billy's direction. "You want to show him, Wabash?"

Again that wide grin. "Sure, Doc." Jack turned and touched his midriff. "Right here," he said to Billy.

"Huh?" Billy asked.

Bannon stepped aside. "Go ahead. Hard as you can," he said, enjoying himself.

"He won't—"

"Nah. Jack enjoys this." Doc Bannon tapped Wabash Jack's abdomen with one knuckle. "I've heard about you boys who are Texas-born. Show us your stuff, lad."

Someone guffawed. One man held up a twenty-dollar gold piece and offered to bet it against a shot of whiskey that Billy couldn't double Wabash Jack over, but there were no takers. Insulted, Billy decided what the hell, stepped forward, planted his feet, and swung from the hips.

"Aaiihhh!"

The Flying Dragon exploded with laughter. His face

white, Billy stepped back and cradled his right hand with
his left. It felt like he'd slammed his fist into an adobe wall,
like he'd driven his knuckles up into his elbow. "Je-*sus!*"
he exclaimed. He stared at his fist, made himself flex his
fingers.

Wabash Jack roared, clapped a monstrous, meaty paw
on Billy's shoulder. "That's a pretty good hit," he crowed.
"I felt that one. You're a good man. *Good* man. Now drink
with Wabash, eh?" The giant turned to French. "Set up a
Wabash special, huh, French."

Bannon saved the young Texan. "Another time, Wabash.
I'm going to buy him some breakfast." He nodded to Saul,
who set to work repacking the medical bag. "And put on
that damned shirt. Wouldn't want you to catch a cold," he
added over his shoulder, already on his way to the door.

The doctor refused to eat at Openeer's and directed Billy
on to Wick's. The hotel restaurant was a pleasant place,
open and airy, with white lace tablecloths, sparkling clean
silverware, and an abundance of windows.

"All I have to say," Billy remarked as he dug into a
plateful of Hangtown fries, a meal of potatoes, eggs, and
oysters, "is that Wabash Jack is one hell of a way to start
a day. Where'd he come from, anyway?"

"Out of the north woods, near as anyone knows," Bannon replied, lacing his coffee with brandy, surreptitiously
poured from a flask he carried. "I've read about men like
him. He's the most remarkable specimen I've ever seen. I
personally know of eight slugs and two knifetips that are
still in him, and I'd lay odds there are a few more I don't
know about. I've sewed up seven major knife wounds.
Don't even bother with the ones like you saw today. Amazing recuperative powers. Look at that wound the day after
tomorrow, and you'll swear it was a month old. Never
ceases to amaze me."

"What I can't understand," Billy said, "is why that

bunch was damned fool enough to light into him. It's like a pack of jackrabbits takin' on a grizzly. You'd think they'd know by now."

Bannon shook his head in agreement. "They do. Problem is, he actually lost a fight once, two years ago. He took on half a dozen real roughhousers. Someone still had to lick him over the head with a four-inch-thick club before he went down. The six men it took are looked up to as heroes. So now it's a challenge. Of course, Wabash thinks it's all a big game. He actually enjoys these brawls."

"In that case, I believe I'll stick to checkers, you don't mind," Billy said. He checked his hand once more to make sure it worked. "I've never hit anything that hard in my life."

"As good a way as any to break into Calamity Bay society," Bannon commented wryly. "Not counting, of course, your highly celebrated run-ins with the Creeds."

Billy arched one brow. "Word sure gets around."

"Ever see a small town where it didn't? We're no better or worse than the rest."

"I reckon." Billy polished off his meal and finished his coffee. "So what'd you think of Rhodes? He going to be all right?"

Bannon pushed his plate away from him, leaned his elbows on the table. "Goretti did a good job. The rib'll heal soon enough, but Hank'll have to learn how to shoot left-handed for a while. His biggest problem will be how to use a crutch and, if the need arises, shoot with the same hand. Good thing you're around, I'd say." He eyed Billy. The doctor was a shrewd judge of character, a talent he'd developed over the years of patching wounds, delivering babies, and holding death at bay in countless hovels, mining camps, and fine hilltop houses. Bannon liked what he saw in this young man from Texas.

"I told Hank I'd stay till he healed. And now that Wabash Jack has shown me how many ways a man can amuse himself around here, I might not want to leave."

"I know what you mean." Bannon grinned.

"Right." Billy's smile disappeared as he glanced around the dining room and lowered his voice. "About Goretti."

Bannon caught the change in mood, and tensed.

"I've been nosing around, talking to folks. I'd like to see things from your side."

"They woke me up about five-thirty a week ago Thursday morning. A dockworker had found her body in Creed's Number Two lumber warehouse, which was under repair after a fire." Bannon wiped a hand across his mouth. The fingers trembled, a signal that it was time for another drink. He licked his lips and continued. "Just a girl, they said at the time. Any rate, Saul and I hightailed it down there. Still dark, of course. A handful of men, by that time, with lanterns. She'd been beaten, horribly bruised."

He closed his eyes as if willing the image into focus, an image he'd been trying to forget. "Her skirts were bunched around her waist, and she was bloody . . . so I checked when I got her body back to the office." His voice was as grim as the look on his face. "She'd been raped, of course."

"And?" Billy asked when the silence stretched out.

Bannon came back from wherever his mind had wandered. "You see a lot of fights up here, like this morning. Lot of accidents in the woods and mills. First rape for me, though." He shook his head sadly. "I knew that little girl. Pretty, smart, sweet as can be. A terrible thing, Anthem. Terrible."

"Yeah." Billy looked out the window. The town was awake. The streets were alive with miners and lumbermen on their way to work. A trio of seamstresses were hurrying to their shop. Life went on as usual in Calamity Bay. Life as usual, except for an innocent girl named Melinda.

"Was it Goretti? How the hell am I supposed to know? I wasn't there. Ah!" Doc shrugged. "Sorry. Not your fault. The Creeds think Goretti's guilty, of course."

"I know what the Creeds think," Billy said, keeping his voice calm. "I asked what you think."

Bannon massaged his eyes with his fingertips. "I don't know. He claims he was elsewhere and never went near that warehouse in his life, but he won't say where he was, so . . ." He paused, shrugged. "He could have, I guess. It's possible. Yet he seems like such a gentle man."

Billy considered his options. He'd heard opinions ranging from innocent to guilty as hell. Anthem found it hard to believe the artist could be guilty of so horrible a crime; on the other hand, from what he'd seen of the Creeds and the way they acted, Goretti was as good as hanged. If push came to shove, the odds were on the Creeds' side. So it was up to Billy to see if he could clear the artist's name. Goretti certainly wasn't being much help.

"Believe I'll go take a look at the warehouse myself," Billy said. "Want to come along?"

"Me? I've got a man needs sewing up back in my office. Besides," Bannon said, throwing a silver dollar on the table and rising, "there's no sense riling up certain people more than necessary."

"Up to you," Billy said, pushing away from table.

"Yes, it is, isn't it?" Bannon watched Billy weave his way through the tables on his way out, quickly caught up with him at the door, and caught him by the sleeve. "One thing," he said before Billy could leave.

"Yeah?" Suddenly, Billy had the distinct impression the doctor suspected a lot more than he was willing to let on.

Bannon held up three fingers on his left hand, one on his right. "Four of the girl's fingernails were packed with skin and blood. I checked Goretti real close. Not a scratch on him."

Billy looked up and down the sun-drenched street. He saw a peaceful, pretty town with an ugly secret lying unseen, just below the surface waiting to erupt.

11

★

The morning was still young when Billy made his first stop at the jail to check on Rhodes and bring breakfast to the marshal and his prisoner. They'd already heard the story of the fight at the Flying Dragon from Krait, who had dropped by to pick up a coat he'd left behind. The fire in the potbelly was built up and a pot of water was boiling, thanks to the ex-deputy, so all Billy had to do was add coffee grounds.

Goretti sat huddled in his cell. He seemed withdrawn, lost in his own thoughts. Rhodes was in a foul mood and getting grumpier by the minute.

"You could've got your head busted and I'm lyin' here like a damn useless . . . useless . . ." He tried to think of a damn useless what, and sputtered to a stop.

"We could always put you down," Billy suggested. "They shoot horses, you know."

The marshal's face fell. "Dad burn it," he grumped. "I swear, but there's times when I think that'd be the best—" He stopped short, glared at Billy. "You reckon you could get that coffee ready sometime before the turn of the century, or am I gonna have to wait 'till I can walk fer some?"

Marshal and prisoner had their morning coffee and watched Billy oil and clean his revolver. He worked the cylinder, checked the hammer action, and finally loaded the weapon with a .45 center-fire cartridge in each chamber.

"I been down to the warehouse, twice," Rhodes said, watching Anthem work. He appreciated a man who took care of his weapon. "But you might as well go look around fer yourself, if you're bound to. Won't help much, far as I can see, but can't hurt."

Goretti hadn't said a word since the conversation had turned to Melinda's murder.

"What about it, Angelo?" Billy asked softly. "Still don't want to tell who you were with that night?"

The Italian stared at his plate and didn't say a word.

"Stubborn as that damn mule of mine," Rhodes grumbled. "Dumber, too. At least Absalom's got enough sense not to kill itself."

"I do not want to die, Marshal," Goretti said. "I will if I have to, but I want very badly to live." His eyes filled with anguished pleading, he looked at each of them in turn. "Maybe I'll change my mind when I stand in the shadow of the noose. But maybe, maybe, you can find another way to save Angelo Goretti's poor scrawny neck, than at the expense of someone's reputation."

"Ahhh!" Rhodes gave up, snorting in disgust.

Billy rose and dropped the weapon into its holster. "You do make it hard on a man, Goretti."

"I'm sorry. I—"

"Never mind. Don't bother," Billy said. "I'll be back in an hour or two. Keep off your feet, Marshal. I'll stop by Bannon's on my way back. And the least you can do," he added, pointing at Goretti, "is clean up the place. And for God's sake, keep an eye out and lock yourself up if anybody comes by."

Warehouse Number Two was at the far western end of Water Street where it crossed the bedding for the narrow-gauge rail track connecting Creed Number One coal mine to the new coal ship docks farther out the bay. Water Street petered out into a dirt path that led to a cluster of shacks belonging to the poorer workers' families. Billy walked down Mount Olive, turning left on Water at the cedar-shake plant. The sawmill, the largest of the buildings on the waterfront, was going full blast. Clouds of smoke spewed from the top of the furnace and trailed off toward the hills.

Beyond the sawmill lay Number One Warehouse, still in use, and beyond it, Number Two, where the murder had occurred. Billy nodded pleasantly and spoke to workers he passed. They were a grungy lot on first appearance, but beneath the grime were simple, honest men who'd heard how he'd saved Hank Rhodes' life, sent Tim Creed packing out of Sophie's, and shut down Wabash Jack's party. These were deeds that had won the young Texan a modicum of respect. He took pride in the achievement.

Repairwork had ceased on Number Two Warehouse while the men concentrated on laying the tracks and finishing the coal dock. The place was empty and the main entrance barred. A sign warned intruders to keep out, but Billy figured that didn't mean the law, so he tossed the sign aside, unbarred and pushed the huge double doors open to let in the light, and stepped inside.

One set of doors, no matter how large, wasn't enough. The vast warehouse stretched away to darkness at his right, and to light, at least thirty paces away, on his left where the fire had burned through the west wall. A high roof intensified the gloom. The body had been found about halfway along the north wall, Bannon had said, almost directly across from the main doors. Billy made his way in that direction.

It was hard to tell much. Left there, for some reason, were a pile of barrels, a stack of ties suitable for a narrow-guage railway, and some rotting tarps. Billy nosed around in the dim light, found a panel in the wall, and opened it. The light that flooded in seemed gray, prompting him to look out and up at the rapidly darkening sky.

He returned his attention to the warehouse floor. Nothing indicated that a crime had been committed. There were smudges where the dust had been disturbed, true, but they could have been put there by someone moving ties.

Hunkering down, he moved one of the tarps aside in the hopes of finding something hidden underneath. Nothing again, except scurrying water bugs and a round, dark, and caked spot that might, and might not, he told himself, have been blood. Rhodes had been right. He wasn't going to find anything.

"Guess you didn't read the sign," a familiar voice said behind him.

Billy swiveled on his heels. The light in front of him had washed out the shadows of the men approaching from behind. All ten of them, he counted as they fanned out to either side. And not friends, from the looks on their faces.

"Or can't read," Timothy Creed snickered. "That it, Texas? The sign said, 'Keep out.' "

"Just looking things over. No harm intended," Billy said, seeing no point in starting a fight. "Didn't figure that sign meant the law."

"Only problem is, you aren't the law."

"Oh?" Billy stood and turned so the light caught the badge he wore. "Believe you're mistaken there, Creed. This badge says so. Given to me by Hank Rhodes himself."

"And doesn't mean a hill a' beans," the youngest Creed sneered. "Not until the city council votes on you, and they don't meet until tomorrow."

So there was going to be a fight, after all. Billy could feel it in his bones. The gun he wore wasn't worth jack straw under the circumstances, since three of the men facing him had shotguns leveled at his belly.

"Guess you boys got the drop on me, then," he said, holding his hands out to his side for benefit of the ones who were armed. "Which means I reckon I'd just better apologize for buttin' in where I'm not wanted, and mosey on outa here."

"Abe. Martin," Timothy said. The hammers on two scatterguns, one on either side of him, clicked back with a deadly sound.

The thought of two twelve-gauge scatterguns cutting him in half was daunting, but Billy figured the men wouldn't shoot without Creed giving them the command. Nonetheless, with a good four steps at a run between him and Creed, and the possibility that his first step might be his last, he froze.

"Not real smart, Creed," he said, careful not to move. He was bluffing, but given the reputation he'd gained in the last couple of days, the bluff might work. "Your boys know the city fathers won't stand still for cuttin' down a man who hasn't done anything. And I don't imagine y'all want to hang for a murder, even for a Creed. 'Sides."— this was no bluff, he decided as his gun hand lowered ever so slightly—"I reckon I'll get off one shot no matter what happens," he told the men with the scatterguns. "And that'll be between Tim's eyes here. Now, what do you suppose old Noah will do when you carry his boy home on a plank?"

Doubt worked across the gunmen's features. Their knuckles whitened where they gripped their guns. These were miners, not gunmen. And Billy had succeeded in rattling their nerves.

"I'm walking out now," Billy said. Knowing—betting— that the men wouldn't fire, he took one step, then another. "If you're smart, you'll stand aside."

Tim's eyes narrowed as Billy Anthem neared. He already owed the deputy marshal for embarrassing him once in public, and he was damned if he'd walk away a loser twice in a row. The price was too high. Creed or no, every man in Calamity Bay would call him a coward and laugh at him behind his back. And that, above all else, he could not bear.

Four steps. Three, two, one. Billy watched Timothy Creed's eyes and read in them the confusion and hatred, the fear, and suddenly, the determination. And in that same instant, sensed and then saw the bunching of muscles and the shift of weight.

The first blow was clumsy and easily avoided. Billy merely leaned back an inch or two, waited for the fist to whistle past his face, then dipped, dug his feet in, and went for the belly.

Timothy took a right and a left, short, vicious jabs that cut like knives into his gut. Blocking the third with a forearm, he doubled over and charged, and caught Billy under the chin with the top of his head.

His jaw felt like it had been torn off. Billy gave a step, slipped sideways, clubbed Creed with a short right as he stumbled past.

The watchers quickly formed a circle. Would they let Creed fight his own battle, Billy wondered, or was it more likely they'd make damned sure the boss's son didn't lose? He worked his jaw to make sure it wasn't broken. Billy knew he had to put Creed down and out before his men stepped in to help.

Creed spun, returning to the attack. Billy darted in with a left to the midriff and right to the jaw before Tim could get his bearings. Creed appeared to crumble, but it was a ploy. In an instant the quick-footed youth drove Billy back with a rain of blows to the belly.

Billy gave way, planted, countered to the face. Blood flew like rain from a cut over Creed's eye. Tim backed away, shaking his head and blinking away the pain. Before he could recover, Billy was into him again, this time with a combination of chest and body blows that drove his opponent backward and knocked the wind out of him.

Creed groaned, tripped on a piece of wood, and went

down to one knee as a haymaker right cut the air over his head. Just able to see, he grabbed a length of two-by-four and swung it. Billy jumped back and dodged the attack as Creed fell on his face down in the dust.

It should have been all over. Creed was at his mercy, struggling to stand. Billy cocked his right for the knockout blow, but at that moment, instead of continuing to rise, Creed leaned forward, grabbed Billy around both knees, and pulled his legs out from under him.

Billy hit hard on his back, struggled for breath. Catlike, Creed scrambled to his feet and dropped, driving one knee into Billy's midriff and clawing for his throat. Billy drove a fist upward, flat into Creed's nose, and was rewarded with a howl of pain and a shower of crimson. Quickly, before Creed could recover, Billy rolled and slid out from under the knee that ground into his gut. He bounced to his feet.

Creed went for the knees again, but Billy was having none of it. Knocking Tim's arms aside, Billy reached down, caught Creed by the front of the shirt, and pulled him erect. Creed twisted violently, trying to free himself. Billy felt the material give, and Tim's shirt tore down the front as the two men separated.

Creed was hurt. His right eye was swelling closed. His nose was badly broken and bled profusely. Billy hadn't begun to feel any pain yet, but he knew he would. His jaw felt odd, his right hand was swollen and throbbing, and his gut burned from the punishment inflicted by the knee. It was not time to hold back, though. Creed was about out on his feet, and one or two good—

And then, through the mist of fatigue, the deputy saw them. Saw the barely healed scratches, the faint white lines of new scar tissue on Creed's chest. "You sonofabitch!" Billy gasped, the fury rising in him.

Tim saw the look in Billy's eyes and knew something had changed.

"Take him," he gasped, sagging to his knees. He spat a gout of blood. "Take the bastard!"

There wasn't a lot of taking to be done. Billy fought like a wildcat, but he was no Wabash Jack. The four men who closed in on him landed two blows for every one he managed.

Beyond pain, he felt his head snap to one side, then the other, felt the air driven out of him as blow after blow cut into his ribs, gut, and kidneys. A minute after it began, it was over. He wanted only to fall, but they were holding him on his feet.

And then, through the veil of blood, Billy saw a face loom in front of him and he dimly made out a club rising, floating through the air. It was Creed. He was going to finish the deputy here and now. For good.

The blow never came. Instead, a hand floated into view and caught the club as it started forward.

"No," a voice said. "That's takin' it too far."

"The hell you say!" Timothy Creed's voice was faint, and strained. "Mind your own damned business!"

The man took the club from Creed, threw it aside, and before Tim could react, relieved him of his gun as well. "You can have this back when you come to your senses. Now go home and lick your wounds. You can take this Anthem fella another day, if you're man enough."

Creed looked around the circle and read in the eyes of the men standing there that it was all over. There was nothing to be done for it. He spat at Billy's feet. "Let that be a lesson, Anthem," he snarled. "Stay out of my way or you'll get more of the same."

Another face materialized where Tim's had been. "You all right, son?"

The question was funny, for some insane reason, but he'd begun to hurt too much to laugh. "Yeah," he managed to croak. Did he know the man? Had he seen him before? Nothing made sense. "Aw 'righ'. I'm aw 'righ'."

"Good. Let him go, boys."

"He's a real heller, ain't he?" another voice said.

Billy was floating. Dropping through air as thick as cane syrup. He could see the ground coming up at him. And then it was right under his face and he could feel it, not hard, but soft as a down-filled pillow.

"Thanks," he mumbled, fading fast. " 'Preciate the party, boys."

Strange, he thought. Four lines swam across his vision. Three and one, slanting diagonally from top to bottom toward each other. Now what did they mean? he wondered. Scars! The son of a bitch. It was him. It was Tim Creed. He had to . . . had to . . .

And then there was no more wondering. No more planning. Nothing he had to do but tumble into sweet, sweet darkness.

12

★

Darkness. A roaring sound. Cold. And only then, pain.

Billy opened his eyes slowly, tried to place himself. Pain vied with memory. He closed his eyes, willing the pain to a distant place. Memories filled the void. Laura was dead. Billy had been captured by Varela's raiders and taken to Mexico. He'd been beaten, imprisoned, and starved, but he endured. He had lived with pain and survived. He never lost faith in the family that would ride through hell itself if need be to rescue one of their own.

Images faded, darkness returned.

He woke again, an hour later, his eyes roamed the gloom, and this time he remembered Creed and the men who had beat him. He was in Warehouse Number Two. And he hurt in more places than he could count.

The first thing to do is stand. No. The first thing to do is get to your knees. Then stand.

He willed his hands underneath him, rolled onto his belly, and pushed upward. So far, so good. Head swimming, he somehow tottered to his feet.

The very act of standing made him feel better. He took stock. His jaw felt like it had been taken off and haphazardly glued back on. His gut ached fiercely. A knife of pain stabbed his chest with every breath. His right hip throbbed from the way he'd been lying on his gun. But what the hell. He was on his feet. And if a man could stand, he could walk.

The first few steps were the worst, but with each the pain receded a little. His head cleared. Now he recognized in the dim light the spot on the filthy floor where Melinda had met her fate. The panel he had opened was closed, and he couldn't make his arms reach high enough to unlatch it.

The main doors were on the far side of the warehouse. Billy lurched across the vast emptiness and pushed weakly against the doors. When they didn't move, he stooped to peer through the crack between the doors and saw they were barred. He made his way back into the interior warehouse. A fire had eaten a hole through the rear wall. It was his only way out.

Billy walked like a drunkard, staggering across the pebble-strewn floor. At last, he reached the charred section of wall, pushed aside one dangling plank, and looked out upon a wall of rain.

"No time like the present," he said out loud, testing to see if his mouth worked.

The rain was cold but refreshing at first. He let it rinse the dried blood from his face as he got his bearings. The ground was littered with debris from the fire. Billy picked his way carefully to the front of the building and stopped under a shallow halfroof to lean against the wall and take a breather. How far was it to the jail? A half-mile? No matter, whatever the distance, it was too damn far.

He didn't dare fall. Because if he landed facedown and unconscious in the ocean of mud that stretched as far as he could see, he might easily drown before anyone came to his rescue.

A wind gusted and chilled him to the bone. Gritting his teeth against the pain, shivering like a puppy, Billy waded through a drainage ditch and half-slipped, half-scrambled up to the relatively easy footing of the road.

He knew no tricks to overcome pain, so he relied on pure raw determination. What did Big John Anthem call his sons? Texas-born. He had lived and worked in heat that could suck a man dry as a corn shuck, he'd driven stock and ridden herd in blizzards so cold that once he'd frozen to the saddle. As a prisoner, Billy Anthem had existed on pain and slops in Varela's cave in Mexico, and had lived to exact vengeance. He'd be damned if a half mile of rain and mud was going to do him in.

To Penelope Swain's way of thinking, education was Bradley Norman's only hope. His father was doomed to a life of backbreaking toil in the coal mines, but Bradley was blessed with a keen mind, and with an education he could look forward to a real future.

Penelope had driven to Mill Hollow because she believed in the boy's future with all her heart. And it had nearly broken her resolve to find his mother drunk, his father gone, and his little sisters, only a year old, cold and hungry. No wonder the poor child hadn't been to school, and no wonder he hadn't told her why. The ten-year-old was proud, and the only one to earn the pennies they survived on. Bradley Norman, she feared, was a lost cause in a world full of lost causes.

Her horse shied. Penelope reined in and barely missed trampling the man staggering up the middle of the road. "If you don't mind," she called.

The man seemed oblivious to her. She steered the little mare to the right and tried to pass. No sooner had the carriage pulled even with him, though, than the man swerved to the right too and stopped dead in his tracks, again blocking the way.

"Would you let me pass, sir?" Penelope said, alarmed now by this stranger in the rain. The man made his way toward the woman in the carriage. He used the harness to keep himself from falling and drew close enough for her to recognize him.

"Billy Anthem! Is that you, Billy?" Penelope set the brake, jumped down, and ran to him. Mud splashed her ankle boots and the hem of her gray dress and hooded cape. "Dear heaven, but what has happened to you?"

"Hurt," Billy said, swaying dangerously and then pulling himself erect. "Not bad. Jus' a li'l."

Both of them slipping and sliding, she led him to the carriage seat and wrestled him in. "Just sit still," she told him. "I'm taking you to Doctor Bannon."

"No," Billy slurred. "Nothin' broke. Jus' fine. Jail."

"Very well," Penelope lied. She climbed up beside him. He leaned against her, water dripping from his hair and battered features onto her neck and shoulder. Billy grinned, enjoying the closeness. Penelope hurriedly released the brake and slapped the reins on the little mare's back. "What happened? Who did this?"

He offered no explanation and replied by closing his eyes and nestling against her.

The rain slacked, which was no improvement, for a heavy mist moved in. The carriage rumbled across the bridge over Klallam Creek. Penelope turned up Helena and down Pine to Bannon's office, jumped down, and ran to his door, only to discover that both he and Saul were out. "Damn!" she cursed, most unladylike, stamping her right foot in a puddle and splashing herself.

She returned to the carriage and considered taking him to the jail, then ruled out such a course. He'd be sure to catch pneumonia in that drafty old building. That left only one other place to take him. Penelope sighed. Billy snuggled against her again. The schoolteacher, muttering a prayer of gratitude for the concealing mist, wheeled the little mare about in the middle of the street and headed for home.

* * *

Billy was soaked, of course. Badly beaten, too, but she had no idea how badly until she lit a lamp and took a closer look at him. The left side of his jaw was swollen, his upper lip was split. His right eye was almost closed, and the cheek below it was turning an ugly black and blue. The knuckles on both hands were split and raw, so he hadn't been completely defenseless and had probably given a good accounting of himself.

Billy opened his eyes and looked around at the sitting room. "Where are we?" he asked, thankful to be out of the rain. His arm was draped over her shoulder.

"My house. Here. Come along," she coaxed.

Shivering violently, he let her lead him into the small but cozy bedroom, and sat dutifully on a straight-back chair. Lace curtains framed the tightly shuttered windows. A wood stove had been set in one corner. The rest of the room was dominated by a big brass bed.

"We need to get you dry and warm," Penelope said, opening a chest and removing a heavy wool Hudson Bay blanket. "Get your clothes off," she commanded, speaking to him as she might a child, "and wrap up in this. I'm going to heat up some coffee and will be back for them in a minute."

Stripping was easier said than done, but Billy was in no condition to protest. His muscles screaming, he eased out of his coat. Unbuttoning his vest was nigh impossible. His fingers could barely push the small buttons through the thick fabric. The boots were easy, but he had to sit to remove his trousers because he couldn't bend over far enough.

"Feeling better?" Penelope asked a few minutes later when she entered and found him wrapped in the blanket and huddled in a chair.

"I think," Billy said, his teeth still chattering.

"The fire's down and will take a while to build up," the teacher said. She moved to the bed and turned down the thick down comforter. "In," she said in a no nonsense manner.

"Wouldn't be proper," Billy protested.

"Don't you dare tell me what is or isn't proper. You'll do as I say, Billy Anthem." She helped him off the chair and into the brass frame bed and pulled the down comforter up to his chin. "Sleep, if you can. I'll be a while."

She took the lantern and closed the door behind her, leaving the room dark. Billy stretched his legs, then straightened his arms at his side and flexed his fingers. His abdomen was tender. Higher up, he winced when he touched his ribs. Hell, he'd never in his life hurt so many places at once.

The wool and down caught his body heat, reflected it back to him. Soon he stopped shivering. He was tired and felt like he'd been riding for a week without sleep. It was no time to sleep, though. Had work to do. Get back to the jail, let Rhodes know he was all right. Creed . . . What? He struggled to keep his eyes open. Something about Creed's what? . . . Fingers? That didn't make sense. But what did? Safe and dry and warm, he succumbed to the sweet laziness that stole over him, and he fell into a deep sleep.

Laura was alive. Her death had been a cruel hoax. And now she was better and had come to him. Her hands were soft and tender when they brushed the hair off his forehead. Her lips were cool, a sweet balm, a great and healing gift. Hungry for her, his heart nearly bursting with joy, Billy reached for her and . . .

"Billy? Billy?"

It wasn't Laura's voice at all. Billy opened his eyes, saw a vision of peaches-and-cream skin, of pale lips, of a cascade of ash-blond hair falling to touch his cheek, lips the color of rose wine.

"Billy? Are you awake?"

His mouth was dry and he licked his lips. "Yeah. I

guess." He studied the woman seated on the bed beside him. How proudly she held herself. Her small, firmly proportioned bosom rose and fell with every breath. "Yes. Definitely," he amended. "You think you could do that again?"

"Do what again?"

. He reached to touch her cheek, to wind his fingers gently in her hair. "This," he said, pulling her to him.

Their kiss was gentle, but insistent. "You're a rogue, Billy Anthem," Penny whispered in his ear. She pushed herself upright and gazed fondly down at him. "Or an ogre. One or the other," she said, noting his battered face.

"Neither," Billy said, grinning as widely as his split lip permitted. "Just a man who thinks you're a beautiful woman." He reached for her again. "Come here."

"No." Penny laughed. "No, sir, Mr. Billy Anthem." She stood and arranged her skirt. "I've gone to a great deal of trouble to fix some soup for you. I'll not be dissuaded by a kiss. Especially," she made a mock serious face, "by a man who looks as if he's just been through the business end of a sawmill." She started for the door. "I'll be in the other room."

Billy crawled out of bed and looked into the mirror on her bureau. He did look pretty bad, he admitted. He felt better, though, and that was what counted. "All in one piece, I guess," he said a moment later, joining her in the front room. He wore the blanket wrapped about his body and felt rather silly for it. But at least it was warmer than prowling around bare-assed and buck-naked.

He took his place at Penny's table and studied his surroundings while she served him. The diningroom wall was cheerily covered with a fleur-de-lis print. Lithographs and original oil paintings adorned two of the walls. A nearby hutch displayed a row of china that probably had been handed down from mother to daughter.

"I hope it's filling," Penny said as she watched him hungrily empty his soup bowl.

"I'm tempted to lick the dish clean," Billy replied. He grinned, cocking an eye toward her.

"You look like a cat watching a mouse," he observed dryly. Suddenly embarrassed for having concentrated so hard on eating and, in the process, totally ignoring her, he set aside his spoon. "I do something wrong?"

"No." Her smile was warm and friendly. "I'm just wondering, is all."

"About what?"

"How a man beaten so badly that he can hardly walk can, only a few hours later, be up and about and eating like a horse. I'd be flat on my back for a week."

Billy nodded. "I look worse than I feel. Now, don't get me wrong. I hurt like blazes and I'll be sore for a few days, I warrant." He stopped, hit by a sudden thought.

"What?" Penelope asked.

"Just dawned on me." His frown of concentration turned into a split lip grin. "I don't believe those boys think too highly of Mr. Timothy Creed. If their hearts were really in their job, I'd be in a lot worse shape than I am."

Penny shook her head in awe, looked up sharply as the clock on the mantel in the sitting room began to chime. "Good Lord! It's eight o'clock." She got up, went to the door and looked out. "And the weather is clearing. We have to get you out of here. If someone sees you . . ."

She didn't need to finish the sentence. Billy had seen how a town's matrons could hound a schoolmarm out of a job, home, and reputation after a man had been caught in her house after dark.

Penelope fetched his clothes from the kitchen where she'd hung them on a makeshift rack by the stove. She'd dried his boots as well. Billy, clothes in hand, headed back to the bedroom. The feather mattress looked inviting, but he put it out of mind. Warmth and a meal had returned his strength, and he managed to dress without undue trouble. As he sat on the edge of the bed to pull on his boots, he glimpsed the corner of a painting on the floor, hidden behind the bureau.

Paintings belonged on walls, not hidden behind bureaus. Curious, knowing it was none of his business, Billy tiptoed to the bureau, quietly moved it away from the wall, and pulled out the framed canvas.

"Well, well!" he softly exclaimed, gazing at the oil painting and its alluring subject. "Miss Penelope Swain." And he didn't need to guess who had rendered it. Goretti had even signed the corner. Captured on canvas, Penelope was dressed in a shimmering white cotton gown. She stood in front of the bureau. The view was of her back, painted from the bed where Billy had lain. A candle placed on the bureau lit her features.

Head tilted slightly to the left, a faint, mysterious smile on her lips, she looked with sleepy eyes into a handheld mirror at the artist who painted her. Her right held a brush that lifted the hair so the candlelight glowed through it like a sunrise through mist. Her gown was unlaced in the front, but the material and her right arm, where it crossed her chest, hid all but a modest hint of her breasts.

"Billy?" Penelope called from outside the door. "Are you about ready?"

"One minute," he called back. Quickly, he replaced the portrait, moved the bureau back to the wall, then loudly stomped into his left boot despite the fact that it sent a stab of pain up his left side. "You see my hat?" he asked a moment later when he emerged from the bedroom.

"You didn't have one."

"Damn! Uh, sorry." He grinned at her. "You have a back door?"

It was almost eight-thirty, and Penny was nervous. "Of course," she said shortly. She dimmed the lamps and led him to a blanket-covered door in the back of the kitchen and into a cold, windowless storeroom filled with firewood.

"I'm sorry it has to be this way," she said. "You do understand?"

"Of course." That hair, that mysterious smile, and the swell of her breasts . . . Billy cupped her chin, leaned to meet her lips in a soft and lingering kiss.

"I . . ." Penelope began. Then frowned. "I don't know what to say."

Her hand touched his cheek, traced a line down his jaw, then lowered to her side.

"I'll be back," Billy replied. He opened the back door of the cottage and felt a rush of damp, cold air. "I am in your debt." He kissed her once again, then vanished into the night-blackened yard. "Good night," he softly called to her.

To which she answered, in a whisper of regret as she closed the door, "Good night, Billy Anthem."

It was dark and Calamity Bay had shuttered its windows against the cold rain and mist, so no one saw him leave or pass through the town. His gut ached and the cold made his face and hands smart.

The storm had passed, the sky was clearing. Brief bursts of moonlight lit the scene. He didn't pause to watch their display; he was in a hurry to reach the jail.

"Billy!" Goretti called out as Anthem shoved the door open and entered the marshal's office. The breeze followed him in and rustled the wanted posters on the oak desk by the wall. "We've been worried about you."

Billy ignored him, hung up his coat, and marched into Rhodes' quarters, where he held his hands to the stove.

Rhodes looked him up and down, decided there was no point in repeating Goretti's statement. "You look about as bad as I figured. You won't be asked to no church socials for a while."

"You heard?"

"Hell, yes, I heard. Kid named Sam Burden, whose

daddy was killed over to Creed's sawmill a few months back, brought the news. I pay the boy two bits to tidy up. He comes by now and then."

Billy nodded. "Maybe I could hire Wabash Jack to be *my* deputy."

"Not a bad idea," Rhodes said, his voice heavy with sarcasm. Irritation turned to concern. "You all right?"

"I've been better, but I've been worse, too. No broken bones, at least." Lazied by a full stomach and the heat on his back, he gingerly stretched and yawned. "Been a long day." He sat on a stool near the black iron stove.

"Longer tomorrow," Rhodes said. "Your presence at the city fathers' monthly meeting has been respectfully requested. Which means they want you there so they can boot your ass out in person." Rhodes chuckled. "Oughta be fun."

Billy didn't understand. "Fun?" he asked. "What are you supposed to do for help after they take my badge away?"

"That's easy," Rhodes said. "Anyone I hire is on until the city fathers' next meeting, right?" The marshal scratched his stubbled jaw. His eyes positively twinkled.

"Well, then, they take your badge tomorrow, you bow to their infinite wisdom, and then I hire you again Thursday morning." He leaned back and laughed aloud.

Billy stared at him. "You think that'll work?"

"It's worth a try, ain't it?"

"I guess." Billy yawned, stretched. "You don't mind, I reckon if I turn in."

"Be my guest. Stoke the fire and blow out the lantern on your way, will you?"

Stoke the stoves, pull in the latches on the doors, blow out the lanterns. Nothing was ever as easy as it ought to be, even going to bed. Groggy with fatigue, Billy hobbled about, at last collapsing on his cot in the office and pulling the blankets over him. He stared at his bruised knuckles. Well I gave Tim Creed as good as I got, he thought. Tim

Creed! He bolted upright. The scars, my God, how could he have forgotten.

"Rhodes?"

A snore filtered through the walls. Billy lay back on his pillow. Tomorrow would be soon enough to break the news. The marshal was hoping to avoid a confrontation with the Creeds. Now Billy had news that would have just the opposite effect.

If things were nasty before, they were fixing to get downright deadly. Calamity Bay was a kettle about to boil over, and Billy was fixing to fuel the fire.

13

★

The smell of coffee woke him. Confused, his brows knotted, Billy lay without moving.

"Marshal says time to wake up, Deputy."

Billy opened his eyes. It was morning. A wisp of steam floated upward from the spout of the coffeepot on the stove. A young man, little more than a boy, thin and with a mess of freckles and a shock of bright-red hair, stood by his cot.

"Who are you?" Billy asked. "What're you doing here?"

"Sam Burden. You can call me Red, like ever'body else. Coffee?"

The name rang a bell. Still groggy, Billy tried to fit it with a face and then realized it belonged to the boy Rhodes had hired. "Yeah," he said. "How long've you been here, Red?"

Sam looked at the clock on the wall over the desk. "A little over an hour. You were really sawin' it off. Doc Bannon came by with a wheelchair. He took the marshal down to Ah Sing's Oriental Baths. Said it'd do him good. He wouldn't ride in that chair. He used his crutches."

It was going on eleven o'clock, Billy noted with disgust. He was alarmed that he could have slept so soundly and for such a length of time. He tried to sit up, fell back with a groan. "Jee-sus!"

"Somethin' the matter?"

"No. I'm fine. Fine." They could have sawed him into planks, he was that stiff. Slowly, he worked his feet over the edge of the cot and sat up in time for Sam Burden to hand him a cup of coffee.

"Careful. It's hot."

"Right. Thanks, Red."

The coffee helped. Piece by piece, Billy put himself together. He managed to pull on his woolen trousers. Socks were a problem because bending over that far was nearly impossible, but the boots were easy. He washed his face in the basin the boy brought him. Putting on his clean shirt, one of two he owned, was a chore, but his vest and coat were relatively easy.

"You amused?" he asked Goretti, who had watched the ordeal without comment.

The Italian leaned on his forearms on the crossbar on the door of his cell. "Not at all. Impressed, rather. Your recuperative powers are amazing."

"Yeah. Look at me. I can stand up and get dressed," Billy glumly replied. He had wanted to alert Rhodes as to Tim Creed's curiously scarred chest.

Sam Burden announced he was going home and sauntered out the front door with a perfunctory wave of the hand.

Billy noticed a packet on the desk. A telegram lay on top of the desk.

"Hank wanted you to read that. It came up from Port Angeles," Goretti said. "While you slept," he added.

"Appears everything happens while I sleep," Billy noted. He picked up the telegram and read it.

ARRIVE MONDAY NEXT. APRIL 24. PLEASE SET ANY COURT CASES READY FOR TRIAL. YRS., GEO ROBBINS, CIRCUIT JUDGE, NORTHERN WASHINGTON TERRITORY.

"That sort of clears the air," Billy said, and sat in the chair behind the marshal's desk. He tilted back in the chair, put his feet on the desk, and continued to stare at the telegram. He tried to decide what his next step ought to be and couldn't focus on any one recourse other than to push and prod and stir, poking his nose where it didn't belong just to see what happened.

"Don't move, please?" Goretti said suddenly.

Billy had started to get up, but froze, and cut his eyes wildly from side to side. "What?"

"Don't move. I'm nearly finished. Another minute . . ." Goretti was laboring at his sketch pad. His hands practically flew over the paper.

"What the hell are you doing, Goretti?"

"No, no. Don't ask. Another minute . . ."

The next three minutes seemed more like ten. At last, the Italian called Billy over to his cell and turned the easel so he could see it. There, in charcoal, was Billy, his feet on the desk and his hat pulled down over his face. "What do you think?" Goretti asked.

Billy shook his head in admiration. "Sure wish I could do that," he said wistfully.

"There's no time like the present for a lesson," Goretti said, removing the top sheet and handing it through the bars. "Put that somewhere, and come on in." He made a mock bow. "The studio, *signore*, is open."

Billy hadn't had a piece of charcoal in his hand for over a year, but it would pass the time until Rhodes arrived. "What should I draw?" he asked a moment later, suddenly ill at ease in front of the blank sheet of paper.

"Why, whatever you like."

"Well . . ." He looked around, couldn't find anything. "You?"

"A face?" Goretti frowned. "Perhaps something a little easier to begin with, eh?" He surveyed the office. "Perhaps the stove, eh? The lines, the proportion, the shading, many problems to solve, but not so hard as a face, I think." He gestured with one hand. "Well, begin, eh? And light lines, so we may chalk them out if need be."

The charcoal felt like a lump of coal, his bruised right hand like a haunch of beef. Quickly, though, the touch returned, a natural talent he had hidden in his youth but gave him great pleasure now that he was on his own.

Line by line, some chalked out and redrawn not once but two or three times, the stove took shape. Goretti coaxed, teased, demonstrated, praised. And at last he pronounced the work complete and made Billy step aside.

"Very good," the artist said, looking from stove to paper. "Very, very good, especially for a beginner! Somewhat hasty and impetuous, but you will learn patience in time. You have a fine, raw talent, my friend, and that is rare in one who is also a man of action."

"It does look kind of like a stove," Billy admitted.

"Of course it does. Like *that* stove. But . . . the way you perceived it. A thousand artists would draw it a thousand different ways, because each would perceive it differently. Draw it again and even your own work will change. You notice more, you learn. See here, the smokestack, you've defined it with such a hard line. Now use shading to give it substance and depth. And the firebox . . ."

"I wanted to capture the lamplight reflected in the metal, but I didn't know how," Billy said.

"I'll show you," Goretti replied. "Don't be afraid to let the natural whiteness of the paper show through. Let it work for you. Only darken what you need and no more. It's the same for watercolors. My razor is just as important as my brushes. I apply the color. Then, after it is dried, I use the razor to scrape the color away. A simple mud puddle becomes a pool of captured sunlight." He unrolled a small watercolor of a wheel-rutted road after a rain shower. The puddles looked real enough to splash in.

"I'll remember," Billy said, impressed by the simplicity

of the work. "I doubt I'll ever be more than a student."

"Bah. We are all students, my friend. Pity the man who thinks he has learned it all." Goretti tapped a finger on Billy's drawing. "You have talent. And you have the gift of seeing, these are things more important than anything else. But . . ." He paused as the clock chimed the noon hour. "Enough for one lesson, eh?"

Noon? The hour had flown. The meeting of the city fathers was at eight. He hoped Rhodes didn't take all day hobbling back up the street from the baths. He started out of Goretti's cell.

"Billy." There was a tearing sound as Goretti pulled the drawing off the pad. "Your stove."

Billy took the drawing and rolled it up as an idea came to mind.

"Tell me, Angelo, were you, uh, satisfied with that portrait of Penelope Swain? You know. The one of her in her, uh, bedroom?"

"She showed it to you?" the artist asked, taken aback. He spoke without thinking.

"No." Billy explained briefly why he'd been in her bedroom and how he'd found the portrait.

Goretti's expression grew clouded. "I would rather we leave Penelope out of this, Billy."

"You didn't answer my question."

"Penelope is a sweet and gentle soul who doesn't need trouble," Goretti said, his voice rising nervously. "Leave her out of it, I beg of you. My reputation is jaded enough. Why ruin hers?"

"You're in love with her, aren't you? And that's where you were the night Melinda was killed."

Angelo retreated to his bunk, sat heavily, and covered his face with his long graceful hands. "Ah . . . you are a very clever young man."

"And you can't tell anyone you were with her because she would be driven out of Calamity Bay if people even suspected her of impropriety." Billy closed in on the cell, his fingers curled through the bars.

"I came to her house late one night. No one saw me. We talked of literature and art. And love. Yes. I told her I loved her and it did not matter that she could only think of me as a friend." Goretti looked up at Anthem peering in through the cell door. "What did I expect? I am a wanderer, a ne'er-do-well, an itinerant. But I begged her to let me paint her, and at last, against her better judgment, she allowed me to."

Billy wasn't convinced. "And that was it?"

"Five times I visited her and she sat for me. Five long, secret evenings to put my love for her on canvas."

"Which you don't even own."

"The canvas was for her. Painting it was all I asked." He threw his head back and sighed deeply. "Leave her out of it, Billy, I beg of you."

"Even if it means your life?" Billy asked.

"Yes." A spasm of coughing racked his frail body. "Yes. Even if it means my life."

There had been a time, Billy thought, when he too would have died for a woman. He would have pleaded and begged, as Goretti had, to give his life to save hers. "Very well, Angelo," he said, hoping that Penelope would not let it go that far.

He returned to the desk, set his drawing aside, and poured a cup of coffee.

"Fill a cup for me," Rhodes said from the doorway. The burly old man, his face red from exertion, hobbled into the room. He limped across the office and headed into the backroom and slumped with a groan of relief onto his bed.

The marshal's hair was slicked down and he smelled of both soap and hair tonic. The expression he wore dared anyone to make fun of him.

Billy followed the marshal into the room and handed him a cup of coffee he'd laced with whiskey. Rhodes nodded and gulped the steaming brew. He wiped his mustache and lips on his shirt sleeve, then looked up at Anthem.

"Don't worry, younker. I ain't about to die on you." Rhodes studied the Texan's bruised and battered features. "Wish I could say the same for you. I told you not to bother with the warehouse. I knew there was nothing to find but trouble."

Billy sat on the stool across from the marshal. He hunched forward, resting his elbows on his knees. "You were wrong," he said quietly. "Bannon gave you all the details on the Crenshaw girl, didn't he?"

"Yup. Besides, I was standing alongside him when he looked her over."

"Good." Billy lowered his voice. "Remember anything special about her fingernails?"

The marshal's nose flared, as if, like an old and wise tracking dog, he smelled something coming. "Three on her left hand, one on her right, packed with skin and blood."

"Right." Billy nodded. "Now, me and Tim Creed had us quite a set-to before his boys joined in. And I managed to rip his shirt open."

"Go on."

"He tried to pull his shirt together, but I saw them. The flesh was streaked like he'd been clawed by a wildcat. Or a girl fighting for her life."

Rhodes lay back, exhaled slowly. "I shoulda guessed. Especially after the trouble with Angelina."

"Who the hell is that?" Billy asked.

"Angelina One Punch," Rhodes answered matter-of-factly. "One of Sophie's whores. Found her in a crib one night. Her neck was broke. She'd been worked over pretty good. Talk was Timothy Creed had been spending a lot of time with her. Didn't want her running with nobody else. But business is business to a whore. That didn't prove nothing. What could I do?"

The two men sat quietly a moment, each chewing on his

own thoughts. "You want me to bring him in?" Billy asked.

Rhodes thought a second. "Easier said than done. Noah's liable to have something to say about it. And even if we managed to take his boy, what jury would convict him here? If you don't work for the Creeds, then you don't work, period. Peoples' lives here are tied to that old bastard's coattails." Rhodes tugged at his mustache, a habit he had when thinking. "When's that meeting tonight?"

"Eight o'clock."

"I'm not goin' because I don't want to give 'em the chance to tell me not to pin that badge on you again. When they see what I've done, well, they might call another meeting to dismiss us both. Meanwhile it'll buy us some time. Maybe I can catch a few of the town fathers on the side and talk some backbone into them. Doc Bannon's on our side. He knows what to say for tonight."

"What do you want me to do?" Billy asked. His admiration for the old marshal grew with every passing day. "Stir the pot and see what floats to the top?"

Hank Rhodes grinned. "Just remember. Tim knows you've seen them scars of his. He may be a crazy son of a bitch, but he ain't stupid. Watch your back." The marshal stretched out on the bed.

Billy Anthem nodded and rose from the stool and walked out into the office. He crossed to the window and looked out at the bay in the distance. Then he realized what a splendid target he made and ducked back. It was going to be a long day, he realized with sinking heart. And the night, longer still.

14

★

Billy planned to go in style. Cleanly shaved, he was dressed in his best: black woolen pants, pale-gray shirt and string tie, and a frock coat he'd borrowed from Rhodes, who insisted the coat was too small for him now. The coat fit loosely, but Billy didn't mind. At seven-thirty, feeling ready for the worst Creed could throw at him, he adjusted his gun belt, checked the loads in his Colt revolver, and set out for the meeting.

His horse stood with head down and tethered to the hitching post in front of the jail. Sam Burden had brought the animal up from the stables early in the afternoon. Billy wiped the saddle dry as best he could, mounted, and headed down Pine for Broadway.

A heavy mist had rolled in from the Pacific for the second night in a row. The town was quiet, the mare's hoof-beats muffled by the thick, damp air. A wisp of a breeze carried hints of cedar and spring grass, of salt water, and mud.

The calm before the storm, Billy thought, and kept the mare to a slow walk. The darkness, the enveloping mist dulled his senses, and for a moment, in the muffled stillness of the hour, Billy felt as if he were all alone, amid an illusion of ghostly buildings and shrouded streets.

His reverie ended with a wink of light and the dull report of a rifle. Almost simultaneously, the mare studder-stepped backward and Billy's saddle twisted violently to the right as a .45-caliber lead slug slammed into the horn. Billy followed the motion of his saddle, kicked free of the stirrups, twisted in midair, and hit the ground running, his Colt in hand.

He kept his head down, ran low, skidded through the mud, and gained the boardwalk. Billy slid to a stop by the corner of Franklin's Haberdashery. The shot had come from ahead and to his left. Somewhere up on the flank of Cameron Bluff.

A shutter banged open across the street. Billy whirled and, his revolver at the ready, crouched and aimed in the direction of the noise.

"What the blazes is goin' on out there?" a voice called out from the shanty.

"Keep your head in, man," Billy shouted. "Or lose it." His heart hammered in his chest. His mouth was dry as a bone. He hurt like hell from the sudden exertion.

"No need to tell me twice," the voice answered, and the shutter banged closed.

Billy sidled to the edge of Franklin's, ducked low, chanced a look, and saw nothing but the fog rolling in from the bay and thick as chowder. In the distance, he heard the solitary clanging of a bell buoy that warned ships away from the rocks jutting out from the land on the western edge of the bay into the strait.

He considered making a dash for the other side of the street and working his way up Cameron Bluff. But the chances of finding anyone in this soup-thick mist were next to nothing. Anyway, his attacker had probably given it up as well.

"Was that a shot?"

Billy turned, made out Doc Bannon approaching down the side street, Hemlock, on his ancient black gelding. The doctor would never know how close he had come to a bullet in the brisket.

"It *was* a shot," Bannon continued, answering his own question. "Did you get elected?"

"No, but I came near to being nominated," Billy replied. He could still feel the tug of the bullet striking his saddle. "You on your way to the meeting?"

"That's right." Doc heeled his horse in the ribs and nudged him forward. "Ride along with me."

"Might not be safe for you, Doc," Billy warned, following the man back onto Broadway.

Doc dismissed his concern with a wave of his hand. "Nobody gonna shoot the town's only doctor," he said, turning to catch up the reins to Billy's horse. "Come on."

The city hall faced Broadway and had been built across the street from the Congregational church. It was here that the city fathers met at eight on the third Wednesday night of every month.

Noah Creed had been the first and only city father twelve years earlier. Calamity Bay was his dream and his town.

He'd begun with cedar shakes that he shipped to the growing San Francisco, more than nine hundred sea miles to the south. Four years later, when the sawmill opened, Calamity Bay boasted three hundred residents.

And then the dream that was growing into an empire hit a snag. Finding himself short of capital for the ships he needed to transport the thousands of board feet his mills cut, Noah was forced to ally himself with a San Francisco bank.

On the very day he signed the papers that brought outside money into Calamity Bay, he no longer owned the town and its inhabitants lock, stock, and barrel. He was still the king, but a king who was forced to share his power, at least in some measure, with his subjects.

In 1870, a group of citizens drew up a town charter, and

the city fathers became a force to be reckoned with. Six years later Noah Creed now shared authority with six other men: Abner Tremain, banker; Rufus Hollander and John Ratliff, merchants; Clyde Brinton, the Congregationalist minister; N. J. Garner, the publisher of the Calamity Bay *Courant*; and Dr. Bannon.

These six men wielded their limited power in such a way as to not offend Noah because they understood that their well-being depended on his. They were likewise unwilling to be his lackeys, because they were proud men and knew his well-being depended to no small extent on them. It was a workable, if uncomfortable, alliance.

The town hall was a modest single-story wood building some twenty feet wide and forty long. Whitewashed, it glowed in the light of the lanterns hung on either side of its double front doors. Inside, two rear offices housed the mayor, Noah Creed, of course, and the town secretary, one Mr. Paxton Mullins, who kept the census and collected the taxes. A third, and by far larger, front room served as a courthouse and meeting hall.

Somewhat subdued after his jaunty start, Billy dismounted and tethered his horse just as the bells on the Congregational church tolled the hour.

Billy and Bannon entered together. Bannon strode to the head table, whispered briefly to Mr. Mullins, a bookish little man wearing pince-nez eyeglasses, and took a seat. Billy looked around and decided that no one there looked like an assassin. The men noticed his mud-spattered attire, exchanged glances, and tactfully refrained from comment.

"The hour is eight and all members in good standing are present, Mr. Mayor," Mullins began. He nodded in respect toward Creed and continued. "I have been informed by Doctor Bannon that Marshal Rhodes, who normally attends these meetings, is still weak from his wounds and unable to attend. He sends in his stead"—he glanced at Billy as the Texan took a seat on one of the benches provided for spectators—"Mr. William Anthem, his deputy. I believe all is in order, Mr. Mayor."

The council sat at three tables arranged in a U shape directly under the main chandelier: Creed and Mr. Mullins at the head table and the other six members split three on each side. Creed gaveled the meeting to order and instructed Mr. Mullins to read the minutes of the prior month's meeting. The secretary's voice was frail and reedy.

Creed busied himself reading a document, Tremain and Ratliff held a whispered conversation, and the Reverend Brinton appeared to be praying. He was a corpulent man, balding and obviously ill with a bad cold. Doc Bannon pared his nails, and the last two men, if their eyes were to be believed, napped.

N. J. Garner was not one to waste time. "Move the minutes be adopted as read," the editor said, miraculously coming to life and speaking before Creed could ask for a motion.

The treasurer's report followed. The balance in the city treasury was $432.71 after an expenditure of $200 for replacement of the boardwalk on both sides of Hemlock, and another $50 for Mr. Mullins' salary. The treasurer's report was accepted, and Billy found himself wondering how long they would need to get around to him.

Old business was considered at length. Many of the town's women were agitating for the Sunday closure of all Water Street businesses: a committee of three was studying the issue, and a special meeting with the women and the owners was scheduled for the next Thursday night at seven. The water board was waiting on the report of the engineer who had been commissioned to compare the costs and benefits of drilling three new wells as compared to running an aqueduct from Elk Lake.

A nearby clock set back against the wall chimed eight-thirty, and then nine. A few of the spectators who had entered shortly after Billy began to drift away. Still, there were some who remained, and one of these, a miner, began to snore. He was abruptly awakened by Mullins, who requested that all spectators either remain awake or leave.

Billy studied the clock, watched the time pass, and noted that if the town council took much longer, he could retire before they'd get around to kicking him out.

"And now," Noah Creed intoned, "is there any new business?"

Billy sat up. Doc Bannon winked at him, leaned forward in his chair. The whole hall, city fathers and the lingering spectators alike, perked up. Everyone knew what came next.

Creed himself didn't begin the discussion. Instead, he glanced meaningfully at John Ratliff, who everybody knew was deeply in debt to him. Ratliff was of average height, wearing his middle age well. He patted the wrinkles from his frock coat, smoothed his already slicked-down hair, and began.

"Mr. Mayor."

"The chair recognizes Mr. Ratliff."

"Thank you, sir." Ratliff cleared his throat. The man didn't enjoy bowing to Creed's will, but had no choice. "As called for in our town charter, this council ratifies the selection of all town employees, including our deputies. Thus, we ratified the selection of Mr. Krait, who has recently resigned, and his two predecessors. Normally, Marshal Rhodes' choice is accepted without question. However, it is my solemn duty to inform this council that I have encountered certain expressions of discontent concerning this appointment."

"Go ahead, Mr. Ratliff."

Here it comes, Billy thought.

"Yes, sir." Ratliff glanced down at a piece of paper. "As you all know, Marshal Rhodes was grievously wounded this Friday past by scoundrels unknown. His life was saved by Mr. William Anthem here, who claims he chanced upon

the scene of the crime. If that were the whole story, I have
no doubt this body should today be unstintingly expressing
its gratitude to Mr. Anthem. However, certain rumors and,
as I said, expressions of discontent have lately arisen, which
I feel compelled to bring before this body."

Long-winded, for a hardware store owner, Billy thought,
biding his time. Ratliff spoke with the sureness of a play-
actor reciting his lines. In this case, the playwright was, no
doubt, Noah Creed.

"You mentioned rumors," Noah Creed interrupted. "I
myself have heard none."

"Yes, sir. The most damaging comes from a salesman
who was in my store the day before yesterday. He saw Mr.
Anthem in town and expressed his amazement at seeing
him here and wearing a badge. When queried, he told me
Mr. Anthem was, to his knowledge, a notorious gunman
and troublemaker, the bad son of a good family who is
wanted for questioning in connection with the death of a
gentleman back in Texas."

"A serious charge indeed," said Abner Tremain, the
banker. He was a pale-skinned, tired-looking individual
with a solemn worried expression.

"Beg your pardon," Billy interrupted, "but is this man
available for me to question?"

"Why, no," Ratliff said, somewhat taken aback. "I, ah,
believe he sailed for Seattle yesterday."

"I see," Billy said dryly. "A handy departure."

"Your comments will be solicited in due time, Mr. Anthem," Creed snapped. "Until then, please remain silent.
The council will take into account the fact that the charges
are unverified, but I will also note that I find them ex-
tremely interesting, under the circumstances. Proceed,
please, Mr. Ratliff."

There was more. A woman of ill-repute, who worked at
an unnamed bordello on Water Street and who feared retribution if her name became known, had also recalled see-

ing Billy in San Francisco, where she knew him as a con artist. A sailor enjoying a bath at Ah Sing's claimed to have been roughed up by the new deputy.

"In addition," Ratliff went on, "it has become common knowledge that our deputy has displayed a suspiciously close friendship with Angelo Goretti and has even allowed this murderer to wander freely outside his cell. He has also, which you know better than I, Mr. Mayor, trespassed upon private property and attacked your own son."

Creed shook his head sadly. "Grievous charges, Mr. Ratliff. Grievous indeed. Does anyone else have anything to add to or detract from them?"

Billy watched without comment as Creed fixed each of the other men with a brief stare. Each, in turn, silently shook his head "no" while they avoided looking at the patriarch.

"Any discussion?" Creed asked.

Again the silent, shaking heads, and Billy's gorge began to rise.

Mayor, king, and empire-builder, Noah Creed reached for the paper Ratliff handed him, let the tension build as he glanced over it. "I am not one to pass judgment lightly, or without due cause, on any man," he began at last. "The evidence against Mr. Anthem, with the exception of the trespass and attack, and of his conduct regarding the prisoner, Goretti, which I know to be fact, is circumstantial and unsubstantiated. This council, however, is responsible for the safety of the citizens it represents. When a man delegated to ensure that safety threatens the same, then we should get rid of him."

Creed paused, regarded Billy with a mixture of contempt and victory. "My sentiments are clear. Do I hear a motion on the matter?"

"You do, Mr. Mayor," Doc Bannon said.

Billy held his breath, hoping Bannon remembered the exact wording Rhodes had given him.

Creed appeared surprised by Bannon's response, but could only recognize him. "Dr. Bannon."

Doc's voice was firm and purposeful. "I move that this council release the present deputy from his duties on the instant, and instruct Marshal Rhodes to fill the post with a suitable candidate at his earliest convenience."

It was time to stoke the fire under the pot. "That's it!" Billy said, rising and interrupting before anyone else could speak. "I've had a craw full. Marshal Rhodes told me to take whatever you folks dished out, but damned if I'll let this pass without having my say." He turned on Ratliff. "A mysterious gentleman, an anonymous whore, and an un-named seaman. Very good. And the rest of you people be-lieve him?"

"Now see here!" Ratliff sputtered, his face turning red.

Billy went on. "What you ought to be asking, if you had any backbone, is why people are so damned anxious to get rid of me?"

He stopped, moved in front of N. J. Garner, keeping his bruised and swollen features in the light. "You're a news-paperman. Are we going to see in your paper how I stopped Timothy Creed from carving up one of Sophie Barrett's girls?"

Garner coughed, looked pleadingly to Creed.

Billy wasn't finished with him yet. It was time to play his hole card. "Here's another question, Garner, after all, you're a reporter. Why don't you ask Timothy Creed how he got a chest covered with deep barely healed scratches? Was he clawed by a mountain lion, or a girl fighting for her life?"

"Enough!" Noah Creed knocked his chair over when he stood. His face was red with fury and his finger trembled as he pointed at Billy. "You, sir, are a villain and a scoundrel. I will not sit here and listen to my son accused of—"

"Of what?" Billy asked, knowing full well everyone had heard of the way Melinda had tried to defend herself.

"There is a motion on the floor, gentlemen," Creed snarled, stepping away from the table and clapping his hat on his head. "You know where my sympathy lies. I suggest you dispose of this matter immediately, and in a manner consistent with your own best interests. As for me, I will not remain here and listen to another word from this detestable . . . contemptible young lout."

Nobody moved to stop him as Creed stormed out of the meeting. The city fathers and the spectators sat as if stunned. No one knew what to say.

Billy broke the silence. "Well, you heard the man," he said, his own contempt evident. "Better vote, if you know what's good for you."

"Ahem!" Mr. Mullins cleared his throat uncomfortably. "Mr. Tremain, as assistant mayor—"

"Do I hear a second?" the banker asked, not waiting for Mullins' formalities.

Rufus Hollander seconded, Tremain called for the vote. "Six for the motion as moved, none against," he announced scant seconds later, to no one's surprise. "And now, if there is no other new business . . ." He paused in deference to the rules, then went on. "I will entertain a motion—"

"Move we adjourn," Doc said dispassionately.

Reverend Brinton's second was greeted with a chorus of "ayes." The councilmen adjourned. They left the table and the room as quickly as their dignity allowed. But to a man they were visibly shaken by Billy's revelation. In silence, the remaining spectators departed, leaving Mullins to finish the minutes.

The two men strolled out of the town hall and walked to the hitching post. "You carried it too far, Billy," Doc warned, his hand on Billy's arm. "Noah Creed will never forgive you."

"I'm not looking for forgiveness," Billy countered. "Oh, hell, Doc, it had to come out sooner or later."

"That's right, but sometimes folks have to swallow a bitter medicine a spoonful at a time. Not the whole damn bottle at once!"

Billy glanced at the man, surprised by his outburst. "I thought you were on our side."

"This town owes its livelihood to the Creeds," Bannon said, wiping a hand over his face. "You practically called Tim Creed a murderer. That kind of talk makes folks jittery. Goretti's their man. He spent time with the girl and won't say where he was that night, so he might have done it."

"You aren't supposed to hang people for something they 'might' have done."

"It wouldn't be the first time," Doc snorted. "And it won't be the last."

"The line's been drawn, Doc," Billy said. "Which side do you aim to stand on?"

Doc mounted his gelding nag. "I don't know," he answered in all honesty as Billy swung up onto the saddle. They turned their horses back through the center of town. "Word will have spread to one and all by midmorning." Bannon chuckled. "How the Creeds won again."

"The lot of you have sold your souls to the devil," Anthem snapped.

"You're too young to be so bitter," the doctor replied, his homely face grown gentle. "Besides, when push comes to shove, I think you'll find plenty of folks are on your side."

"I haven't seen any of them. Except you, I think," Billy mentioned. And he wasn't sure about the doc. He cocked an eye in the direction of the bluffs and tensed, though common sense told him the fog was his protection.

"And N. J. and Brinton, to name two more," Doc said.

Billy's eyes widened. "The editor and the preacher? For Christ's sake, why didn't they speak up?"

Doc shrugged. " 'Cause they knew voting you out didn't mean anything. And they've been doing what Creed wanted them to do for so long, it's hard to even think about standin' up to him. They're scared, Billy. Hell, I'm scared. We've all seen how Creed can grind a man under his thumb. Nobody wants to be ruined." Bannon guided his animal closer to Billy and lowered his voice. "Give us a chance, Billy. You know, as far as most folks are concerned, the guilty man is in jail, and if Creed wants his scrawny neck stretched, so do they."

They turned together down Mount Olive and stopped at the mouth of the alley leading to the stable.

"Only one thing," Billy asked.

Doc paused before he rode off. "Yeah?"

"Whose scrawny neck are they going to want stretched when the next girl is raped and dies?"

Billy kept his mare to an easy gait and cut a solitary figure in the mist. Silent, shrouded silhouettes emerged from the thick gray clouds that had drifted over the bay to cloak the town in its ghostly raiments. The passersby, glimpsed briefly, disappeared without acknowledging one another. Indeed, they were all but unrecognizable in the gloom.

Now and then Billy rode past a patch of pale amber, glowing wanly against the night, someone keeping a late hour or perhaps hoping to wait out the fog. Anthem was grateful for the obscure conditions, however treacherous. It hid him from scrutiny. And he wanted no one to see him or discover his destination. When he tethered his mare, it was not by the jail but in a shed behind Calamity Bay's only schoolhouse. He found a bait of oats and gave it to the mare. His mount taken care of, Billy left the shed and followed a recently memorized crushed rock path that lead from the school to the cottage a little farther up the slope.

He caught the scent of wood smoke, heard the distant lap of waves, the lonely tolling of the bell buoy, and the faint, plaintive song of a fiddler playing somewhere down by the docks. Magic ruled a night like this, Billy mused.

He paused to listen, to experience, to take it all in, and afterward, he hurried on, letting desire lead the way.

Penelope had a dozen reasons for not opening the back door to Billy Anthem, but for the life of her she couldn't think of a one. She was dressed in a thick cotton house gown that covered the thinner chemise she generally wore to bed. Her ash-blonde hair, unbound, flowed past her shoulders. One cheek was smudged with flour and the interior of the house smelled of fresh-baked bread.

"I thought you might have a pot of tea on," Billy mentioned. "And with the fog as thick as it is, an elephant could walk up Broadway and no one would be the wiser."

Her worried expression relaxed and she lead him into her sitting room, lit only by the cheerful blaze aglow in the fireplace. Sure enough, a brown stoneware teapot was set on the hearth.

"I'm glad to see you, Billy," Penelope Swain replied as she went about checking the front windows. "Forgive me, but I have to be as cautious as a nun," she sighed.

"I guess it wouldn't do for the schoolmarm to have an unchaperoned male visitor after dark?"

"I have to protect my reputation in order to protect my job," Penelope said. "But you know that."

"I've just come from the council meeting," Billy explained, stretching out on a bearskin rug by the fire. The first glimpse of her had already taken most of the chill out of him. "They dismissed me. Seems the town fathers are all afraid of Creed ruining their livelihood."

Penelope knelt beside him and poured a cup of tea for her visitor. She was listening, but the subject made her uncomfortable.

"How much is your job worth, Penny? An innocent man's life?"

The question caught her off guard. Her eyebrows arched, then as quickly, a knowing expression replaced her startled glance. She handed Billy a cup and sat back on her haunches.

"You know, then. Angelo was with me." She pursed her lips a moment, watched the dancing flames in the fireplace. "How simple a fire is, giving off warmth. Lights our way. Sometimes it burns us when we aren't careful. Not nearly as confusing as life with all its subtleties and shadings. And yet, there is a right and wrong. And we hope to know the difference." Penelope set her own teacup aside. "No. When Angelo comes to trial, I fully intend to speak up for him. And tell the truth, no matter what the cost. Do you believe me, Billy?"

"The way you look tonight, I'd believe the stars were cat's paws if you said so." Billy leaned forward and took her in his arms.

A simple room, lived in, warm, smelling of fresh-baked bread. A small room, with drawings on the walls and lace curtains drawn across shuttered windows. A rolltop desk by the wall is crowded with readers and textbooks and progress reports on each child.

A homey comfortable room and more, a place of trysting. Two shadows on the wall meld together and sink to the rug as hands fumble for buttons, untying bows until at last flesh meets naked flesh.

"Let me," Penelope whispered out of concern for his bruised torso. She rolled atop and straddled him, gasped as he entered her. She sank forward. His mouth found her breasts, his hands cupped her hips, and he moved with her. Their mutual hunger for each other fueled them to a quick and glorious climax.

A shuddering last spasm, followed by an all-engulfing sense of completeness, then Penelope whispered his name. Words failed her. But then, the oneness of new love spoke volumes for them both.

*   *   *

Billy woke when the clock on the mantel chimed twice. He knew he couldn't stay the night and must be leaving soon. But for the moment, he enjoyed holding Penelope in his arms, listening to the soft whisper of her breath, her cheek nestled in the crook of his neck.

The fire crackled; a swirl of sparks spiraled up the chimney. He studied the pulsing coals, the shimmering flames, and glimpsed in the orange-blue depths the face of another love, a long-ago love, or so it seemed. She was lost to him. And a part of his heart had died with her, but only a part. Life remained, to be savored, each precious moment, brimming with existence. The image faded and he bid the past farewell. A silken hand traced a gentle path along his neck.

"A penny for your thoughts," the woman in his arms asked, and smiled, enjoying her pun.

Billy grinned. "Best offer I've had all night," he replied, and his mouth covered hers in the first of many languorous kisses. He knew he had to leave, Penelope knew he had to leave.

But not just yet.

15

★

It was amazing how fast a man could find and lose a job in Calamity Bay. It took about four days, just long enough to ride to Luminaria's nearest neighbors to the west, and back.

Billy lay quietly and reveled in the smell of morning coffee. He was getting lazy, he decided, listening to the clock chime seven. Of course, he'd only had four hours of sleep.

Slowly, he came to life. Goretti was coughing out his lungs as usual in the morning. Rhodes was thumping around on his crutch in his quarters, clumsily dressing himself.

Billy swung out of bed, pulled on his britches and boots. "Need to take a walk, Goretti?" he asked.

"Went already," the artist answered. "The marshal told Sam to let me out."

"Hell of a way to run a jail," Billy snorted. He wandered through Rhodes' quarters, paused to watch the marshal practice a cross draw while leaning on his crutches.

Rhodes glared at him. "Another hour I'll have it down," he growled. "Where the hell were you last night?"

"None of your business," Billy retorted on his way to the privy.

By the time Anthem returned to the jail, young Sam had returned with breakfast, which the three men lost no time in gulping down.

"Well," Rhodes said, pushing back his plate after finishing the last of the flapjacks. "Reckon it's time you got back to work. Where's that badge?"

Billy nodded toward the office. "On the desk. Been thinking, though. You don't mind, there's somebody I need to talk to before you swear me in again."

The marshal's eyebrow rose in a question he didn't need to ask. "If you're thinkin' about Noah Creed, you must be crazy."

"That's what you said the last time," Billy said, rising from the table. He removed his gun belt and lay it on the table in front of Rhodes. "I want you and everybody else in town to see me ride out unarmed."

"Look, younker . . ." Rhodes stopped in midsentence, realized he was wasting his time, and gestured toward the office. "Goretti, lock yourself up. Just in case we have any more visitors."

Goretti, like Rhodes, realized it was futile to ask questions. The artist entered his cell, locked the door, and tossed the key across the room to Billy. "Be careful, my friend," he said as the young man clamped his hat on his head and started out. "I've already lost one student. I shouldn't like to lose another."

Billy stopped at the door, turned, and looked back at Goretti. He touched the tip of his hat and walked out.

The air was crisp, rain washed and heavy still with moisture. The smell of seacoast and pine trees was a heady mixture. In truth, the northwest coast was working its magic on him.

His mare gained back some of the weight she'd lost on the long trip north. Her coat had come up, and she was frisky and ready for a ride. Billy rounded the jail, but reined in when Rhodes called to him through the open window.

"Believe I'd rather not have the judge's arrival mentioned."

"Won't say a word about it," Billy replied.

"You watch yourself, son," the craggy-faced marshal cautioned. "I'm damned if I want some idiot Texas kid on my conscience."

Billy grinned, waved, and rode away.

As he guided the mare through town, Billy went over his plan. Noah Creed had been genuinely shaken by the news about the scratches on Timothy's chest. He obviously hadn't known about them, and that realization had led Billy to believe he had to talk to the man before things got completely out of hand.

Creed was even more like Billy's father than Rhodes. Both Noah and John Anthem were big men, physically powerful. Both had begun with nothing and had built an empire. Both would defend their empires with furious resolve, both were fiercely loyal to their families, and both were stamped with a pride as hard and durable as granite.

Such men were not rare, for it was their kind who had built America, who had tamed and made the land productive all the way from Texas to Washington Territory, and the thousands of miles between.

But there the similarities ended. For as much as they were alike, their characters were as different as night and day. John Anthem was a hard man, but his very soul and heart were carved of yet a sterner stuff than the granite of his pride, and that was unassailable honesty and indomitable courage. He expected those same standards from his sons and daughter.

The Noah Creeds of the world possessed a meanness of spirit that must succeed at any cost. Perhaps because their courage was flawed, they feared the loss of their empires, and so compromised their honor. And lacking courage and honor themselves, they passed on neither to their sons.

Fathers and sons alike faced the world from behind a

brittle facade they were forced in desperation to maintain, for it masked the hollow emptiness that was the essence of their true selves. Billy had seen little to respect in Noah Creed. Instead, he pitied him, and it was this pity that led him to Creed's Knob, and a confrontation neither of them wanted.

The day, he thought, should have been gloomy, rainy, to match his mood. Instead, the spring sun bathed the road and cast shadows so hard they seemed to bar his way. Billy tipped his hat to a pair of ladies coming out of Ratliff's, and exchanged greetings with Garner, who paused as he unlocked the *Courant* for the day. The congenial newspaperman noticed Billy was unarmed as he rode up Broadway. By heaven, it looked as if Anthem was heading for Creed's Knob, the editor thought, frowning. He locked up again and headed back down Pine toward the jail.

Broadway curled up the flank of Creed's Knob through scrub hemlock and cedar, cut a shallow channel through a wide meadow where sheep grazed, and became Creed's drive as it passed through his gate. The house looked bigger from this angle, Billy thought, taking the left-hand fork that led to the main entrance. The bright-white paint was splashed with color where quilts hung from the sills of upstair windows. The blue trim matched the color of the water in the bay, and the sky itself.

The house was quiet, with no sign of life. Billy tethered his mare and walked up the wide steps and across the bare and spacious porch. The wide double doors inset with leaded-glass windows, each depicting identical seascapes in delicate shades of blue and green, announced entrance to a castle rather than a regular house. A bellpull hung to the right of the doors. When pulled, a pair of bells sounded dimly. Scant moments later, a shadow appeared behind the glass and the doors opened.

Chi Lo looked so deeply into Billy's eyes that he appeared to be looking straight through him. His expression was an impenetrable mark, hiding his feelings. "I may help, please?" the servant asked in a deferential voice. He wore a brown frock coat and brown wool trousers. But his shirt was heavily ruffled with coarse lace down his chest.

"Yes. Is Mr. Creed in?" Billy asked.

"One moment, please." The door closed, the shadow faded and reappeared moments later. The door swung wide. "This way, Mr. Anthem. Master will see you in the front parlor."

Did the Chinese servant know him? Possibly, Billy thought. More likely, Creed had noted his arrival, used his name, and ordered his servant to open the door.

"That will be all for now, Chi Lo." Creed stood in front of the fireplace, legs spread, hands behind his back. "You surprise me, Anthem," he said, forgoing the courtesy of a greeting. "I should have thought you would know you are not welcome in this house."

"Morning, Mr. Creed," Billy said, accepting the man's remarks. "I expected as much," he added, undaunted.

"But here you are." Creed wasn't about to bend an inch. "You are a very brash young man, Anthem."

"Yes, sir, I expect I am." Taking the liberty, Billy walked to the front window and pulled the curtain aside to look out over Calamity Bay and the strait beyond. "Nice view." He let the curtain drop, turned, and looked around at the exquisitely japanned furniture, the decorative Oriental pitchers and vases arranged on tables and shelves. A huge, very English-looking painting of a landscape peopled with lords and ladies and framed with thick, heavily worked walnut burl hung over the fireplace. The whole room glowed with the aura of wealth. "Nice house, too. I'm impressed."

"I doubt," Creed said acidly, "that you came here to be impressed by my house. If you wish to state your business, please do so quickly, or I shall have you thrown out."

Billy Anthem bridled for a moment. He had enough foolish pride to rise to the man's challenge but managed to suppress it. He hadn't come looking for trouble. "I wanted to talk to you," he said calmly. "Without a badge, before—"

He was interrupted by the clatter of boots on the stairs. A second later, to Noah Creed's obvious displeasure, the door flew open and Timothy stormed into the room. "Chi Lo said—" His eyes darted around the room, found Billy. "You!"

Noah Creed's voice was ominously tight. "That will be quite enough, Timothy."

Tim's face clouded. His shoulders tensed and his fists curled as he stepped toward Billy. "Get out!" he hissed. "You're not wanted here!"

"I said—"

"My God, Father!" Timothy raged. "You let him in our house? After what he told the council?"

Noah Creed was no fool. He had not yet checked his son's chest, and he didn't want to. Nor did he want to give Billy further cause to interfere. He had seen men like Anthem before, and they could be dangerous. "I am well aware of what he has said and done. And you will kindly leave us and allow me to handle this in my own way."

"The hell you say!" Again, he started toward Billy. "I want you out of here, Anthem."

"I didn't come here to fight anybody," Billy said, noting that Timothy's face was as torn up as his. He held out one hand and stepped behind a chair. "Mr. Creed?"

Noah moved much, much faster than Billy had believed possible. Three steps, and he was between Timothy and Billy. "Go to your room," he ordered, wasting no words. "Now."

"This is my house, too, Father, and I—"

"Chi Lo!" Noah roared, towering over his youngest son. His voice seemed to rattle the walls. Even Billy cringed despite himself.

The servant appeared as if by magic in the doorway.

"Take him to his room and keep him there."

Chi Lo didn't so much walk as glide. Without seeming to move, he was at Timothy's side, with one hand on the youth's arm.

Timothy's face, the bruises livid, twisted in hatred as he glared over Noah's shoulder at Billy. "Father, I . . . I . . ." Abruptly, he shook Chi Lo's hand off his arm, whirled about, and stalked out the door and down the hall.

Noah gestured, and Chi Lo pulled the door closed behind him and glided off in pursuit of Timothy.

"My apologies, Anthem," Noah said, returning to his spot at the fireplace as if nothing had happened. "A son with a mind of his own can sometimes be a trial. But that is something your own father knows full well, I imagine."

Billy had openly defied Big John precisely once in his life, and had regretted it ever since. "Yes, sir," he said, letting it go at that.

As if he suddenly remembered that Billy was an enemy, a frown played briefly across the older man's face before it set in the same cold, emotionless mask as before. "Be that as it may. I am a busy man, Anthem. You have two minutes to state your business and then you will be excused." The patriarch folded his long arms across his chest.

"Very well. You have a problem, sir."

Noah appeared amused. "Oh?"

"One that will only get worse the more you try to avoid it. Goretti is innocent of Melinda Crenshaw's murder. As I believe you know full well."

Creed bristled. "I know nothing of the sort. The fiend lusted after her, as anyone can tell you. He cannot account for his whereabouts at the time of the murder, and his victim's bloodstained blouse was found in his room."

Billy shook his head. "Not good enough, Creed. Goretti was nowhere near that warehouse at the time of the murder. I know that for a fact, and I will bring it out if I have to in order to keep you from stretching his neck." Billy drew closer to the man, knowing his time was running out. "As for the blouse, it was found in a room that was never locked. Anyone could have entered unseen at almost any hour of the day. Give way, Mr. Creed. Goretti might be different than most, but he's not idiot enough to leave evidence like that lying around in the open. Whoever killed Melinda put it there."

"I think I've heard quite enough. Your two minutes are up." Creed moved toward the door. "I'll see you out myself."

"Not yet, Mr. Creed." Billy took a deep breath and stood his ground. "Your niece was beaten viciously, fought her assailant, and scratched him. Rhodes has told me Goretti bears no recent scars. I cannot say the same for Tim. He killed her, Mr. Creed, sure as my life."

Noah Creed turned and walked to the window. He raised a gnarled fist aloft, then slowly lowered it to his side.

"Do you know who I am, Anthem?" Creed asked, his voice a hoarse whisper. The knuckles on his clenched fist turned white.

"I know, sir," Billy softly said. "You own this town and the people in it. You're its life's blood. When you say 'jump,' folks answer 'How high, Mr. Creed?' "

"I am the power in Calamity Bay," Noah said, slowly facing the younger man. Creed's features were livid with rage. "The power of life . . . and death. Do I make myself clear?"

Billy took a deep breath, eased it out, remained calm. "I'm my father's son, Mr. Creed, and he taught me that all the power in the world—and he has plenty—doesn't give a man the right to own another man. My father has laid his life on the line for me. And would do it again at the drop of a hat. But if I crossed the line like Tim has, he'd turn me in himself, though his heart would break."

"I will protect my own. And you may mark my words, Anthem. Judge Robbins will find Goretti guilty, come Monday, and the scoundrel will hang Tuesday morning."

Billy couldn't hide his surprise. "Robbins?" he said. No secret was safe from the patriarch of Calamity Bay.

"Hell, I knew he was coming before you and Rhodes did," Creed sneered.

"Then the judge will have an interesting story to hear, about a whore named Angelina and another named Carolina Jenny," Billy replied. "And after the court takes a look at the fresh scars on Timothy's chest, we'll see who hangs on Tuesday."

Noah Creed took one step sideways, reached into an open drawer on the table next to his chair, and pulled out a Navy Colt revolver that he leveled at Billy. "Do you think," he asked flatly, "that I would hesitate to use this?"

Billy slowly opened his coat. "No weapon, Creed, and I made sure there are those who know that. Don't make things worse for yourself."

Creed's hand tightened on the trigger; Billy braced himself and prepared to dive to one side. To his great relief, Creed suddenly lowered the revolver.

"Leave town, boy. You have till Monday. You cannot stop what is going to happen. Leave."

"I'll see you in court, Mr. Creed," Billy answered.

"You'll lose, Anthem. You hear me? Everything!"

Billy paused at the door. Memories exploded from the past. A blast of thunder, a flash of lightning. Driving rain, and Laura, his bride-to-be, bloody and broken on the rocks, lost to him.

"I've lost everything before, Mr. Creed. But I'm still here." Billy left the way he came, knowing the battle lines were drawn. He'd done all he could. There was nothing else save the waiting and the wondering and, be it tomorrow or the next, the killing.

16

★

"Dammit, Chi Lo! I am not a child. I won't be treated like one."

Chi Lo didn't answer, didn't twitch a muscle. His eyes were half-closed, he appeared as relaxed as a cat taking the sun. Noah had told him to keep Timothy in his room, and to disobey was not only out of the question, but unthinkable. The young master was too impetuous. Let him rail and shout all he wanted, but he would not be allowed to leave his room. Timothy Creed had yet to learn that a wise man listens and learns and waits for the right time to act. The young master was a fool.

Timothy strode from bed to bureau and back again, three steps this way, three that. Who did Noah think he was anyway? Tim fumed, Lord and Master? Probably so the way Chi Lo obeyed him.

"Father's getting old and soft," Tim said aloud. He continued to pace, like a cat, smooth and quick; though he might appear to be a delicate youth, there was strength in his motion. He tugged at his brocaded vest and searched his pockets for a cigar. "Five years ago, he would have squashed Anthem like a bug and the hell with the consequences." Well, Tim Creed hadn't been afraid to settle things once and for all, with Anthem in the front parlor and no goddamn mist to block his shot.

Earlier, Timothy had stormed out of the parlor, but instead of returning to his room, he had headed for the library and the gun rack. He would have made it, too, and returned to blow Anthem's brains out if it hadn't been for Chi Lo.

Silent as a snake—Timothy hadn't even heard the man coming—Chi Lo slipped into the library behind young Creed and plucked the Winchester out of his hands before he could lever a shell into the chamber.

"How dare you!" Timothy had blurted out, reaching for the gun.

"The old master said you go to room," Chi Lo replied in that soft, accented voice that Timothy hated, and replaced the rifle in the rack.

"My father be damned! He doesn't—"

He got no further. Chi Lo spun the young man around and propelled him backward across the room. Tim slammed into the wall. His shirt was bunched in the smaller man's left fist, and the cold point of a dagger pressed lightly against Tim's throat.

Chi Lo twisted his left hand, pulled, and Timothy's shirt ripped open to reveal his chest. Sweat beaded on the young man's forehead as the double-edged dagger traced the thin white lines on his chest.

"Go to your room, pup cur." Chi Lo stepped back. The dagger disappeared. "This loyal servant who knows guards your shame. But you will burden your father with no more grief."

Timothy had been shaken. Chi Lo had never laid hands on him before. He pulled his shirt closed and lowered his head. His secret was like a tapestry of deception becoming slowly, inexorably unraveled.

The damned bitch! If she hadn't fought him, she'd still be alive. It was all her fault. Chi Lo had no right to blame him.

"I will wait out in the hall," Chi Lo said, bringing Tim out of his reverie. The Oriental left and closed the bedroom door as Tim sat sullenly on the edge of his bed and changed his shirt.

What were Noah and Anthem talking about? "Me, no doubt," Tim muttered.

And Melinda. Blaming him for her teasing ways, always preening herself and showing herself off to Tim and his brothers. But mostly Tim, because Aden and Eb were usually up at the mine. The muted sound of their voices rose through the house. After a while, he couldn't stand it. The longer they droned on, the more frayed his nerves became. Soon, he could sit still no longer, and was up on his feet, pacing, pacing again.

The front door closed with a thump. Timothy froze and listened. Moving quickly and quietly, Timothy tiptoed to his closet, pulled out an old Remington cap-and-ball revolver he kept hidden on the top shelf, and hurried to the window.

I'll show them all, Tim thought. He knew what had to be done.

Billy paused on the porch, looking over the panoramic view before him. How strange, he thought, that so much hatred and greed and fear lived and thrived in the presence of such great natural beauty. How ironic that a man should work, build, dare, and at last succeed and achieve neither peace nor love.

The mare lifted her head and watched him as he stepped down to the moist dark earth. The animal whinnied.

"Right, old girl," Billy crooned, and loosing her reins, patted her on the neck. "We're on our way." She balked as he tried to lead her onto the drive. On a whim, Billy rode around the eastern side of Creed Manor and found nothing out of the ordinary, only a carefully tended flower garden, and, beyond the yard, a row of buildings. The servants' quarters, set well away from the house, appeared neat and clean. A smokehouse he'd missed seeing from the ledge on the mountainside when he'd ridden up the bluffs stood in the lee of the stables.

He rounded the mansion, stopped briefly, and looked up and studied the wooded slope. Yes, there was the small clearing where he'd stood. His curiosity satisfied, he nudged the mare into a walk, and rode down from Creed's Knob.

The gall of him! Noah had never been subjected to such insolence, much less under his own roof. Creed tried to pour himself a brandy, but his hand shook and he sloshed the liquid over his coat sleeve. The suggestion, the very idea, that his son might have murdered Melinda was simply beyond consideration.

At least he tried to convince himself that was the case. But the possibility that Timothy might have committed the crime, once voiced, took root and grew. Noah tried to shrug off his suspicions, to no avail. He hurled the snifter to the floor and stalked out of the parlor and up the stairs.

Chi Lo, slouched outside Timothy's door, straightened as Creed approached. He wished Noah could face the truth. This pup was a mistake that should be gotten rid of, but the old master was as loyal as he was blind.

"Stay here. I may need you," Noah ordered as Chi Lo stepped aside.

Noah paused at the door, steeled himself, and entered. Timothy was at the open windows, stepping onto the balcony. He held the cap-and-ball revolver in a two-handed grip and sighted along the barrel.

"No!" his father ordered, rounding the bed.

His attention distracted, Timothy had yet to bring the sights to bear on the retreating figure heading townward. "Yes!" Tim hissed. There was still time.

"Chi Lo!" Noah called as he sprang toward his son. He caught Tim's arm and forced it up. Timothy fired straight up into the air.

The distant gunshot alerted Billy, who swung his horse about. He saw father and son struggling on the balcony and watched as Noah grabbed the Remington revolver and tore the weapon out of Timothy's hands.

Tim wrestled briefly with his father, but the older man prevailed and sent his son spinning through the open doors into what Billy figured must be the youngest son's bedroom, toward the left-rear corner of the house. Anthem slapped the mare's rump and the animal galloped down the hill, quickly distancing itself from the mansion's peaceful environs.

The scene in Timothy's room was far from peaceful, however. Near tears from anger and frustration and fear, Timothy crouched by the bed where he had fallen. Noah stalked inside, throwing the revolver across the bed to Chi Lo. "And what kind of damned-fool idiot stunt do you think that was?" he demanded.

Timothy glared up at his father and staggered to his feet. "Bastard spread lies about me like that! He deserves to die!"

"You'd kill him, unarmed, and on our own property?" Noah thundered. He exhaled slowly and willed himself to calm down. Finally, under control, he added, "Where's your common sense, boy?"

"You would have done exactly the same thing if he'd called you a murderer."

"I would have acted, yes. But not acted stupid."

Timothy swallowed, felt the sweat trickle down his sides from his armpits. "I know what he said at the meeting. He's trying to pin Melinda's murder on me. Why would I want to kill Melinda? I wouldn't do a thing like that! How would you like it—"

A great calm descended on Noah as he listened to his son rave on. And in the center of the calm, the seed of doubt planted by Anthem took root and grew to a size that Creed could not deny. "Your shirt," Noah said when Timothy wound down. The patriarch's mane of silver splayed out as if charged with electricity. His long beard flashed silver in the lamplight.

Timothy blanched, glanced sideways at Chi Lo. Had the chink told him? His father would kill him. Kill him if he knew. "What?" he asked, his voice faint.

"I want to see those scars."

Timothy's mind raced with a speed born of desperation. "You believe him!" he whispered, taking care not to lie. It was not difficult to feign shock. "My own father believes that Anthem lout? You believe him!"

"I do not want to believe," Noah said, "but—"

"You believe your own son could commit a crime . . . a crime . . ." He was overwhelmed by his father's lack of faith in him, and his face fell and his head drooped. "Very well, Father," he whispered, his voice barely audible. Praying, praying that the ploy would work, his fingers moved to the top button of his shirt. "If that is the way it must be."

One button. Noah's eyes widened and his breath quickened. Two buttons. He had to know, couldn't bear to learn. His mouth was dry, too, but from fear that his doubt should destroy his son's love and respect for him.

"Stop!" Noah closed his eyes, breathed deeply.

Timothy hid his smile of victory.

"Tell me." It was not a command, but a plea. "Just tell me it is not true."

"It is not true," Timothy flatly stated.

Noah looked into his son's eyes and saw past them to the sickness they hid. He knew his son lied. But he could not bring himself to accept it. Let Goretti pay the price. And afterward, somewhere, somehow he would find help for his poor, sick, youngest son.

Strength returned, and with it resolve. "Quickly, then, Timothy. Ride out to the mine. Find Aden and Eb. Tell them to be here for dinner tonight. We have important matters to discuss."

He was gone, tramping down the stairs.

Chi Lo paused on his way out the door and looked back at Timothy, a smug expression on his face. "The cur pup is clever," Chi Lo admitted in a voice Timothy alone could hear. "But don't think you have fooled him." The Oriental vanished past the edge of the door.

Timothy shrugged and began to dress for his ride up to the mine. His father had finally been roused to action. Things were finally taking a turn for the better. With Noah and brothers Aden and Eb at his side, nothing and no one was going to stand in Tim's way. Anthem would pay. Just like the others, that whore bitch Angelina.

And just like Melinda.

Tim hurried out into the hall and in his haste never noticed the silent figure of a woman who had waited and watched and listened. Eudora Creed Crenshaw drifted back into Melinda's bedroom. Her fingers brushed across the bed where her daughter had slept. She stopped, looked in Melinda's mirror, and thought for a fleeting second she saw the sweet face of her child. No. Only her own wishes, never to be fulfilled.

She had crouched, silently, with her ear to the door, and had heard every word, her brother's questions and Tim's reply. And she didn't believe him any more than Noah.

She should have known all along. There had been so many little things. The hungry look she had seen in Timothy's eyes as he watched Melinda at work or play. One night she had discovered him standing in the hallway. Melinda's bedroom door had been ajar and the fifteen-year-old girl visible in her bed. And Melinda had always tended to avoid Timothy, but Eudora had never known why.

The woman's long hair was stringy as it hung unbrushed about her shoulders. She pulled absentmindedly at the tangled strands. Her skin was pale, the lines deeply etched by grief. With dull eyes, she stood at the window and stared, unseeing, at what was once her favorite view overlooking the bay. Then she returned her attention to the darkened bed.

"Did you kill my daughter?" she asked of the shadows and the ephemeral image of Timothy Creed that plagued her mind.

"Oh, my darling, Melinda," she moaned, clutching her hands to her stomach. She sank to the bed and stifled her sobs with the pillows that still carried her daughter's rose-water scent.

17

⭐

Billy had wasted no time in making his way to the jail. The light in the windows had been a welcome sight; an open door and a cup of black coffee among friends were even better.

Rhodes sat at his desk, his left leg propped up on the nicked, smooth-worn top, his crutch by his side. Goretti was in his cell, the door ajar. Billy sat on a chair by the desk. Doc Bannon sat on Billy's cot with his hands clasped beneath his chin, elbows on his knees, his expression intense as he listened to Billy's accounting of his visit to Creed Manor. N. J. Garner stood with his back to the room, gazing down Mount Olive to the shake factory. He hadn't liked what he'd heard.

"Sure looks like Tim is our man," Rhodes growled, and shook his head. "My God, his own cousin, too."

"You think maybe he's the one who took that shot at you last night, too?" Garner asked in a tired voice.

"Could be," Billy said with a shrug. "What bothers me more is what happens next."

"You can bet Creed ain't gonna just sit tight an' do nothin'. Not with his boy headed for a hangman's noose," Rhodes remarked in the silence that followed.

Garner turned and nodded to Bannon. "He is not a man

to trifle with," the editor said. "I learned long ago what to print and what to leave out of the paper." He lowered his gaze to the floor. "Much to my shame," he added.

"We've all done our share of bowing and scraping to Noah Creed, N. J.," Bannon interjected. "But we're standing now and that's what counts. And there's others ready to stand with us."

"The way I see it," Rhodes spoke out, "we gotta take a look at who we're dealing with. Tim's a dangerous hothead. He's quick with a gun too, you mark my words. Noah's proud, he won't bend. Now, Aden's got a good head on his shoulders, but the only thing he's interested in is owning the whole damned coast. I can't see him risking his future for his younger brother. And Eb, well, he don't drink or fight, gets along with his men, works hard, and generally minds his own business." Rhodes rubbed his jaw and considered the possibilities. "I like Eb, but he'll do anything his pa tells him to."

Billy noticed the dull metal tin star on the desk. Well, here was something he could do, one action he could take. Marshal Rhodes needed a deputy.

"I might as well pin that badge on again, unless somebody has a better idea," Billy dryly observed.

"Can't think of a better man to wear it," Rhodes gruffly conceded. He struggled to his feet and propped himself on his crutch. "I reckon there are no objections?" he asked, checking briefly with Bannon and Garner, who nodded in accord.

"It's fine with me," Bannon said.

"Just watch your back," Goretti called out.

"I learned to do that a long time ago," Billy said. "Marshal?"

"Right." Rhodes tried to raise his right arm, gave up, and lifted his left. "You swear to uphold the laws of Calamity Bay to the best of your ability, so help you God?"

"I do," Billy said simply.

"Good. Then consider yourself a deputy again."

Billy grinned, pinned on the badge, and headed for the hatrack. He made a stop at the gunrack on the way.

"Where you goin'?" Rhodes asked.

"Thought I'd take a little stroll." Billy headed toward the door. "Water Street is as good a place as any to let folks know Calamity Bay has a new deputy." He winked and disappeared into the night.

"What about me?" Goretti called out to the marshal. "Am I still a prisoner?"

"As long as you are, Creed can't touch you without stepping into real trouble," Rhodes said. "Stay put and you got a chance of staying alive."

"How much of a chance?" Angelo inquired.

"Oh, about as much as me," Rhodes said. He didn't sound confident.

In the house on Creed's Knob, dinner might as well have been a wake. Noah was stonily silent. Aden's face looked as if it had been chiseled out of stone. Timothy sulked, Eudora remained upstairs. Only Eb, newly arrived from the sawmill, had come to the table in anything remotely like a good mood, and that had dissolved quickly in a matter of minutes.

Noah fumed in silence. Krait had brought the news that Anthem walked the streets wearing a badge once more. His reinstatement was an affront and a challenge. Creed had spent the afternoon pondering his response. Clearly, he couldn't let Rhodes get away with it unless he wanted to lose the town's respect immediately and forever. Something would have to be done, and before Monday, when Judge Robbins arrived.

"Enough," the elder Creed announced suddenly, after tasting his coffee. He rose, threw down his napkin. "We'll be busy tonight." He glanced at his sons. "Eb, Aden, Timothy? Come to the library."

Chi Lo appeared in the hallway and hurriedly preceded his master to the library and began lighting the lamps within. By the time the four Creeds entered, the room was awash in light. Noah went immediately to his desk. "Sit!" he commanded as his sons filed in behind him.

Aden sat in the leather armchair he had long ago claimed as his own. Eb chose the horsehair sofa, where he sat placidly and attacked the large bowl of peach cobbler he'd brought with him from the dinner table. Aware he was in deep trouble, Timothy sat as far as possible from his father, in the corner by the window that looked out on the spiny southern ridge of Cameron Bluff.

Noah leaned back in his chair, his left arm crossing his stomach and his chin cupped by the thumb and forefinger of his right hand. The only sounds were the quiet crackle of flames in the Franklin stove and Eb's spoon clicking against his plate. "Do you mind?" Noah snapped.

At peace with himself and the cobbler, Eb ate on.

"Ebeneezer!" Noah barked.

"Huh?" He looked around at his brothers, realized his mistake. His big, rawboned frame shifted uncomfortably and the sofa creaked and groaned beneath his weight. "Sorry." Eb reached forward and set the nearly empty bowl on his father's desk.

They waited in silence, but not for long. Soon enough, Noah, prophet of old, his stern, leathery features and white shock of hair in complete disarray, spoke.

"You," Noah barked, his eyes pinned Timothy to the wall. His heart ached with anguish for what he had to do, but he was resolved. "My son, whom I loved—And fool that I was, pampered and over-indulged, and made a monster."

"Father, I—"

"Shut up." Noah hadn't been able to look at Timothy's chest because he had known in his heart what he would see there. But he could not hide the truth from himself any longer. "To think that a son of mine could have done that . . . those things . . . to that poor child . . ." His fist crashed onto his desk and his soul cracked.

Why couldn't Timothy have been more like the hated but admired Anthem? A young man of pride, and honor, and courage. "You make me sick. Be grateful that I accept part of the blame and be at least man enough to accept your portion of it. Chi Lo."

The servant, stationed just inside the door, took a step forward and bowed ever so slightly.

"Do you know if Krait is in town?"

"I saw him at market today, Master."

"Please pay him a visit. Tell him he'll have to take a few days off from the freight office and that I want him here ten minutes ago."

"It is done, Master." Chi Lo turned and hurried away.

Creed returned to his son. "You know what kind of man Krait can be, Timothy. His instruction will be to ensure that you remain within this house until this trouble is resolved."

Timothy was outraged. "Jared Krait!" He sprang out of his chair. "What am I? A prisoner in my own house?"

"Call it what you like. You'll dance to my tune or to the hangman's! Now go to your room!"

Tim paled. He looked to his brothers, found only shock and, afterward, contempt in their eyes. He meekly left the room.

Aden and Eb watched him leave, exchanged glances, and then returned their attention to their father. Aden was already working through several scenarios as in a game of chess. He was determined not to lose this game even if it meant sacrificing Timothy.

Noah sat and rubbed his eyes with his fingertips. "Very well," he finally began in a subdued voice. "Our reputation and our power are at stake. If Goretti doesn't hang for his crime, we stand condemned. It could have repercussions. Later, we will wash our own dirty linen, but quietly and privately. With Goretti dead and buried, this unpleasantness is closed. The people here will believe what we tell them to believe. Of course, we may have to rid ourselves of Rhodes and Anthem. Are you with me?"

Aden fished a cigar from his coat pocket and lit up. "I'll do what you say, Father," he said through the smoke. Up to a point, he mentally added.

"Ebeneezer?"

"Yes, sir," Eb said, but his heart wasn't in it.

"Good." He abruptly rose and went to the window. Outside, dusk was giving way to darkness and a fresh north wind was thrashing the trees.

"Eb, round up some men from the mine, your best and hardest men, each willing to take orders without question. They're to be at the shake plant at five tomorrow morning."

"Yes, sir."

"Aden. You must make the arrangements. The men will have to be fed. But see the saloons stay closed for the next few days. An army of drunkards is no good to us. Also we will need weapons . . . rifles and plenty of ammunition. Get a count from Eb."

"What are we planning to do?" Aden asked.

Noah grinned. But his eyes glittered like the blade of a cutlass. "Calamity Bay belongs to the Creeds. I intend to prove it."

Rhodes was practicing with his crutch when Billy returned. The Texan racked his shotgun and slumped wearily in the nearest chair while the marshal proudly displayed the addition he had made to his crutch, a holster he'd lashed to the wooden grip.

"Not bad," Billy admitted, trying to sound impressed. He'd had one too many beers at Sophie's. "Is there any coffee?"

"Hell, yes, there's coffee. Ain't there always? Where've you been? It's damn near ten o'clock."

"Out and about. Nosing around." Billy helped himself to a cup of coffee and eased back into a chair. "Goretti all right?"

The marshal tucked his revolver under the bandages that immobilized his right arm, and began to load it. "For the time being."

"You expecting to use that any time soon?" Billy asked.

"Little Sam come by about half an hour ago. Word is Creed is bringing in his men. Plenty of them. We oughta see 'em come sunup."

"We could take Goretti and head for Port Angeles," Billy suggested.

"Creed'll have the trail covered. No, whatever happens, I want this whole blasted town to know. I'm hoping it'll help some folks find enough backbone to take a stand." The marshal holstered his revolver and hobbled across the room until he stood in front of Billy. He looked Anthem straight in the eye.

"It ain't your town, Billy, and it ain't your fight. So ride if you want to. While you're in one piece, and can. Be no hard feelin's on my part, and that's the Lord's truth."

Billy stood, stretched, and yawned again. "I got a better idea," he said. He tried to sound braver than he felt.

"Yeah? What's that?" Rhodes asked.

Billy downed the last of his coffee and headed for his cot. "Get some sleep," he said. "Gonna be a big day tomorrow."

18

★

Five o'clock. Morning mist lay heavy on the land as the final stragglers entered the west-side door to the shake plant. In the northeast corner, over forty men milled about in the middle of the warehouse, vacant since a huge load of shakes had been shipped to San Francisco. Wondering what the day would bring, the men talked quietly among themselves, stomped their feet to keep warm, and waited. It was the hardest job of all, waiting.

A makeshift platform made of heavy planks laid across sawhorses angled across the corner of the warehouse. Behind it, a dozen coal-oil torches lit the men's faces and threw giant shadows into the gloom beyond them.

A door opened and a breeze harried the torches. The men quieted without being told at the sound of muffled footsteps on the packed-dirt floor. A moment later, a figure stepped onto the platform. The figure's back was to the light, so his face was in shadows, but there was no mistaking the silhouetted shock of white hair and the commanding presence of Noah Creed.

"We are here to see that justice is served!"

A rumble of agreement ran through the crowd.

Standing alone, statuelike, his feet spread and planted firmly, Noah presented his case simply and to the point.

His niece had been foully murdered and there were those who would free the dastardly, cowardly scoundrel who had committed the crime. By what right did such a fiend deserve a trial? If the likes of this perpetrator went free, no man's wife or child was safe.

"We know what must be done," he finished, his voice soaring. "Are you with me?"

"Aye!" the men roared as one.

"What say you? I heard you not!"

"Aye! Aye! Aye!" the voices thundered, their echoes resounding throughout the vast warehouse by the bay.

Again Noah spread his arms for silence. "You all know my son Aden." He gestured, and Aden leapt onto the platform to stand at his side. "He speaks with my authority. Listen to him and heed him well. I will rejoin you later."

Noah stepped down and Aden took over with the details of how the men would cordon off the streets surrounding the jail. If Goretti was released immediately, Creed's men could all take the day off with full pay. If not, the job would take longer, perhaps two, perhaps as many as three days.

Under Ebeneezer's command, six men were named to hold the lumber road up Hurricane Ridge, four the coalmine road, another half a dozen to patrol along Cameron Bluff. Men were assigned to the waterfront to guard the piers and to make certain no one left Calamity Bay for Port Angeles, where a squad of the territorial militia was quartered.

Under Aden's command, five men, hard cases all, were assigned to key points in town to assure peace and quiet, while the remainder of those Ebeneezer had brought would mount a siege on the jail until Angelo Goretti was handed over. A hangman's noose dangled from a cross beam in the warehouse, its ghastly purpose evident to one and all.

The stage was set. There would be no turning back until Noah Creed's version of justice was served.

* * *

William Michael Anthem, deputy marshal of Calamity Bay, Washington Territory, woke to darkness. Somewhere in the distance, a dog barked. The dog was answered by a rooster, who crowed in irritation at being startled awake. Billy listened as the sound died only to be replaced by the rhythmic ticking of Rhodes' pocket watch lying with its case opened on the desktop.

Billy yawned, enjoying these first few minutes of inactivity. Back home in Luminaria he might be tempted to loll around in bed till daybreak. Of course, it was a luxury ranchlife seldom allowed. The thought occurred to Billy he might never see home again. He forced such a notion from his mind.

The lantern that burned all night long in the office was turned down to the merest hint of a flame, just enough to illuminate the face of the watch. Billy padded to the desk, palmed the watch, and by lamplight read 5:10. Any notion of returning to his cot died aborning. Guests were no doubt on the way. It wouldn't do to be caught abed. Not this day.

Goretti coughed himself awake as usual. Rhodes was up and out to the privy. Billy poked down the fire, added kindling, opened the draft, and put on a pot of water. Somehow the little day-to-day chores helped to ease the tension.

Life goes on, Billy thought, philosophizing. A man has to pull on britches and socks and boots before he confronts his fate. He makes coffee the same way he makes coffee every other morning of his life. As he stood there buttoning his shirt, his eye chanced on the drawing Goretti had done of him Wednesday afternoon. Was that the same man who before the sun rose to burn off the mist might have to face down the mob Creed had assembled?

Goretti emerged from the cell. He carried a shotgun in his trembling hands. His reed-thin frame seemed more frail than usual and his black frock coat clung like an oversized bag to his torso. He waved to Billy and followed Rhodes out the back door.

Creed and his men arrived at six. Torchlight preceded them, a soft and dancing glow in the mist closing in from north and south on Mount Olive, and east and west on Pine. A handful turned into the alley and secured the stable. And the privy, which hardly seemed fair. Judging by the gloom, it promised to be a cold, drizzling day.

"Rhodes? Anthem?"

The rear door and all the shutters were closed and barred. Billy took stock of the half-dozen jugs of water behind the desk. They had plenty of ammunition, three rifles, and a shotgun.

Rhodes squirreled his way into a new vest, black leather and only slightly wrinkled, twisted the tips of his mustache, and slipped his revolver in and out of its holster. He wanted to look his best. "Well, this is it, Anthem. You ready?" He tossed a twelve-gauge shotgun to his deputy.

"You're a vain old goat" Billy chuckled.

Rhodes scowled and together they opened the door and stepped out onto the boardwalk.

Noah and Aden, flanked by a pair of men carrying torches, stood in the middle of the street immediately in front of them. Noah and his son both wore heavy coats that hung to their ankles. Aden's hat was pulled low and concealed his features. Noah wore no hat, as if wanting everyone present to know who exactly had come to the jail.

" 'Mornin', Noah. And is that Aden?" Rhodes drawled. He glanced to the east, leaned on his crutch. "Kinda early to be up and about."

"You know what we want, Rhodes," Noah said. "Hand him over and save yourself a lot of trouble." Torchlight cast a flickering orange pall to his features. He looked like a man afire.

"We'll keep him, if it's all the same to you," Rhodes said.

"Don't be a damned fool, Rhodes," Aden soothingly

added. "You've friends out here. People you know. You aren't going to fight them."

"Whatever they're paying you boys," Rhodes interrupted, his voice rising over Aden's, "it ain't enough for what you've got into." He squinted through the gloom. "Is that Tom Keller out there? And Burk Tillis? I see your brother, Alvin, too. Seen most of you others, too. You're good men. Roughhousers, but fair. So I'll say this once. Me and my deputy are sworn to uphold the law. You stand against the law and someone's gonna get hurt." Rhodes spat into the street. "Go home, lads. *Now*."

The grim semicircle of men grumbled and shuffled their feet; they seemed to waver for a minute, then, by mutual consent and inspired by the likes of Noah Creed, they stood firm.

"You've said your piece," Noah replied. He turned, gestured with a wave of his arm. "Let's go, men."

Billy had his belly full of talk. The shotgun leapt in his grip as he emptied one barrel right into the ground at Noah's feet. A great gout of mud erupted and spattered the Creeds. Aden faltered and retreated a step. The men with the torches balked at the shotgun's fiery blast. Billy leveled the shotgun at Noah. "Just so you know, the next one's for you."

Noah's face turned red, then white, not with fear, but with fury. "I should have let Tim kill you, Anthem," he hissed in a voice trembling with rage.

"You could have let him try," Billy said. He glanced at Rhodes, who seemed as startled as everyone else by the gunshot.

"Looks like rain," he finally said. "Better go inside." The marshal limped through the doorway. Billy followed, but he never took the shotgun off Noah Creed until he closed and barred the door.

* * *

"It's too early for them to be dangerous," Rhodes said, checking his pocket watch. Three hours had passed. "Like any mob, they got to work up to ugly. Five dollars a day don't hardly seem fair recompense 'fer bein' shot. So they'll have to think about it. Right now all this is a party. The longer it goes on, the more they get paid. And they don't have to dig for it."

"A party," Goretti muttered, peering through the gun port cut in the shuttered windows. "Sweet Jesus, but I don't think I can take this too much longer."

"You don't have a choice in the matter." Billy sat at his desk, his chair tilted back, his feet up, the reloaded shotgun across his lap.

Noah had disappeared shortly after seven. Aden held command now behind a buckboard blocking the intersection of Mount Olive and Pine. The men out front stood in loose knots of threes and fours, talking, joking. It was the same out back and down the side alleys. Four men huddled out of the damp breeze inside the open stable doors. Using barrels for stools and a table, a lively game of poker had ensued. Nearby, a couple more miners were taking turns throwing a knife at a tree stump.

"Nothing to worry about," Rhodes muttered. Suddenly a roar of guns filled the air. Rhodes dropped his cup of water. Billy almost went over backward in his chair.

Slugs slammed into the front door, rattled the shutters on the front and side windows. "Jesus!" Billy shouted when one ball screamed through a crack in a shutter, clanged off an iron cell bar, and whined into the wall.

Goretti dived behind the Franklin stove. "A party!" he shouted. The gunfire was coming from the front of the building. Only the front.

"Damn," Billy cursed, and headed for the backroom. He ran into Rhodes' quarters, plastered himself against the rear wall, and chanced a look through a gun slot in the heavily planked door.

Rhodes got the idea the second he saw Billy running across the room. "What'd ya see?" he called above the din.

Gunfire at last opened up from the rear. Billy crouched and darted to Rhodes' side by the bed. "A couple of men running off with a ladder and a length of planking. All that crap out front was a diversion. I don't know what they're up to."

The roof sloped evenly from front to rear. The marshal jerked his head toward the rafters. Billy, as if reading the man's thoughts, jumped and caught a rafter and swung up into the open framework, then inched his way toward the front of the building where he could stand upright.

Sure enough, he felt more than heard the roof creak. Suspicions confirmed, he dropped to the floor as light as a cat and hunkered down by Rhodes. "Someone's up there, all right."

"The roof's too thick to shoot through and the wood's too damp to burn," Rhodes observed. He scratched his stubbled jawline. "I sure hate to have them up atop us, though. Gives me the willies."

The gunfire trailed off. Rhodes and Billy quickly returned to the front windows.

"Rhodes!" Noah Creed called from his vantage point. He stood in the doorway of the farrier's shop directly across the street from the jail. "We can keep it up until a stray bullet finds one or the both of you. Be reasonable, walk away. Go have a beer at Sophie's. Let us do what must be done."

"I'm thinkin' on it, Creed," the marshal shouted back. "Keep your dogs at bay a minute." Rhodes turned to Billy. "I want them boys off the roof."

"If we can't swat them off, we'll at lcast give them something to think about," Billy said, patting the scatter-gun. He peered through the gun slot. The shop window across the street was almost opaque with dirt. Billy squinted and thought he could make out in the reflection a couple of figures squatting on the jail's roof, facing the street.

"They'll jump us as soon as we step down from the boardwalk," the Texan observed. Sweat stung his eyes. He mopped his face on his shirt sleeve. "Goretti, best you stay put."

"My sentiments exactly," the artist replied. The panic had left him now and he seemed resigned to his fate.

Billy glanced at Rhodes, who nodded he was ready. He wore a crazy kind of a smile, as if he were enjoying himself. Perhaps it was the tension, but Anthem had to admit he felt a little giddy himself.

The deputy removed the bar on the door, swung it open, and stepped onto the boardwalk. Behind him, Rhodes took a stand in the open doorway. "Maybe we can work some kind of deal," he announced.

Billy ambled to the corner of the jail, staying on the boardwalk. He counted the men by the farrier's, no easy task in the fine misting rain. He figured a dozen rifles spread out behind barrels and buckboards and shacks and shops lining Pine Street. There were men on the roof of the farrier's shop as well, crouched below the sign that read SAMSON FREER, PROP.

"No terms," Creed said. "Anthem goes. We don't need his kind here. Then you step aside."

One of the men on the roof edged toward the corner of the porch roof. If he leaned out, just so, he'd have a clear shot at Anthem, just for a second. A second was all he'd need.

"We'll take care of the rest," Creed continued, his gaze inadvertently centering on the man on the roof.

Billy heard the hammer click on the gun above him. He leapt forward and landed in the street just as the man above fired. A bullet shattered the roof post and ricocheted into the mud. Billy's right hand brushed his holster, the Colt filled his hand, spoke once, twice, a third time. One of the men jumped from the roof; the other, his own gun smoking, tumbled to earth, seriously wounded.

Billy spun and fired the shotgun at the men in front of Freer's shop. Wood splinters filled the air as buckshot spattered the men. Rhodes was firing from the doorway.

Billy ducked low and headed for the door. He fired his shotgun again and emptied his revolver at the men in the midst. Bullets fanned the air around him, plucked his shirt sleeve, and slapped the walls of the jail. Even the men down the street opened up, but picked the wrong target.

The second man from the roof of the jail was caught in the cross fire. He was beefy, a bull-strong-looking miner who shrieked and held his hands up as if to ward off the hail of lead that pummeled his big frame and dropped him facedown in the muddy street.

Rhodes fell backward through the door, Billy dived in after him, and Goretti slammed the door shut and dropped the bar in place.

The marshal lay on the floor, feeding shells into his revolver. Billy crawled to the right of the door and collapsed against the wall. "Jesus!" he panted.

The fire from outside quieted. A voice called for help. Someone shouted for help. Another man was sent for Doc Bannon.

Billy counted two holes in his shirt, his hat was history. A bullet had nicked his boot heel. His foot ached from the slug's impact. "How much did you reckon Creed's paying those men?"

"Five dollars a day, is what I heard."

"And how much does a deputy marshal make?"

"Two," Rhodes said, hitching over to inspect his bullet-gouged crutch. "Plus found, of course."

Billy stood, tested his foot. He peered through the gun port in the door at the army Creed had brought against them. "I wonder if it's too late to switch sides."

19

★

One man dead riddled by Creed's own men, another four with wounds grave enough to take them out of action. They had been loaded on a buckboard and taken to the shake plant, where Bannon could tend their wounds.

Noah was beside himself. This was as bad as a mutiny with the mutineers in control of the helm. Creed's own men were grumbling and discontent. The grim reality of the situation tested their loyalty. No one wanted to die. It had ceased to be a party.

"Mr. Creed! Mr. Creed!"

Noah looked up to see a young man running down Mount Olive. "What, now?" he snapped, meeting his man partway.

The young man skidded to a halt in front of his employer and touched the brim of his cap. "There's a boy tryin' to bring food to the jail. Sam Burden's his name. The men stopped him, wanted to know should we let him through."

"Under no circumstances," Noah ordered. "No food, no water, nothing. And no one gets in or out of that building unless I say so."

Rhodes finished lashing a chair rung to his crutch for better support. He stood and warily eased his weight onto it.

"That'll have to do," he observed when the repair held. He maneuvered his way across the office to where Billy was holding the fort. "Anything new?"

"No. I've been thinking. We've seen Noah and Aden. So where are Eb and Timothy?"

"Good question," the marshal said. "Up to no good is my guess." His stomach growled. "I don't imagine Creed'll break for ham and eggs."

Billy didn't answer. He continued to watch the street. The next move was probably Creed's.

It was high noon. Outside, another lumber wagon had been brought up, unhitched, and tipped on its side. Riflemen quickly moved to position themselves behind the new partition.

Goretti had volunteered to watch the back. He sat, perched on a stool by the window, and busied himself with his sketch pad. Billy marveled at the calm that had come over the man once he had charcoal and paper in his hands.

"At least we can have some coffee," Rhodes grumbled. He'd begun to add timber and crumpled paper to the firebox in the stove.

"Forget it," Billy said from his place at the front of the jail.

"Huh," Rhodes turned to stare at him.

"They covered the chimney," Billy said. "I saw it from the street."

"Damn," Rhodes muttered, fuming at their plight. "That just ain't fair." He shook his fist at the shuttered window. He knew Creed couldn't see him. But he didn't care. It made him feel better.

"Anybody for a cup of nice cold water?" Goretti asked from the backroom.

Rhodes shuddered and limped back to his desk.

Calamity Bay had never known such a situation. For some, the siege was better than a medicine show, and they gathered as close as possible to watch and talk and laugh and drink and make bets on whether Rhodes or Creed would prevail.

But there were others who gathered on street corners out of harm's way and talked in hushed and angry tones. Creed was wrong. His course could only lead to disaster. However, no one had the courage to tell him.

Doc Bannon, on his way to treat the wounded, took time to rail against the unwarranted use of force by the Creeds. Wabash Jack, newly arrived from Sophie's, his breath still reeking of alcohol, stood silent, hands thrust into the pockets of his overalls. Reverend Brinton, standing in the shadow of this giant, decried the harsh power of evil, and N. J. Garner, his hands black with printer's ink, swore his note to Creed be damned, he would trumpet this day's news to the entire length of the northwest coast.

"We must act. We must," Garner said. One of the men nearby, a nay-sayer, spoke up in derision. "Aw . . . you're full of, uh, it." The speaker corrected his language as Penelope Swain approached down Helena Street.

Back up the street, the school stood empty. Mothers kept their children home this day. And Penelope was glad for it. She nodded as the men doffed their hats, acknowledging her presence.

"Better not go any farther," a one-eyed sailor named Cage opined. He fumed to the men in the group, "We oughta march down there, take their guns, and toss the Creeds in the bay."

"Along with your job," another man spoke out. "But go on. I'll watch."

"I didn't say I'd go *alone*," Cage protested. "We all need to stand together."

Bannon and Garner and the rest lowered their heads and stared at the ground. Only Wabash Jack studied the jail, but he made no move. Whiskey dulled his thoughts. Penelope had heard just about enough. The men might be afraid but not Penelope Swain, not Calamity Bay's most eligible schoolmarm.

Without so much as a by-your-leave, Penny walked right through their midst. Doc Bannon called to her, but she ignored him and headed right for Wick's Hotel, where another crowd had congregated to argue and complain and in the end do nothing.

A half hour later, carrying a basket laden with two baked chickens, a loaf of bread, a canister of fried potatoes and onions, and a large jug of coffee, she marched right back up Pine and, without hesitating, crossed the bridge and headed for the jail.

"That'll have to be 'bout fur enough, Miss Swain." A man of average height wearing homespun clothes blocked her path. The rifle looked incongruous in his hands.

"Hello, Allister Atwater. Your boy Gary Dean is a second-grade pupil of mine," Penny said.

"Why, uh, yes, ma'am."

She looked him straight in the eye. "Good. A nice boy. Now, either let me pass or explain to your sweet boy why you shot his teacher."

"Well, now, ma'am—"

Penny brushed him aside. She continued on toward the jail. Aden Creed left his position by the buckboard and fell in step alongside her. Aden had escorted her to a number of church socials and hoped to do so again.

"See here, Penny," Aden protested. He reached for the basket. She avoided his grasp and pulled her cloak tightly about her shoulders. "Look, we have a problem."

Penelope's smile was charming, but her voice was crisp, and hard as steel. "*We* don't have a problem, Mr. Creed. I imagine you will though, if you try to manhandle me any further."

Aden looked nervously at the spectators just across the bridge, then back up the street, where Noah and Chi Lo were approaching. "She's trying to bring food to them," he explained in answer to his father's unasked question.

Noah Creed was brusque and to the point. "Turn back now, Miss Swain, or you will be dismissed immediately from your position."

"I won't," Penny bristled.

"I am tired of this nonsense." Wasting no more time, Noah gestured to Atwater and his companions. "Take her back across the bridge," he ordered. "And make sure she stays there."

The men saluted awkwardly, and in that instant Penelope surprised them all by simply walking past Noah and continuing on toward the jail.

"Now, damn it all! Grab her," Noah thundered.

Distracted by the schoolmarm, none of the men saw the giant form of Wabash Jack stride across the bridge. He was an ominous apparition dressed in woolen pants and a thick cotton shirt, its sleeves rolled up past his enormous biceps. Not to be deterred, he caught up with Aden, spun him around with one hand, and picked him up by his shirtfront with the other.

"Hey!" Aden gasped. Choking for breath, suspended a foot above the ground, he clawed for his revolver, then dropped it when Wabash Jack's free hand closed like a vice on his wrist.

"Let her go," the giant growled.

Noah stared dumbstruck at his son's predicament. He yanked a Navy Colt from his pocket. Chi Lo drew a stiletto.

Wabash Jack was undaunted by the weapons arrayed against him. "Put them things away or I break his neck." He tightened his choke hold and Aden groaned aloud.

Chi Lo sheathed his knife; Noah holstered his pistol and told his men to release Penelope. "Put him down, Wabash."

Wabash Jack shook him lightly instead. "Soon. First he takes a walk with Jack and Miss Penelope," he said with a grin, and nodded toward the jail. "They ain't afraid to stand alone. Like me. So maybe I'll even the odds, huh?"

"You'll have a dozen rounds in you before you reach the front door, Wabash," Noah warned.

"Maybe," Wabash Jack said. "But you have to shoot through him to get me." He shook Aden like a child his toy doll. "C'mon, schoolmarm." And unconcerned by any further threats, the giant brushed Noah aside and escorted Penelope down the street.

"What the hell?" Billy snapped out of a doze, grabbed his shotgun, and sat upright.

"Billy? It's me, Billy. Penny. Let me in!" The door rattled beneath her fist.

"Cover me," Billy told Rhodes as the lawman stumped into the front room. "Goretti, watch the back!"

Billy checked through the gun port, saw Penelope, and opened the door. She hurried into the jail, forcing Billy out of the way. Wabash Jack loomed right behind her. He turned on the boardwalk and hurled Aden back toward the street.

"I throw this little fish back." Wabash laughed. He leapt to cover and slammed the door as Aden skidded halfway across the street and emerged from the mud, wild-eyed and cursing.

"Now, why'd you do that, Wabash?" Rhodes asked, checking the men in the street. He gazed longingly at Aden. "He would've made a good bargainin' chip."

The giant frowned. The thought had never occurred to him. But Billy glanced up, the simple remark had given him an idea.

"Ah, never mind," Rhodes continued. He clapped Wabash on the back. "Thanks for helping the little lady. I hope that basket ain't full of chalkboards and primers." She didn't answer. He sniffed the aroma of baked chicken, looked around, and noticed that Billy and the schoolmarm had embraced. It looked like Billy had skipped the meal and moved right to dessert.

* * *

While they ate, Penny recounted all she had heard, be it rumor or true, of Noah Creed's intentions. Billy wasn't surprised to learn Creed had control of the town.

"Most of the townsfolk are on your side," Penelope said. "They just need some sort of . . . well, a catalyst to rouse them to arms."

"A what?" Wabash Jack interjected.

"A kick in the ass," Angelo Goretti answered, polishing off a chicken leg.

"I can do that," Wabash Jack replied.

"What do you hear about Eb and Timothy?" Billy asked, his brows furrowed in thought.

"Eb is in charge of the men guarding the roads out of town. Nobody has seen Timothy all day, but I heard rumors that he's locked up under guard in his room at Creed Manor."

"I heard the same thing," Wabash Jack said from the window where he was keeping an eye on the street.

The marshal's brow furrowed. "That's strange."

"I, for one, hope Mr. Creed keeps him there forever," Penny said. "He's a terrible man. He made certain suggestions to me," the teacher admitted. "I never said anything about it . . ." She glanced sheepishly in Billy's direction. "I didn't want anyone to come to harm on my behalf."

Rhodes checked his pocket watch. "You'd best be getting on back. Be dark soon."

Billy stood, touched Penelope's arm, and despite the inquisitive glances of the other men, led the teacher into the backroom.

He closed the door, took her in his arms, and kissed her. What they felt for each other needed no words. For one single sweet moment in time they had eased each other's loneliness. The memories were all. Billy placed his hand in hers. She nodded, knowing there was nothing to say, only something to feel in her heart and treasure forever.

* * *

Rhodes stood with Penny at the front door and nodded to Billy Anthem, who cracked a shutter open and called out. "Hold your fire. It's Miss Swain comin' out. Alone." Penny hesitated.

"Go on," Billy said. He waved her on. "Last chance to leave with her, Wabash."

The giant shook his head no. He rubbed one ham like a fist into the palm of his hand.

"Be careful," Rhodes told Penny, handing her out the door. "We thank you for the food." He closed the door, and the bar dropped into place with a final sounding thud.

"And now, what?" Goretti said. He held up a hastily sketched portrait of Wabash Jack, who beamed with approval.

Before Goretti could protest, Wabash grabbed the portrait, folded it, and placed it in the pocket of his overalls.

"I keep this for good luck. You're my good friend, too." He clapped Goretti on the back and sent the whip-thin artist sprawling.

Billy Anthem and the marshal laughed despite themselves. The grimness of the situation was, for the moment, temporarily dispelled. Wabash Jack threw back his head and had a real belly laugh. Even Goretti had to smile wanly and rub his shoulder.

"See," Wabash Jack exclaimed. "We have a real good party."

"Too bad we can't invite Noah Creed." Rhodes chuckled.

"Or Tim," Billy said. Something in his tone of voice caught Rhodes' attention. He glanced at his deputy and the laughter faded. Billy's expression was dead-serious. "I'll personally deliver the invite," said Anthem. "Tonight."

20

★

"It's time, Wabash."

Wabash Jack was as much at home on a jail cot as in the woods. He had fallen asleep the instant he had stretched out, and now woke as quickly. The giant of a man stood, rubbed his eyes, stretched, and shook his head violently from side to side. "Yup, Billy," he said, his thick homely features split in a grin.

It was three in the morning. Goretti and Rhodes had traded off on watches. Creed's men were likewise standing guard. Now and then one of the miners shifted his stance and revealed himself in the fitful glare of sheet lightning.

The early morning had turned even more miserable than the previous day. The temperature had dropped another ten degrees and the air was laden with moisture. Time became measured in blocks: when it rained, when it threatened.

Goretti huddled on his cot and hacked and coughed almost constantly; two blankets weren't enough to keep out the cold.

Rhodes wore his heavy sheepskin coat and kept his hands in his pockets to keep warm. "Wish to hell I could go with you," the lawman grumbled.

"Wish you could go *instead* of me," Billy countered. He tied down his holster and checked the loads in his .45. He grabbed the sawed-off shotgun, considered taking it, then opted for a second revolver he tucked in his gun belt. It rode butt-forward on his left side. He paused and listened to the night. It had begun to rain in earnest now. Good, all the better to escape unnoticed.

Everyone knew his role. Goretti unbarred the rear door. Rhodes waited at the back window, shotgun in hand. Wabash Jack took his position to one side of the door. If Billy went down, it was Jack's job to bring him back into the jail. Behind him, Billy blew out the lamps and allowed his eyes to adjust to the gloom. "Remember," he said while they waited, "I'll be back as close to seven as I can make it. Straight down Pine. Be ready."

"You can count on it," Rhodes grimly promised.

"Right." Billy took a deep breath and, when Rhodes edged the door open, slipped through and ducked down by the back step. He waited, crouched in the rain, expecting an outcry. But he might have been alone in the night. He knew he wasn't, however, and stole quietly away. The rain soon had him drenched. A block from the jail and Billy was soaked to the skin. He didn't mind. There'd be plenty of hot lead to warm him later.

Creed Manor rose above the fog. Billy paused at the gate, his breath clouding the air, and ran silently through the low, sheep-cropped grass to the rear corner of the house. He sneezed and blew his nose on a bandanna. "Oh, God," he muttered. "Not now." There was a light in the Creed stable, but he couldn't see anyone moving. He worked his way across the front of the house, peering through the windows, to no avail.

Halfway down the east side of the house, he dropped to the muddy ground as a woman emerged from the servants' quarters, and shielding herself with a coat held over her head, she hurried to the rear of the house and disappeared inside.

So the cook was up and working in the kitchen. Good. Any noise he made might be attributed to a servant. Billy clambored to his feet and quickly checked the rest of the windows facing east. He remembered Timothy had fired at him from what must be the west corner bedroom. But was it his bedroom?

There was only one way to find out. Billy trotted back to the front of the house, climbed over the rail onto the porch, and tiptoed to the front door. A lantern burned in the hall, outlining him against the glass, but that was the least of the chances he had to take. Slowly, he twisted the knob.

"Nothing like well-oiled hinges," he muttered when the door opened silently. Noah Creed was so confident he hadn't even bothered to lock the place. Slipping inside, Billy closed the door, then waited, contemplating the stairs.

A clock chimed to his right. A formal parlor, he recalled from his previous visit. If Noah had returned . . . The thought was interrupted by the sound of a door opening and a brief flood of light on the upstair's landing. Quickly, Billy stepped into the darkened parlor and ducked behind the door.

Krait! The ex-deputy descended the stairs, turned, and went down the hall into what was probably the kitchen. Billy heard the sound of voices and laughter. What to do? Go upstairs immediately? Or wait until Krait came back?

A door opened. ". . . hell when it's ready," Krait said, walking back into the hall.

The question answered for him, Billy held his breath while Krait came down the hall and started up the stairs. Seconds later, he heard a door open and close.

There was no time like the present. Gun in hand and one eye on the kitchen door, Billy followed Krait's path. His shadow lengthened as he climbed. A portrait of a woman, her eyes following him, seemed to watch him as he passed. He paused when his head cleared the second floor, cautiously looked around, and found the upstairs hall empty.

So far, so good. A narrow beam of amber light bled through a crack at the bottom of the door to what he thought was Timothy's room. Voices, Timothy's and Krait's, rose in disagreement, then fell.

Billy couldn't stand there forever. Moving catlike, he climbed the last steps, crossed the hall to Timothy's door.

What of Jared Krait? He was just a hireling. Would he back down?

Billy crept to the door, flattened himself against the wood panel, and listened. The soft chime of a bell sounded within. Immediately, Billy ducked back. A second later, when a key turned in the lock and the door began to swing open, Anthem was waiting.

Billy kicked the door wide open, darted inside, and collided with Jared Krait. He drove his shoulder into Krait and knocked him backward.

If Timothy was caught by surprise, he didn't pause to show it. The youngest Creed came up off his bed and hurled a metal washbasin at Billy's skull.

Anthem ducked, moved inside Timothy's reach, and drove his left fist into Creed's solar plexus. Tim gasped and fell to his knees. Billy spun, saw Jared Krait in a half-crouch, rising from the floor. And he held a gun. Flame jetted from the muzzle of the Colt, but his shot went wide, punching a hole in the wall behind Billy. Before he could try again, a second deafening gunblast shook the room.

Billy Anthem stared at the dead man sprawled on the floor. He felt sick to his stomach. But he didn't have time to mourn the waste.

"Son of a bitch," Timothy gasped.

"Shut up," Billy replied. He dragged the fallen man to his feet. They entered the hall together.

An Oriental servant paused halfway up the stairs, decided Tim's fate was none of his business, and retreated to the floor below.

Billy gave Creed a shove toward the stairs. Anthem glanced over his shoulder and saw Eudora Creed Crenshaw watching him from across the hall.

Her flesh looked pale as porcelain. Her silver-streaked hair was drawn tightly back from her face, though a single strand had pulled loose and dangled like one of Medusa's snakes down along her cheek.

"He killed my daughter," she said, her voice higher-pitched than normal, almost lilting in its tone. The way she spoke gave him the creeps.

"Yes, ma'am," Billy said. He caught Timothy by the arm, jabbed a gun barrel in his side. "Let's go."

"Where are you taking me?" Tim asked, his voice rasping in his throat.

Billy fixed him in an icy stare. "To hell," he replied.

21

★

"He what!" Noah roared, his fist slammed the desktop. A row of books fell over on a nearby shelf. Men who had huddled half-asleep in their coats outside the farrier's suddenly bolted awake. Creed rose from the big leather chair he'd been dozing in and towered over the stablehand who had brought him such dire news.

The poor soul could hardly speak, so great was his fear. "He . . . the deputy . . . t-took Mr. Timothy away," he stammered.

"When? You there by the door. Fetch me Aden. Hurry!"

Terrified, the stablehand recounted the events at Creed Manor as best he knew them, and retreated gratefully when Noah stormed past him and out the door.

"What's wrong?" Aden asked, out of breath as he met his father on the boardwalk. Rain dripped from the eaves of the roof overhead.

"Anthem has Timothy! Killed Jared and took him."

Aden blanched. "My God." His features were puffy, his eyes slightly sunken. The tension had taken its toll.

Noah briefly retold the stablehand's story. "What do you think he did with him?" he asked, at a loss for the first time in years.

"I can't imagine. He'd have to be insane to bring him here. Port Angeles?"

"A possibility. Or hid him somewhere in town. We need Eb."

A rider was sent to the outpost on the lumber road that wound up Hurricane Ridge. Other men were dispatched to alert the contingents on Cameron Bluff and down by the docks.

"As for you," Noah told Aden, "gather your men. All of them. I want Goretti in my hands in case Anthem shows up with Timothy."

Aden had never questioned one of his father's orders, but this one was ill-considered. The revelation that Timothy had murdered Melinda, the besmirching of the family name, the long ordeal of the past two days, had aged Noah and clouded his judgment. "That's not a good idea, Father," he said.

"You dare question —"

"Yes," Aden interrupted. "Let's not make things any worse than they are already. If Rhodes or Goretti are killed . . ." He let the sentence trail off, a warning without words. "There has been too much bloodshed already."

Noah's shoulders sagged. In his mind he knew Aden was right, but in his heart he could think only of his son. His son, who was a murderer, but whom he loved. "What do we do, then?" he asked meekly.

"Wait," Aden said as gently as possible. "We wait."

Timothy didn't look much like a Creed. Creeds weren't gagged and bound hand and foot to a chair in the schoolmistress's house. It seemed a new day was dawning in Calamity Bay, and it was beginning with Timothy Creed.

Billy checked his handiwork, decided that it would take a better man than Timothy Creed to work out of his bonds.

"You look like a regular drover," he said as he entered the front room, where Penelope Swain waited. "A bit too round in places for a cowpuncher. But I'm not complaining."

Penny didn't like her man's apparel, but was nonetheless pleased by the compliment and repaid the favor with a cup of fresh hot coffee. In men's clothes she hoped to make her rounds unnoticed.

"Thanks," Billy said. He burned his tongue on the scalding liquid, added even more brandy, and drained the contents of the cup. "You know what you have to say?"

"The Pine Street Bridge, seven A.M.," she repeated. "And they'll come, when folks hear you have Timothy Creed."

"I hope so," Billy said.

"Whether they stand and fight is another matter," Penelope added.

"They won't have to. Not when Noah Creed sees our prize catch." Billy walked over and blew out the lantern. He didn't like leaving Tim alone, but there was nothing else to do. He did not intend to be gone long, just the time it took to reach Bannon and the newspaper office. He leaned over and blew out the lamp and took advantage of the darkness to seek out Penelope for a last kiss. "No time to dry out," he added with a shiver.

"Be careful or you'll catch your death . . ."

Billy vanished through the door. And her motherly admonition was left hanging on the silence, that followed.

22

★

"You see anything at all?" The speaker, one of the men Aden had chosen to patrol the streets of town, emerged from the early-morning mist and stopped on the corner of Pine and Broadway, where one of his cohorts was stationed.

"Hell, no. And ask me if I give a damn anymore."

"I sure as hell don't," the second man, a millworker, replied. "Where the hell is that Chinaman? He said he'd fetch us coffee."

The first speaker spat and fished in his pocket for another plug of tobacco.

"Still an' all. Five dollars a day . . ." He paused and listened intently, took his rifle out of the crook of his arm, and peered down Broadway. "Chi Lo . . . is that you?"

"Hold your fire, Ward."

Three men swam out of the mist in the alley. To Ward's right, three more ran down Broadway toward him. "Give it up, Ward, Piney. Don't force us to shoot."

"Mr. Garner?" the man named Ward with the tobacco asked, taken aback

"None other," the *Courant*'s editor said. He motioned with the shotgun he carried. "Lay down your weapons." Behind the editor, Chi Lo stood, oddly erect, the muzzle of a sawed-off scattergun thrust against the back of his neck.

Ward considered the situation, looked at Piney, who had already made his decision and was lowering his rifle. "Well, shit!" he said, following Piney's lead. "We prob'ly wasn't gonna get that five dollars anyway."

Reverend Brinton didn't have a gun and refused to carry one, but had promised to be at the bridge with some of his parishioners at seven to offer moral support. Billy emerged from the parsonage. Brinton had been the last of the men on his list, and time was running out.

The mist wasn't exactly lifting, but it had thinned. Running, Billy crossed Cedar, darted between two houses, and headed down the alley for Penny's.

Timothy had fought the ropes, had wept, had tried to scream. "They can't do this to me," he howled silently into the gag, and almost choked. It hadn't been his fault. None of it was his fault.

He heard a door open, and footsteps. Seconds later, the bedroom door opened too and lantern light flooded the room. Billy Anthem knelt at his side. Timothy squinted against the sudden light and struggled to see the face of his tormentor.

"Almost time, Creed," Billy told him, untying the knots in the rope that held him to the chair, but not those that bound his limbs together. Tim groaned as some of the circulation slowly returned. He wore only a brocade vest, a mud-spattered white shirt, woolen trousers, and muddy boots. Billy looked even worse. He was drenched to the skin and had wrapped a blanket around his shoulders to keep warm.

"Billy?" Penny hurried through the back door.

"In here," he called "Any luck?"

"Yes. Especially when I told them about Tim."

"How many will join us?"

"Twenty? Thirty? It's hard to say." Penny shucked her coat, held her hands to the stove. "They've disarmed several of the millworkers in town. Most of them were ready to quit anyway. Nobody wants to die for Tim Creed."

"What time is it?"

"Five to seven." She stepped back from the stove, watched the man who had goaded the town into action and who had won her heart. "Billy? I'm glad we're together."

"Me too, Penny," he said, his voice husky.

"You're a dead man," Tim muttered. "My father will see you dead."

"Think so?" Billy said, his tone hardening. He shoved Tim toward the front door. "Let's find out."

With the advent of morning, the darkness gave way to gray light. Soot-colored clouds reduced the sun to a bone-white glow outlining the bluffs. The rain had called a temporary truce, but the day held little promise of drying out. The men behind the barricade across from the jail flapped their arms to get the circulation going and grumbled among themselves. Tempers weren't any better inside the farrier's shop. For the first time in his life, Noah found his sons openly defying his demands.

"Call it off, Pa," Eb said. He thrust his hands in his flannel jacket and shook his head. "I did plenty of thinking up there on the bluffs. It's funny how damn near freezing to death, being cold and wet and miserable, sort of clears a man's head." Eb walked to the window and looked out at the jail. "I figured we'd bluff him out. But Rhodes called the hand. It's time to fold and quit the game."

"And send the men back to work," Aden replied.

"That's all you think about, isn't it?" Noah sneered, disgust in his voice. "The business, ledgers and profit and losses. Nothing about Tim."

"You're right," Aden retorted. "Remember, I had a good teacher, Father." Aden walked up to stand alongside Eb. "I nearly got killed yesterday. Wabash Jack could have broken my neck. For whom? That sick whelp you call my brother!"

"Stop it. Shut up, you hear!" Noah bellowed. "Before I'm through—"

One of the men from outside barged in through the door. He was so anxious he forgot to doff his hat in the presence of Noah Creed.

"S'cuse me sir, but you better come out here! Anthem's coming. Your son, too. And it looks like half the town's following right along."

Noah glanced at his sons. For a moment he balked, torn by indecision, then the color returned to his features, a fierce reddening to match the fire in his eyes. He strode through the door and onto the boardwalk. Across the street, Hank Rodes stood in the doorway to the jail. Noah stared at him.

"You haven't won, Marshal. Not yet," Creed called. "Anthem'll have to get past me."

Noah headed down the street, his sons behind him. But a curious thing began to happen. At the sight of so many armed citizens, Creed's army began to melt away, to disappear into the alleys, to edge toward the nearest buildings and barns.

Noah didn't care. What was to come must be between Anthem and himself.

"Creed!" Billy Anthem's voice rang through the gray dawn.

"You've got my son," Noah roared.

Billy remained motionless. He decided to let Noah get good and close. It drew Creed from the jail, placing him in a cross fire between Anthem and Rhodes if it came to gunplay.

"My father will handle you," Tim said chuckling. "What are you gonna do now?"

"Blow your head off, if I have to," Billy softly replied out of the corner of his mouth. Tim's smug expression faded, the blood drained from his features.

"That's far enough, Noah," Billy called as the patriarch

of Calamity Bay closed to within thirty feet.

Billy stepped forward, away from Doc Bannon and Garner and the other resolute townspeople armed with a motley assortment of rifles, shotguns, and black powder muskets.

"I have arrested Tim for the murder of Melinda Crenshaw, your own niece, Mr. Creed. It is my belief he raped and murdered her." Billy's voice resounded in the heavy dampness. His smaller, wiry frame leaned forward, his muscles hunched. He stood like an Apache, poised to attack. Noah was the bigger man. But there simply was no give in Billy Anthem.

"He'll have a fair trial, Mr. Creed."

"Pa, help me," Tim blurted out. "Aden . . . Eb . . . take him. These others'll back down!"

Noah's hand started drifting toward his coat pocket.

"Don't make me kill you, Noah," Billy called out.

"Papa," Tim cried again.

Aden made a move; Billy tensed and shifted his stance, his hand dropping to his holstered Colt. Aden lifted his coat and with his opposite hand gingerly drew a revolver from his waistband and tossed it into the street. Creed's eldest son turned on his heels and walked back the way he'd come.

"Aden," Tim shouted. "You bastard!" His insult had no effect. Aden continued on up the street. He tipped his hat to Hank Rhodes, who had left Wabash Jack in charge of the jail. The marshal was stumping down the street as quickly as his bum leg, crutch, and the muddy road would allow.

"No," Eb said. "You're the sick bastard in this town."

Billy shifted once again to face Noah. Eb returned his hands to his pockets and left them there. "I ain't very smart, Pa. But I know what's right. And you do, too."

Noah looked at Eb, then back to Tim, from Eb to Tim yet again. And the fire in him died. Tears glistened in his eyes. He lowered his hands to his sides.

"No!" Tim roared, and spun on his heels. He swung a solid roundhouse right fist that Billy tried to duck and failed. The blow caught Anthem in the chest and knocked him off balance.

Tim charged back among the townspeople as Billy drew his gun then held his fire for fear of hitting an innocent bystander. Garner tried to block Tim's path. Young Creed lunged into the newspaperman and dragged Garner's shotgun from his grasp. Tim whirled about and leveled his weapon, not at Billy but at Noah Creed. Billy had no choice. He snapped up his own revolver.

A gunshot rang out and smoke billowed from in back of Tim. He arched backward, fired the shotgun into the air, stumbled forward, and slowly turned.

Eudora, clothed in a hooded black cape, shot him again, before Doc Bannon managed to wrest Jared Krait's gun from the distraught woman's hand.

Tim spun on impact and sank to his knees.

"Little trollop . . . always teasing . . . shouldn't have fought me. I didn't mean . . . mean to . . . kill," he muttered aloud. Pink froth appeared on his lips and he slumped forward in the middle of the wheel-rutted road, his blood mingling with the mud and the rain.

Silence descended, broken only by a woman's sobs. Noah Creed seemed rooted in place. Everything had happened so fast. Then, still in shock, the crowd soundlessly dispersed.

"He would have killed me," Noah muttered weakly. Strength ebbed from his limbs and he leaned on Ebeneezer, the slow, strong son. "Tim . . . tried to . . ."

"Yes, Pa, I saw."

Billy watched Rhodes limp toward him as the rest of the townsfolk ambled back to their homes and shops. A hand touched Billy's. Penelope Swain stood at his side. Billy looked into her soft, sweet face, her countenance mirrored the relief he felt. Penny didn't need to tell him she'd be waiting. Her eyes spoke volumes and promised even more. He nodded, and lifted her hand to his lips, and kissed it.

She turned away then and started for home. Billy intended to join her just as soon as he finished his final act in the drama.

He unpinned the badge from his shirt pocket and placed the tin star on the dead man. Justice had claimed Timothy Creed.

"What are you doing?" Rhodes asked, drawing up alongside Anthem.

"You don't need a deputy anymore," said Billy.

Eb moved in, picked Tim up in his arms, and carried him toward the nearest buckboard. Noah trailed after him, his shoulders hunched forward in his grief.

"Look at them go. Creed besieged the jail, caused the deaths of some innocent men. And tomorrow, I'll bet it will be as if nothing happened," Billy grumbled. "I thought the good guys were supposed to win."

"They do," Rhodes said. "They just don't win everything." The marshal spat in the mud and shook his head. "Noah's punished. Not enough, but folks have got to work." The lawman chuckled. "Bannon, Garner, and the rest, they might bite the hand that feeds 'em. But they won't bite it off." Rhodes sighed. "I'll miss you, Billy Anthem."

"Let's go tell Goretti he's a free man," Billy replied, and started up the lonely street to the jail.

By sunset the clouds had rolled in from the Pacific. The rain returned, hesitant at first, then the wind picked up and the downpour began. Penny listened for the knock at the door. She tried not to be impatient and busied herself with brewing a pot of strong coffee and stoking the fire in the hearth until she had a merry blaze.

Justice had come to Calamity Bay. Justice had shaken the foundation of Noah Creed's domain. She wondered if the town would ever really be the same. She had stopped by Doc Bannon's office to see if there was anything she could do to help. The doctor insisted that Eudora Crenshaw remain in his office. The distraught woman had refused ever to return to the house on Creed's Knob—not that anyone expected her to. A river of blood lay between Eudora and her brother now. And what tomorrow held for the poor woman was anyone's guess.

A rap at the front door and the click of the latch turned Penny's thoughts away from Eudora's future and back to her own. Billy Anthem stepped in out of the rain. He doffed his battered hat and nodded to her. "I saw your fire ma'am," he said with mock deference. When he shrugged off his coat Penny noticed he no longer wore a badge. That was fine with her. Billy had come close enough to getting killed over the course of the week. At least he had sense not to press his luck.

Leaving his coat to drip by the door, Billy crossed the room to stand by the fire. He held out his hands to the flames.

"I don't know if I'll ever dry out," he grinned. Then, glancing down at his vest, he patted the place where the badge had been. "I feel kind of naked."

"Hank will take you back if you change your mind," the schoolteacher replied.

"No thanks," Billy said with a wag of his head. "I've a different calling in mind." He pursed his lips a moment, lost in thought. A sheepish expression crossed his face. He hesitated, as if fearing her ridicule. Finally he realized the foolishness of such a notion . . . Penny would understand more than most.

He turned from the hearth and walked back to the window, tugged the curtains aside and stared out at the storm-swept bay, the slate-gray waves churned by the wind and capped with foam against a backdrop of sheet lightning. He was already analyzing the mixture of shadow and light, framing the scene in his mind, judging what he would keep and leave out.

"Goretti's given me some of his equipment. I might even hang around and study with him a while before striking out on my own." Billy turned toward Penny. "And while I'm learning to be an artist maybe . . . uh . . . we could be together?"

Penny blushed despite herself. She lowered her eyes a moment, as she sorted through her own feelings and emotions. She didn't know if she loved this young man. Well, yes she did, but in a special way. He made her feel beautiful and free and for now that was good.

She opened her arms to him and that was answer enough. Billy returned to her healing embrace while the storm raged outside. In his soul he had at last found peace.